MW00814260

The WRIGHT BROTHER

ALSO BY K.A. LINDE

AVOIDING SERIES

Avoiding Commitment
Avoiding Responsibility
Avoiding Intimacy
Avoiding Decisions
Avoiding Temptation

RECORD SERIES

Off the Record
On the Record
For the Record
Struck from the Record

ALL THAT GLITTERS SERIES

Diamonds
Gold
Emeralds
Platinum
Silver

TAKE ME SERIES

Take Me for Granted
Take Me with You

STAND-ALONE

Following Me
The Wright Brother

ASCENSION SERIES

The Affiliate
The Bound

The WRIGHT BROTHER

K.A. LINDE

Copyright © 2017 by K.A. Linde
All rights reserved.

Visit my website at www.kalinde.com
Join my newsletter for exclusive content and free books!
www.kalinde.com/subscribe

Cover Designer: Sarah Hansen, Okay Creations.,
www.okaycreations.com
Photographer: Sara Eirew, Sara Eirew Photography,
www.saraeirew.com
Editor and Interior Designer: Jovana Shirley,
Unforeseen Editing, www.unforeseenediting.com

No part of this book may be reproduced or transmitted
in any form or by any means, electronic or mechanical,
including photocopying, recording, or by any information
storage and retrieval system without the written permission
of the author, except for the use of brief quotations in a
book review.

This book is a work of fiction. Names, characters, places, and
incidents either are products of the author's imagination or
are used fictitiously. Any resemblance to actual persons, living
or dead, events, or locales is entirely coincidental.

ISBN-13: 978-1635760972

To Rebecca Kimmerling,
for every wonderful book you've helped me with
and a million more to follow.

One

Emery

I rolled my shoulders twice and yawned. I hated being at the office this early. It was mind-numbing, but at least I got to see Mitch. He didn't have class for another hour, and I figured we could use that time to get some coffee...or just occupy his office. I could think of a few things that I preferred to working.

My feet carried me straight down the hallway of the history building at the University of Texas, Austin. I was anxious for that uninterrupted hour alone with my boyfriend. It might be a bit taboo that he was also my professor and the advisor for my PhD, but it worked for me.

I reached his office and opened the door. "Mitch, I thought we could—" I stopped mid sentence and stared at what was before me.

Mitch was seated in the chair behind his desk—the very desk I had been fantasizing about. And a tiny blonde undergrad was sitting in his lap. Her skirt was hiked up; I could tell even from my vantage point.

My stomach dropped out of my body. *This could not be happening. I could not be this naive.*

"What the fuck is going on here?" I demanded.

The girl hopped up and straightened out her skirt. "Nothing," she squeaked.

"I was just helping her with some last-minute… assignments," Mitch said.

"You've got to be kidding me," I said, my voice low and menacing. My eyes snapped to the girl. "You should leave. Now."

"Emery," Mitch said consolingly.

"Now!" I yelled.

The girl grabbed her purse and rushed out of the room. I slammed the door shut behind her and glared down at the man I'd thought I loved for the last three years. But looking at him sitting there, adjusting himself, all I saw was a pathetic excuse for a man.

"God, this is embarrassing," I snapped. "I'm leaving. I'm leaving you, I'm leaving the program, and I'm leaving the university. I'm fucking done."

"You can't leave the program, Emery," he said, not acknowledging what else I had said.

"I can, and I will."

"That's ridiculous," he said, pushing back his messed up hair. "You only have a year left."

I shrugged. "Don't give a damn right now. You fucking cheated on me, Mitch."

"Come now, Emery. Do you really believe that?"

"Um…hello? I just walked in on you with Angela! She's an undergrad!"

"You don't know what you saw."

I snorted. "That's rich, coming from you. I'm well aware of what I saw. I doubt it was the first time, too. How many others are there?"

He stood and tried to reach for me, but I pulled away.

"We can make this work, Emery."

"God, do you think I'm an idiot?"

"Oh, Em," he said, straightening his black suit coat. "Don't act so childish."

I fumed at those repulsive words. "I am not acting childish by accusing the man I loved of sleeping with someone else. I'm standing up for what I think is right, and your bullshit routine is far from that. Are you sleeping with other students?"

"Honey, come on."

"You are, aren't you?" I shook my head and retreated. "Wow, I am an idiot. Not only do I really not want to be in academia, but I also really don't want to be with you."

"Emery," he called as I marched toward the door. "It's been three years. You can't do this."

I whipped around. "Tell me you're not fucking anyone else and that I'm the only girl for you."

He ran a shaky hand back through his long blond hair. He thought he was the cool professor, the one everyone could talk to about not just their research problems, but also their life problems. He'd reeled me in that way, and like a fool, I'd been blinded by the nice suits, fancy dinners, and finally finding a man on the same level as me. Turned out…he was just a rat.

When he didn't respond, I scoffed at him. "That's what I thought."

Walking out of his office was one of the most liberating experiences of my life. He deserved to lose his job for what he had done all these years, but I didn't have it in me to go there just yet. I walked into the history department and filled out the appropriate paperwork to withdraw from the program. Maybe, one day, I would want to go back and finish my PhD, but today, I knew that I had come to the end of the line. One too many panic attacks, my first ever prescription for Xanax, and a dissertation topic that seemed perpetually out of reach had done me in.

Screw academia.

I drove my Subaru Forester back to my one-bedroom studio, cursing Austin traffic the whole way. *How was it possible for there to be bumper-to-bumper traffic at all times?*

Three years' worth of neglect had taken over my apartment, and my head ached from just imagining what to do with it all. At that moment, my life was completely open before me. No obligations. No job. No future.

I rolled my eyes at my own ridiculous thoughts and began to stuff half of my closet into the two suitcases I had. An hour later, I tucked my MacBook into my leather bag, remembered to grab my phone and computer charger, and kissed Austin good-bye. I'd eventually have to come back for the rest of my shit, but for now, all I was going to do was kick up the Christmas tunes and drive the six hours home to Lubbock.

The weird thing about Lubbock was, most people had no idea where it was, and when you told them that it was actually not full of tumbleweeds or overrun by the desert, they'd seem surprised. As if that was all there was in west Texas. It was a city of three hundred thousand people, for Christ's sake!

The four years I had been in Norman at the University of Oklahoma, I'd gotten so good at responding to strangers' questions about where I was from that I still hadn't broken the habit of telling people I was from Texas, even when I'd moved *back* to Texas.

It would inevitably be followed up with a, "Where?"

And then I would have to explain, "Lubbock. It's west Texas. Stuff actually exists there. Texas Tech and Buddy Holly."

People would nod, but I didn't think anyone really believed me since they hadn't been to west Texas.

My sister, Kimber, was waiting for me outside when I pulled up to her brand-spanking-new house. She placed a hand on her swollen prego belly, and her four-year-old daughter, Lilyanne, ran around her ankles.

I put my car in park and jumped out in a hurry to scoop up my little niece. "Hey, Lily Bug," I said, twirling her in a circle before swinging her onto my hip.

"Lilies aren't bugs, Auntie Em. Lilies are flowers!"

"That, they are, smarty-pants."

"Hey, Em," Kimber said, pulling me in for a hug.

"Hey, Kimmy."

"Rough day?" she asked.

"You could say that."

I dropped Lilyanne back onto her feet and opened the trunk. Kimber hoisted the smaller suitcase out of the trunk, and I wheeled the larger one into her ginormous house.

"Em! Do you want to see my new dress? It has dinosaurs on it. Dinosaurs say *rawr*!" Lilyanne said.

"Not now, Lily. We have to get Emery into the guest room. Can you show her where to go?" Kimber asked.

Lilyanne's eyes lit up, and she raced for the stairs at lightning speed. "Come on, Auntie Em. I know the way."

Kimber sighed, exhausted. "I'm glad you're here."

"Me, too. She's a handful. But it's good to have her. How else would I be able to find my way around here?" I joked as we made our way up the stairs after Lilyanne. "Seriously, are we in *Beauty and the Beast*? Is there a west wing I should avoid?" I gasped.

Kimber snorted and rolled her eyes. "It's not *that* big."

"Never too big for a library with ladders, of course."

"Of course. We might have one of those."

"I knew it! Please tell me all the dirty romance novels we read in high school are proudly on display now."

Kimber dropped my suitcase in the guest bedroom, which was approximately the same size as my loft back in Austin.

K.A. LINDE

"Noah would kill me," she said with a roll of her eyes. "Most of those books are on my iPad now anyway. I've converted to e-books."

"Fancy," I said, fluttering my fingers at her. "I could use an iPad. Just throwing that out there in case Noah needs gift ideas for Christmas."

Kimber laughed. "God, I've missed you."

I grinned devilishly. Noah worked at the Texas Tech Medical Center. He worked long, long hours and made Scrooge McDuck–level dollar bills. He and Kimber were high school sweethearts and possibly the disgustingly cutest couple I'd ever encountered.

"Come on, Lilyanne," Kimber called. "We have cookies in the oven."

"Cookies?" I asked, my eyes lighting up. "Mom's recipe?"

"Of course. Are you going to go see her?" Kimber asked, as if she didn't care. But I saw her glance nervously in my direction.

It wasn't that I didn't get along with my mother. It was more like…we were the exact same person. So, when we were together, our stubborn heads butted, and everyone ran for the hills. But there weren't hills in Lubbock.

"Yeah…probably."

"Did you even let her know you were coming into town?"

Kimber picked Lilyanne up and dropped her down into a seat by the sprinkles. The timer dinged for the cookies, and Kimber pulled them out of the oven. Fluffy golden brown Christmas cookies, just the way we liked them.

I shot Kimber a sheepish look. "No, but…"

"Gah, Emery! She's going to kill me if you stay here without telling her you're in town. I do not want to deal with that while I'm pregnant."

"I'm going to tell her!" I said, reaching for a cookie.

Kimber slapped my fingers with the spatula. "Those are too hot. Wait for them to cool."

"You don't want a boo-boo," Lilyanne said.

I sucked my finger into my mouth and made a face at my sister. "Fine."

Kimber dropped the subject, and we spent the rest of the afternoon making cookies. Lilyanne and I got to cut out the shapes with Kimber's cookie cutters, and then she placed them on the tray and into the oven. Once they cooled, we iced and added Christmas sprinkles on top of them.

By the time Noah was home, earlier than usual for him, we were covered in flour with sugary-sweet hangovers.

I pulled Noah in for a big hug. "Missed you."

"You, too, Em. I heard you were having some trouble."

My nose wrinkled. "Yeah. Thanks for letting me stay while I figure things out."

"You're always welcome here. It'll be good to have you around for Kimber, too. She's home a lot with this one, and I know she's ready to get back to work."

My sister owned a kick-ass bakery right off of campus called Death by Chocolate that made the best cookies, cupcakes, and doughnuts in town. But, with the new baby on the way, she'd taken a step back and turned more to management, so she could work from home. But her true passion was baking, and I knew she'd love to get back into the thick of things as soon as she could.

"Thanks Noah."

When it was Lilyanne's bedtime, I finally left their house and went to meet my best friend out for a drink.

When I pulled up to Flips, I was shaking from the bitter December cold that had sprung up out of nowhere. I rummaged through my backseat, extracted a black leather jacket, and then dashed across the parking lot.

I handed the bouncer my ID and then pushed through the hipster crowd to the back of the bar. As expected, I found Heidi leaning over a pool table and making eyes at a guy who thought he was going to make some easy money on a game against a chick. His friends stood around with smirks on their face, as they drank Bud Light. Lubbock was big enough that there were still enough idiots for Heidi to hustle, but the regulars steered clear.

"Em!" Heidi called, jumping up and down at my appearance.

"Hey, babe," I said with a wink.

"Guys, I'm going to have to finish this game early. My bestie is here."

The guy's brow furrowed in confusion. She leaned down and knocked the rest of her balls into the holes, hardly paying any attention. He and his friends' jaws dropped, and I just laughed. I'd seen it happen one too many times.

Heidi's dad had owned a pool hall when she was a kid, and her skills were legit. I was pretty sure pool was the start of her love affair with geometry. She'd gotten into civil engineering at Tech, and she now worked at Wright Construction, the largest construction company in the nation. I thought it was a waste of her talent, but she liked to be the only female in a male-dominated industry.

"You hustled us!" the guy yelled.

She fluttered her long eyelashes at him and grinned. "Pay up!"

He tossed a couple of twenties on the pool table and stormed away like a sore loser. Heidi counted them out and then stuffed them into the back pocket of her destroyed jeans.

"Emery, baby," Heidi said, flinging her arms around my neck. "I have missed your face."

"Missed you, too. You buying?"

She laughed, removed one of the guy's twenties from her pocket, and threw it on the table. "Peter, shots for me and Emery!"

Peter nodded his head at me. "Hey, prom queen."

"That was Kimber. Not me!"

"Oh, right," he said, as if vaguely remembering that had happened to my sister and not me. "You dated that Wright brother though, right?"

I breathed out heavily through my nose. Nine and a half years since Landon Wright had broken up with me on graduation day, and I was still recognized as the girl who'd dated a Wright brother. *Awesome.*

"Yeah," I grumbled, "a long time ago."

"Speaking of the Wright brothers," Heidi said, pushing a shot of tequila and lime toward me and adding salt to the space between her thumb and finger.

"Nope."

"Sutton Wright is getting married on Saturday."

"She is?" I asked in surprise. "Isn't she still at Tech?"

Heidi shrugged. "She found *the* one. It's kind of a rush job. They only got engaged on Halloween."

"Shotgun?" I asked.

The entire Wright family was riddled with scandal. With billions of dollars to throw around and no moral code, it was easy for anyone to get in trouble. But the five Wright siblings took it to a new level.

"No idea really, but I'd guess so. Either way, who cares? I am not missing a chance for an open bar and a swank party."

"Have fun with that," I said dryly.

"I'm taking you with me, bitch," Heidi said.

She raised her shot glass to me, and I warily eyed her before raising mine to meet hers.

After I downed the tequila and sucked on the lime, I finally responded, "You know I have a rule about Wright siblings, right?"

"I know you've been jaded against the lot of them after Landon, yes."

"Oh no, you *know* it's not just Landon."

"Yeah, so they're all a bag of dicks. Who cares? Let's go get drunk on their dime and make fun of them." Heidi seductively

9

placed her hand on my thigh and raised her eyebrows up and down. "I'll put out."

I snorted and smacked her arm. "You're such a whore."

"You love me. I'll get you a new dress. We'll have fun."

I shrugged. *What could it hurt?* "Fine. Why not?"

Two

Jensen

"My whore sister is pregnant again, and this time, she wants to keep it," I said to no one in particular as I expertly knotted the red bow tie at my neck.

"Yeah, that's kind of the point of the wedding today, Jensen," my brother Austin said. His bow tie still hung loose around his neck, and he was already on his third glass of whiskey. At twenty-nine years old, he was already shaping up to be the one who tarnished the Wright name. If he wasn't careful, he'd end up just like our father—a raving alcoholic up until the moment he was buried six feet under.

"Can't believe we're fucking doing this today."

"She's in love, man," Austin said.

He raised his glass to me, and I fought the urge to call him a sentimental dick.

"He's just looking for a paycheck. A paycheck that I'm going to have to provide because there's no way he'll be able to take care of our little sister." I finally got the bow tie straight and turned back to Austin.

"Have a drink. You're being too uptight about the whole thing."

I glared at him. I *had* to be uptight about this shit. I only thirty-two and I was the one in charge of the business. I was the one who had been left with all the money and responsibilities to take care of my four younger siblings. If that made me uptight, then fuck him.

But I didn't say any of that. I just strode across the room and refilled his glass of whiskey. "Just have another drink, Austin. You remind me so much of Dad."

"Fuck you, Jensen. Can't you just be happy for Sutton?"

"Yeah, Jensen," Morgan said. She stepped into the room in a floor-length red dress with her dark hair pulled up off her face. Her smile was magnetic, as usual.

Morgan was only twenty-five and the most normal one of my family. We all had our issues, but Morgan gave me the least amount of grief, which made her my favorite.

"Don't you start in on this, too," I told her.

"Sutton is her own person. She always has been. She does whatever she wants to do, no matter what anyone says," Morgan said. Taking the drink out of Austin's hand, she downed a large gulp. "Don't you remember that time she decided she was a princess superhero? Mom couldn't get her out of a tutu, cape, and crown for almost a year."

I laughed at the memory. Sutton had been a handful. *Fuck, she still was a handful.* Twenty-one and already getting married.

"Yeah, I remember. I'd be happier about the whole thing with what's his face if he wasn't such a completely incompetent dipshit," I told her.

"His name is Maverick," Austin cut in. "And you can't fucking talk, man. Your name is Jen*sen*," he drawled my name out, exaggerating the second syllable. "It's a fucking weird name, too."

"It's not a weird name. Maverick is a douche name, especially since he goes by Maverick and not Mav or Rick or something."

Morgan rolled the big brown eyes she'd inherited from our mother. "Let's just drop it, shall we? Where is Landon anyway?"

As if on cue, my twenty-seven-year-old younger brother Landon schlepped into the room. His wife, Miranda, followed in his footsteps in the same dress as Morgan. My eyes slid over to Morgan. She returned the look, saying a million things in that one glance.

"Hey, Landon," Austin said when he realized neither of us were going to say shit since Miranda was here.

"Hey," Landon said, sinking into a seat next to Austin.

He looked beat.

Landon was the only one of us who didn't work for the company. Austin and Morgan both worked for me at Wright Construction, and Sutton would once she graduated—or that had been the plan before she got pregnant. Now, I'd probably have to hire *Maverick* in her place, so she could take care of that baby.

Landon had graduated from Stanford—unlike the rest of our family who had attended Texas Tech since the school's founding in the 1920s—but instead of putting his business degree to good use, he had joined the professional golf circuit. That was when he'd met Miranda. They'd dated for only six months before he proposed. Just like we were doing with Sutton, we'd all sworn that Miranda was pregnant and using him for his money. But when she hadn't had a baby nine months later, we had all been fucking baffled.

It was one thing to marry a girl like Miranda for a baby. You had to take care of the kid. That always fucking came first. No matter who the mother was. It was *another* thing to marry a girl like Miranda because you liked her—or, fuck, loved her.

"Well, what a happy reunion this is," Miranda said. She eyed us all like she was trying to figure out how to wiggle more money out of the Wright family. There might as well have been actual dollar signs in her eyes.

"Miranda," Austin said. He stood and gave her a quick hug. "Good to see you."

"Thanks, Austin," she said with a giggle.

Austin, the peacekeeper. That used to be Landon but not anymore. Not since the wicked bitch had sunk her claws into him.

As a man who had been through a brutal divorce already, I couldn't figure out why Landon hadn't handed over the paperwork. Being around Miranda for a solid five minutes was too much for me, and it made Morgan lose her shit. I hated that Landon always looked like someone had kicked his puppy.

I'd been there. I knew what that was like. I did not want him to have to go through the same thing I had. Or end up with the same consequences.

"Come on, Morgan," Miranda trilled. "I'm sure Sutton will need us with the other bridesmaids."

"I'm sure. Why don't you head over there and tell her I'll be just a minute?" Morgan said, using the slow voice she typically reserved for small children.

Miranda shot her an evil glare. Or maybe that was her face. I could never tell.

Then, she grabbed Landon's arm. "I'll see you at the ceremony, honey. Kiss?"

Landon turned his face up to her, and she latched on to his lips like a leech.

"I love you."

"I love you, too," he said automatically.

When she was gone, we all breathed a sigh of relief.

"Bless her heart," Morgan drawled.

"Y'all," Landon groaned, "don't."

Morgan started humming the theme song for the Wicked Witch of the West.

"Are you ever going to give it a break, Morgan?" Landon asked.

"No, probably not."

"We've been married for two years now."

"I can't believe you're staying at a hotel," I said.

Landon shrugged and reached for the bottle of whiskey, pouring himself a glass. "Miranda wanted to stay downtown."

"And, before we start World War III by bringing up Miranda," Austin cut in, "I feel like someone should grab Sutton. We're about to suffer through a couple of hours of pictures with eighteen of her closest friends. Might have some time, just the five of us."

"I limited her to nine bridesmaids," I said.

"That's a limit?" Morgan asked with a huff. "I don't think I even like nine people."

"You weren't in a sorority either," I reminded her.

"I don't like people. I certainly wouldn't like to pay for new sisters. Sutton is above and beyond."

Austin and Landon laughed, and that sound finally made me relax. It was nice to have all my siblings back in one place. With Sutton in school and Landon living on some beach in Florida where he could golf year-round, it just wasn't the same. Some people thought the Wright siblings were…odd. They thought we were too close, but we had to be. With both parents gone, we were all each other had.

"You want to go see if she's decent?" I asked Morgan.

She groaned. "This is what I get for being the only other girl."

I opened the door for her, and she hiked up her dress and stormed out. I knew she wasn't happy about having to spend the next twelve-plus hours with seven other girls she didn't know or like, plus Miranda, but there was nothing I could do about it. Trying to convince Sutton to do anything was like trying to move a mountain. She might be tiny, but she was a firecracker.

I grabbed the bottle of whiskey out of Landon's hands before he and Austin could finish it. Leaving the two of them alone with alcohol would guarantee a disaster. Then, I rummaged through my bag and found the group of shot glasses I'd brought with me. I was setting them up right when Sutton returned with Morgan.

"Hey, y'all!" Sutton said, flouncing into the room with a skip in her step. "Morgan said you needed me for something important."

I hefted the bottle of Four Roses Single Barrel whiskey at her. "Your brothers tried to drink the bottle before you got here, but I thought, a toast?"

She sagged in disappointment. "You know I can't have that."

I grinned devilishly and then grabbed a bottle of apple juice that I'd tucked away, knowing she couldn't drink. "How about this?"

"Yes! Make mine a double," she told me.

I laughed and poured out the shots. She was definitely part of the family. Addictive personalities ran in the Wright line. I had my fair share of vices, but I was lucky that alcohol wasn't one of them.

"*Annnd*," Sutton drawled out, "while I have you here, Jensen, I just wanted to run one teensy little thing by you."

She widened her big blue eyes like she was about to ask me for a million dollars. She'd been giving me that same look for years. Once, it was a blowout sweet sixteen to rival that TV show *My Super Sweet 16*. Another time, it was for a trip to Europe with all her sorority sisters. I couldn't imagine what *more* she could want from me right now. We'd put together her wedding in six weeks, and she was flying first class to Cabo for two weeks. Still, she was upset that I wouldn't give her the jet.

"Oh no," I muttered. "What is it?"

"Look, I was talking to Maverick last night, and I *know* that he already signed the prenup, but——"

My face instantly hardened. "No."

"I didn't even ask anything!"

"I know what you're going to ask, and the answer is no."

"But it's silly, Jensen. Really! He's the love of my life. We're going to spend eternity together. A prenup is ridiculous. It's a bad way to enter a marriage. If you're thinking about how it's going to end before it even starts, then what does that say about a person?"

Morgan, Austin, and Landon had all gone still behind her. They could probably read the fury on my face. I didn't want to blow up on her on her wedding day, but I was dangerously close to doing so.

"You are worth a small fortune, Sutton. And I don't give a fuck who you're marrying. You get a prenup to protect yourself *in case* something happens. Thinking about the future is a way to ensure that you are not getting scammed. No matter how much somebody loves you."

"But, Jensen——" Sutton said, trying to reason with me.

"Sutton," Austin said, cutting in, "do you really want to do this right now? I mean, Jensen and Landon both had a prenup. No one marries a Wright without it."

"That's right," I said, silently thanking Austin for his backup.

"Plus, you're only twenty-one," Morgan said. "Who knows what could happen?"

"Oh, wow. Thanks, Morgan," Sutton grumbled.

"I didn't mean that Maverick isn't 'the one,'" she said with air quotes. "I just mean, Jensen didn't think he'd divorce Vanessa under any circumstances and look what happened."

I gritted my teeth at the mention of my ex-wife. Vanessa Hendricks wasn't a name that was usually brought up in polite conversation. But she certainly was a cautionary tale as to why a prenup was necessary.

"If Maverick really wants to throw out the prenup, I'd be happy to talk to him about it," I said to Sutton with raised eyebrows.

She rolled her eyes. "I'm not that stupid. You'd scare him half to death."

"Well, if he's trying to take you for your money, then he'd deserve it."

"Okay, fine. I get it. I just thought I'd ask. Maverick and I had a long talk about it."

"I bet," Landon muttered under his breath.

"Anyway, shots!" Sutton cried.

I passed out shots of whiskey to Austin, Landon, and Morgan and then handed Sutton the shot of apple juice.

I raised my glass high. "To Sutton, on the happiest day of her life and to many more amazing years to come."

We all tipped back our glasses. The whiskey burned all the way down my throat, but I just grinned at my siblings.

The world felt right when we were all together. No matter what challenges we might face, at least we had each other.

Three

Emery

"Heidi, what are you doing to my hair?" I asked.

Heidi laughed hysterically behind me. "I'm making you look presentable, Em. You just wait. It will come together at the end."

She threaded a few more strands of my hair into this crazy braid.

If Heidi and I hadn't been best friends since kindergarten and if I hadn't known all her deep, dark secrets, I was sure she would have dumped me for the cool crowd. Despite her obsession with geometry, her all black attire, and her pool-slinging skills, she had been a cheerleader and obsessed with popularity.

My sister, Kimber, had been the girlie girl—prom queen, homecoming queen, voted most attractive. The whole shebang.

But not me. Though I never had a problem with finding a date, I had not been the typical teenager. I had played varsity soccer my freshman year, I'd skateboarded circles around the dude-bros in town, and I had made up my mind that my dream job was to become a vampire slayer.

At the time, Landon Wright had tested my friendship with Heidi. *Why would the star quarterback have any interest in the loner tomboy?* I hadn't understood it any more than Heidi.

I closed my eyes and pushed the thoughts aside. I was only thinking about Landon because I knew he would be at the wedding this afternoon. He hadn't crossed my mind in a long time, and I hadn't seen him in longer.

"I swear, it's going to be cute," Heidi assured me.

"I know. I trust you," I said. "I just cannot believe that you talked me into going to this wedding with you. Is it going to be like a high school reunion? I don't know if I'm prepared for that."

"It's not a high school reunion," Heidi said. "I got invited because I work for the Wrights and, like, half of the company was invited. It's going to be a big wedding. I doubt you'll even run into him."

"I am not worried about running into Landon. It's been almost ten years since we broke up," I told her.

"Didn't he get married anyway?" Heidi asked.

She yanked on my hair, and I winced.

"I don't follow him. You would know more than I would." I glared at Heidi in the mirror. "Stop giving me that look. Do you know how many guys I've dated since Landon? No, you don't. Because I can't even remember, but it's a lot. And I'm currently sitting right here because of guy trouble."

"I just know you and Landon," Heidi said dreamily. "Perfect high school couple. That was, like, the only thing that you beat Kimber in. You and Landon got Best Couple in the yearbook."

I rolled my eyes. "Please stop reminiscing about high school, or I'll vomit."

"You were cute," Heidi added.

"If you think for a minute that something is going to happen with him at this wedding, you're out of your mind. Not only is he married, but he'll also be there *with* his wife. And, as of today, I'm officially swearing off men."

Heidi laughed. "Yeah, right, Em," she said. "You are boy crazy and always have been. Even when you were our little skater girl."

"Look, Mitch fooled me into thinking that he loved me. He was, like, fifteen years older than me and a total player. I'm almost certain he was sleeping with an undergrad," I told her. "I mean…how bad is my judgment skewed that I ended up with someone like that? I think I just need to be single for a while."

"All right," Heidi said with a shake of her head. Her blonde hair swayed back and forth down against the middle of her back in an amazing wave that she'd somehow created. "More for me tonight."

"All for you."

Heidi stepped back and observed her creation. She messed with my bangs and then added one more curl into the end. "There. What do you think?"

I looked in the mirror and hardly recognized myself. While I wasn't still a tomboy, when I felt down, I'd tend to fall back on old habits, as in no makeup and messy bun galore. But Heidi had practically digitally remastered my face. My makeup was flawless, and the shimmer shadow brought out the green in my eyes. My dark hair was braided into a crown atop my head that wove into a low side ponytail with curls.

"You have a gift," I told her. "You've made me look human again."

"Go put on your dress," Heidi said. "I can't wait to see it all together!"

"All right. All right. I'm going."

I shimmied into the dress that Heidi had picked out for me from a boutique downtown.

I stepped out of the closet. Heidi whistled.

"You're ridiculous."

But I liked the dress. Sutton's wedding was formal attire, and it was hard enough to find a dress I liked, let alone a full-length dress, but Heidi had done it. The dress was black with a gold shimmer layer underneath that accentuated my figure when I walked. Everything came together with cute peep-toes. Benefit of a winter wedding in Texas was that it would reach the seventies during the day if we were lucky. The weather was pretty erratic.

"You are so getting laid in that dress," Heidi said.

I dramatically rolled my eyes. "No boys. This is a no-fly zone."

"You won't be saying that tonight when you're getting fucked. All I'm saying," Heidi said. "Hopefully, it's Landon Wright. That would be so full circle."

"Don't even say that. If I see him, I will run in the opposite direction," I told her.

Heidi grinned, as if laughing at her own inside joke.

"All right, all right," Heidi said when she noticed my glare. "No boys. I got it. If Landon approaches you, I'll distract him. I still have some cheer moves."

She kicked her leg and nearly touched her nose. Then, she spun around in some intricate dance move. I wasn't even sure how it was possible that she was this flexible.

"Oh my God, if you do that in your dress, you are going to be more than a distraction for Landon. You are going to rip your dress in half for the entire party to see."

Heidi laughed and shrugged. "I'm going to get dressed, and then we can go."

A few minutes later, Heidi reappeared in a floor-length mermaid dress in the deepest, darkest purple. She shimmied over to me and winked. "Come on, sexy. You're my date tonight. Let's get Kimber to take a picture of us!"

We hurried into Kimber's bedroom, and Kimber agreed to take the shot. Heidi handed her phone to Kimber. Then, she threw one hand up in the air and placed the other on her hip while making a pouty face. I pointed my finger at the camera while kissing Heidi on the cheek. When we got a look at it, I just giggled with my girls. It was the most ridiculous and the most *us* picture in existence.

"This is so going on Instagram. Damn, it's good to have you back," Heidi said.

"Use a filter," I insisted.

"You just filtered your face," Kimber said, pointing out all the makeup on my face. "You don't need a filter."

"My life needs a filter," Heidi muttered.

Heidi posted the picture and then grabbed her clutch. She stuffed her phone and ID inside. I hated carrying a purse anytime, especially when I had to navigate a dress and heels. So, I gave Heidi my phone and ID, who just rolled her eyes and added them to her bag.

"You really don't mind dropping us off, Kimber?" I asked.

"Not a problem. I just want to hear all about the antics when y'all are done."

"I'll live tweet you," Heidi said.

"Oh my God, you are not going to be on your phone all night," Kimber said. "You should enjoy yourself. Get drunk and make a mistake or two."

"Done and done," Heidi said with a wink. "Let's get out of here."

We all piled into Kimber's car. The traffic around the Historic Baker Building, a venue in downtown Lubbock, was outrageous. And that was saying something because the only time traffic got this bad was on Texas Tech game days.

"How many people did Sutton invite?" I asked, craning my head out the window.

"It looks like everyone she's ever met," Heidi said.

"Or the whole freaking city," I grumbled.

"Maybe we should just hop out here," Heidi suggested.

"Be safe," Kimber said. "Take some condoms for the kids."

Heidi rolled her eyes.

I laughed as I hopped out of the SUV. "Thanks, Kimber."

"Bye, babe!" Heidi called, following in my footsteps.

She slammed the door, and we darted through traffic and onto the sidewalk. The Baker Building was a block or two down the street, and already, I was cursing myself for wearing high heels. They had looked so adorable in the store. Now, they were little torture devices.

Who invented these?

Men.

Men invented these to torture us and make our butts look awesome.

Thank God my butt looked this awesome. Otherwise, I'd be taking these off so fast.

"Stop hobbling," Heidi said, strutting around in her heels like they had been made for her.

"I'm not hobbling. I just don't think I'll be able to wear these all night."

"We'll take them off once we get to the reception. But, right now, you need them to be able to see."

I smacked her arm. "I'm not that short. I can see just fine. You're just super freaking tall."

"Well, we can't both be perfect, Em."

"Oh my God, why are you my best friend again?" I asked.

"Beats me," she said with a giggle. Then, she looped our arms together and strode up to the entrance of the Baker Building.

The place really was packed. At the entrance, a dozen ushers were escorting people to seats, and people milled about as they waited for their chance. I recognized about ten people in the span of a minute and slowly angled my body so as not to have to engage with anyone.

Eventually, it was our turn, and Heidi and I wrangled one usher for the both of us.

"Bride or groom?" the boy asked. He had ice-blue eyes and a real Southern drawl. He was probably in a fraternity at Tech and had gotten coaxed into this with the promise of free booze.

"Bride," Heidi said. "We're friends of the bride."

"Cool. How do you know Sutton?" he asked as he walked us, arm in arm, down the aisle.

"We grew up together," Heidi said.

When I raised my eyebrows, she shrugged.

"Family friend. Got it."

Then, he walked us right up to the third row. I felt myself panicking. *Why were we so close? Couldn't he have given us different seats? I did not want to be this near the Wright siblings. I was here for the booze and had been promised a good time.*

"Family friends up front," he said with a smile, gesturing for us to take our seats.

Heidi smiled brightly at him and then took the second seat inside.

"You're leaving me on the end?" I hissed at her.

"Yeah. Sit your ass down."

"This was not part of the deal, Martin," I spat at her as I sat down.

"Ohhh, using my last name. I'm real scared."

"You owe me big for this."

"Just enjoy it, Em. It'll be over in, like, fifteen minutes, and then we can drink for free all night."

"Right. Priorities," I muttered just as the doors finally closed behind us.

As the remaining guests took their seats, my eyes traveled the room. It was elaborately decorated with flowers attached to every chair and shimmery curtains draped across the entire front of the room. White lights that twinkled down on the attendees were strung on the second-floor balcony.

Softly, a string quartet began playing classical music, and the lights dimmed. I looked back to the front just as the pastor stepped out from a back room with the groom and a long line of groomsmen following in his wake.

My eyes scanned the length of the line. *Nine. He had nine groomsmen. Holy fuck!*

There were so many of them that they had to stand in two lines.

And the last three men in the line were very distinct and downright gorgeous.

The Wright brothers—Jensen, Austin, and finally, Landon.

The party had arrived.

Four

Emery

I purposely turned my attention away from the brothers before me. I really didn't want to look at any of them anyway. Luckily for me, the bridesmaids started walking down the aisle. Then, the traditional "Canon in D" began, we all stood, and Sutton walked down the aisle. I was pretty sure, the last time I'd seen Sutton in person, she was only about twelve years old. But it was shocking to me, now that she was all grown up, how much she looked like Landon.

All of them looked the same—dark hair, pouty lips, athletic figure. Though they had their differences, too. Just not enough noticeable differences. Anyone could see they were related.

Heidi leaned over to me to whisper into my ear, "Ten bucks, she's a crier."

"She's pregnant. She's definitely a crier," I muttered back.

I tried to hold my laughter in as Sutton finally reached the front of the room and immediately burst into tears. Her groom took her hands in his and grinned down at her.

The pastor raised his hands. "You may all be seated," he said.

I dropped into my seat and waited for this whole thing to be over.

"We are gathered here today to join Sutton Marie Wright to Maverick Wayne Johnson in holy matrimony."

My eyes rounded, and I glanced at Heidi. We had an entire conversation without saying a word.

Maverick Wayne.

Maverick?

That's his name?

Holy fuck.

Yeah.

Yeah.

She must be here for his Johnson.

I cracked up and had to cover it with a cough when a few people turned to glare at me. Heidi tried to hide her own laughter by reaching for her purse and digging around for her phone.

The rest of the ceremony progressed just like any other I'd ever been to. If you'd been to one wedding, you'd been to them all.

Yada, yada, yada.

"I do."

Yada, yada, yada.

"Till death do us part."

Yada, yada, yada.

"You may kiss the bride."

I applauded methodically with the rest of the crowd and silently prayed for some really good champagne to make up for this. Champagne cured everything.

The music started up again. The end of their fifteen minutes was up. On to bigger and better things. Like an open bar and a dessert table.

Maverick took Sutton's hand in his, and they strode down the aisle, beaming like streetlamps. Each bridesmaid walked forward in her long, silky red dress, latched on to the arm of one of the groomsmen. With nine people on each side of the bridal party, it was taking forever. One after the other after the other.

The only bridesmaid I recognized was Morgan, who was the maid of honor. She was only two years younger than me and Heidi and had run in the popular crowd, of course. She was easy to figure out because she looked exactly the same as she had in high school. Unfortunately for her, she was on the arm of some leering frat boy. The other girls, I gathered, were Sutton's sorority sisters.

Then, finally, it was on to the Wright brothers.

Jensen moved forward first. He held his arm out for the girl who was blushing as bright as a cherry tomato. She looped her arm in his, and I was trying so hard not to roll my eyes. I had been that girl once. I knew what that was like. Back in the day, Landon had made me feel that swoony, over-the-top, oh-my-God feeling from having the attention of a Wright brother. And I wasn't that type of girl either. Now, it felt ridiculous. Money couldn't buy happiness, and it sure didn't fix shit when the guy broke your heart.

I was so deeply entrenched in my own thoughts that I didn't realize I was staring. At Jensen Wright. And he was staring right back at me.

Why? Why, oh God, did Heidi put me on the end? And why is he looking at me like that?

He hadn't even moved yet. He was just standing there, staring at me with those dark brown eyes. And I didn't know what he was thinking or what he was doing. Except for making a complete fool of himself because, surely, he needed to start walking right now. Like right fucking now.

Synapses must have fired in his brain again because he gradually moved the girl forward. And, just when I thought I'd gotten past that look and away from his penetrating gaze, he turned around. He did a motherfucking double take. Right there in front of everyone at his own sister's wedding, he turned around and looked at me.

What world am I living in?

I didn't think I breathed normally again until he looked away and proceeded down the aisle. By then, Austin had already passed me, and I didn't even get a chance to see Landon and his wife. And that was the only thing I'd been interested in.

So what? I was an ex-girlfriend. I had every right to stalk his wife to see if she was prettier than me.

Heidi shook my shoulder, jarring me back to reality. "Did you just get eye-fucked by Jensen Wright?" she gasped.

An older woman sitting in front of us glared at her for the language. She hadn't exactly been quiet.

"No. Nope. No, I did not," I told her. I was still trying to figure out what had happened. Because nothing I could conjure up was making any sense.

"You so did. You so, so did!" Heidi said.

The two aisles in front of us left first, and then Heidi was pushing me out of the aisle, all while whispering in my ear about how excited she was. "Do you remember mooning over him in high school? He was, like, this hottie college guy, a totally unattainable god. Like Zeus on Mount Olympus. Or maybe we just wanted to get on his lightning bolt, if you know what I mean."

"Heidi, God, you're so embarrassing."

"Em, just think about Jensen when we were in high school. He belonged in a magazine."

"I was dating his brother."

"But *before* that," she insisted.

"Okay. I *might* remember staying at your house a time or two…"

"Or ten."

"Where we talked about him being hot."

"Yes. And he has gone from hot to one damn fine wine. The bottle just gets better with age, honey," Heidi said, knocking her hip into mine.

"Are you really suggesting I hook up with Jensen Wright at his sister's wedding when I *dated* his brother?" I asked with wide eyes.

Heidi laughed. "Getting ahead of yourself, aren't you? I didn't say hook up with him. You said that. Are you thinking about that?"

"No," I spat.

Because, no. Seriously. That would never happen.

I was sworn off of the Wright brothers. None of that was going to happen. No fucking way. Jensen had probably just… seen a bug on my shoulder or something. That was all it had been because his interest would be illogical.

I was his brother's ex-girlfriend.

I was…*me.*

We made it to the reception space a few minutes later. The room was teeming with waiters in pressed tuxedos, handling silver trays topped with hors d'oeuvres. I plucked a fancy crab cake from a passing waiter and headed straight to the bar.

"Champagne, please," Heidi said, flashing the bartender a smile.

I held up two fingers as I took a bite out of the crab cake. *Holy fuck, this was delicious. Wow. Who the hell was the caterer? I glanced around and found my answer. West Table. Of course. Only the Wrights would hire catering from the most expensive restaurant in town.*

"We need more of these," I told Heidi when she handed me two glasses of champagne.

I had no shame as I double-fisted the drinks.

Heidi laughed and nodded toward the tables. "Let's find where we're sitting."

We wandered over to the table with the list of names elaborately tacked up on a rustic window.

Heidi plucked her name off the distressed clothespin. "We're table twelve. My lucky number."

"That's just because Brandon McCain wore that number on the football team all through high school."

"Okay, fine," Heidi said with a shrug. "It's my get-lucky number."

I snorted. "That's rich."

"Here we are." She dropped her purse down right in front of her name. "Heidi Martin and guest. That's you."

"Who else are we with?" I asked.

Heidi and I scanned the names.

I shrugged. "I don't know any of these people."

"Work people," she said. "But at least we have Julia. Julia Banner. She's cool. You'll like her."

"I've never heard you mention her before."

"She's new. You know how it goes with the newbies," she said with a wry expression before downing half of her glass of champagne. "I like to make sure they're going to stick around Lubbock for more than a year. So many burned friendships with people who move here and then relocate immediately. We'll see if she survives, and then I'll decide if we bring her in."

"You act like we're in a gang," I told her with a shake of my head.

Heidi leaned over and conspiratorially whispered, "We are."

I laughed despite myself. God, I had missed her so much. My life had not been the same without her. No matter that I'd spent all those years in Oklahoma and then Austin, I never found a friendship to rival Heidi's. I was certain I never would.

We spent the next forty-five minutes downing glasses of champagne and eating as many of those little crab cakes as we could get our hands on. By the time the family and bridal party were announced into the room and Sutton and Maverick made their big appearance, Heidi and I were each one drink away from wasted. It was good that we immediately launched into dinner so that I could pad my drinking belly with carbs to survive the rest of the night.

By the time they were finished with the regular bouts of wedding festivities, including—*God help us all*—a choreographed dance with the bride and her sorority-sister bridesmaids *for* the groom before launching into a rehearsed first dance, I was ready to hit the bar again. If I ever had to sit through something like that again without another drink, I was sure I would drop dead.

"Bleach." Heidi giggled into my ear. "I need bleach for my eyes."

I laughed hysterically, probably louder than necessary, as we walked back to the bar. Other people had gotten up to join in on the dancing, and that meant one thing—more champagne. I was going to have a killer headache in the morning, but whatever. It would be worth it.

Heidi meandered us back over to her work crowd, and I stood with my back to the dancing catastrophe going on behind me. Julia did seem pretty chill. She was almost as tall as Heidi with mahogany-brown hair to her shoulders, and she had on a pretty green dress. I was just figuring out more about her job as the head of HR when Heidi's face broke into a smile in front of me.

Not good.

"Landon!" Heidi called.

She waved at him, and I wanted to bury my face in my hands and disappear. Sometimes, my best friend was the worst.

"Hey Heidi," Landon said, appearing at my side. He leaned forward and pulled her into a hug. "Good to see you as always."

"Congratulations on your latest PGA win," Heidi said with a smile.

"Thanks. I appreciate that. I've had a pretty good year."

And there I stood as they talked about his normal year, as if I didn't exist. I was less than a foot away from him, and he hadn't said a word to me. He was engrossed in his conversation with Heidi.

With a deep breath, I chanced a glance at him. He looked...exactly the same. Except not.

Same tall body with chiseled features. Same clean-cut look with the dark hair and puppy-dog eyes. But he looked drained and downtrodden. The last time I'd seen him was at the stupid five-year high school reunion party that Heidi had forced me into going to because she had been the student body vice president. I'd gone in protest and reverted to my Vans skate shoes and oversize T-shirt. Heidi had hated it. But Landon had looked as sharp as ever. He hadn't lost his luster then. I wondered what had happened.

I seemed to have missed part of the conversation while staring at him...or maybe it was due to my buzz. But Landon was now holding his hand out to me. I furrowed my brows and stared at it.

"Sorry. I don't believe we've met," he said with his classic nonchalant attitude.

Heidi laughed next to me, but I couldn't even turn to look at her. *Is this happening?*

"Seriously, Landon?" I drawled with disdain.

Landon's eyes widened, and he instantly dropped his hand. "Emery?"

"In the flesh."

He opened his mouth like a fish out of water. It was nice to see a flustered Wright brother. "I didn't even recognize you."

"Um...thanks?" I couldn't decide if that was an insult.

My ex-boyfriend couldn't even recognize me. *Awesome.*

I finally turned to face Heidi. She looked like she was about to combust.

"How much makeup am I wearing?"

"No, I'm sorry. That was rude," Landon said, reeling it back in. "I recognized your voice right away. At least, the way you said my name. I just...wasn't expecting you to be here, is all."

"Yeah, I showed up with Heidi at the last minute."

Landon nodded, but he was still staring at me, as if I were a strange lab rat he was about to dissect. "Are you back in town for the holidays?"

"Maybe permanently."

"Permanently?" he said with raised eyebrows.

I shrugged. "We'll see. I'm just back from college at the moment."

"Huh. Who would have guessed you would come back to Lubbock?"

And, right then and there, I remembered why I'd wanted to punch him in his pretty face. He was the one who had left me and made me feel like a pariah in my own hometown. He couldn't turn the tables around on me, as if I were the one who had left on my own.

But, instead, I just giggled through the champagne buzz.

"I'm pretty sure, no one. Ever," I said dryly.

"There you are, honey," a woman said, walking up behind Landon and latching on to his arm. She was taller than me in heels with a bleach-blonde bob and glamorous makeup. She was good-looking in an overdone sort of way. "I've been looking for you."

"Oh, Miranda," Landon said, his face falling. "I was just talking to some old friends from high school."

"Well, introduce me, lover boy. Your friends are my friends, of course."

I caught Landon's grimace, and suddenly, his downtrodden expression made sense if he had to deal with her every day.

"Y'all, this is my wife, Miranda. Miranda, this is Heidi and"—he cleared his throat and apologetically glanced at me—"Emery."

Miranda eyed me up and down, as if she were sizing me up for a Miss America competition. "Emery. Like...Emery?"

"The one and only," I muttered.

"Your ex-girlfriend is here, and you didn't even tell me?" Miranda hissed.

"He didn't know I would be here," I said, stepping in for him for a reason I couldn't fathom. "I came with a friend."

Miranda didn't seem to hear me, or she didn't care. She turned on her heel and fled in the opposite direction.

Landon rolled his eyes and then scowled. "Sorry, y'all. I've got to..." He nodded his head after Miranda and then jogged to catch up with her.

My eyes widened with shock. Heidi's mouth was hanging open.

"Wow, what a bitch!" Heidi said.

"You're telling me."

"At least we know one thing."

"What's that?"

"You're way prettier!" Heidi said, holding up her glass for a toast.

Five

Jensen

The hardest part of the night was over, and now, I could finally have another drink. Dealing with Sutton had been harder than I'd anticipated, and the whiskey bottle was calling to me stronger than normal.

Or maybe it was that woman who had been seated in the third row. I didn't know where the hell she had come from, but damn! Long dark hair, perfect legs spilling out of the slit in her dress, gorgeous mouth that had been begging me to kiss her. I had decided within three seconds that she was the hottest person in the room, and it had taken everything in me not to ditch the bridesmaid on my arm. I'd wanted to escort her straight out of the room and into my bed.

It had been a while…a long while…since I had that kind of reaction to anyone in Lubbock. Dating here was impossible, and since I did business all over the country, it was easier to meet people on the road. So, maybe she didn't even live in Lubbock. I sure hoped not. Made it much more difficult to date when everyone knew the precise dollar amount you were worth and the dirty business with my ex.

Here was to hoping she wasn't a local I'd somehow missed in my thirty-something years here.

I kept a stash of good liquor with me and poured myself a double out of a whiskey bottle that Austin had almost handled all on his own. He was out in the center of all those sorority girls, probably deciding which one or two or three he should bring home with him. But my eyes were searching out the brunette.

I nodded my head at Morgan, who was talking to Austin's best friend, Patrick.

"Hey, man!" Patrick said.

We shook hands and clapped each other on the back. I'd known Patrick forever. He was practically family. And, if Morgan didn't stop mooning over him, he'd end up as family for real.

"Hey, Pat. What did you think of the ceremony?" I asked.

Patrick cracked a grin. "Typical Sutton."

"That is the damn truth."

"She seems happy at least," Morgan interjected. Her eyes were glued on our younger sister, who was at the center of the dance party.

"She always looks like that," I said.

"Fact," Patrick agreed.

"Oh, shit," Morgan groaned.

I followed her gaze and saw Miranda storming across the room with Landon on her tail. Pretty common occurrence honestly. That was what their relationship always fucking looked like. I still did not understand how that idiot had ended up with her. And I hated that my failed marriage wasn't warning enough for him.

"I'm going to go check on him," Morgan said with a sigh.

"Just leave them," I insisted. "Your hatred of Miranda will only make it worse."

Morgan grinned wickedly. "Will it? Well then, I'll just be a minute."

I shook my head at my evil sister and watched her stalk out of the room toward Landon and Miranda. I wouldn't wish Miranda upon my worst enemy, let alone my brother. But, for a while now, Morgan and I had been on Operation Miranda, which consisted of seeing how far we could push Landon into divorcing her.

But, despite my brother's issues, my mind was still on that girl. There were hundreds of people in attendance for Sutton's wedding. *She* could be anywhere. I just needed to find her.

"Oh no," Patrick said.

I raised an eyebrow in question.

"You've got that look on your face."

"What look?" I asked.

"The one you get in the boardroom. It's the same one you get chasing pussy."

I grunted at Patrick. He wasn't wrong. "I hope she's as big of a challenge as the Tarman merger I'm working on right now."

Patrick laughed in that unabashed way of his. "I doubt it. You're a fucking Wright, man. Girls are not a challenge."

My grin returned at that. "We'll see."

That was when I saw her. Her body was turned, facing the exit. She had an empty glass of champagne in her hand, and fuck, did she look gorgeous. A tightly fitted dress showed off every single curve on her body. Her hair was tugged off to one side, and I almost licked my lips at the thought of kissing down her throat. I couldn't wait to hear her moan my name into the night.

I picked up a tray of champagne on the way over to meet the brunette. I was glad that she was standing with two of my employees so I had an easy in for the conversation.

I knew all of my employees' names who worked at the corporate headquarters for Wright Construction. I personally welcomed every employee and made sure they knew their value. No one was going to work at my company and not feel appreciated. I knew how I had gotten to where I was. I never planned to take it for granted.

"Ladies," I said with a charming grin. I offered the tray to the group of women standing with the brunette. "You looked like you could use a refill."

"Oh, look at that service," Heidi said, winking at the other girl.

"Not every day you get champagne from the boss," Julia said. She took a glass herself.

"Thanks," the other girl said. She exchanged her empty glass with one from the tray.

A waiter immediately snaked over and removed the tray from my hands.

"Are y'all enjoying the party?" I asked.

"It's nice," Julia said.

"Your sister sure likes to dance," Heidi said.

The brunette girl's lips thinned, and she stared down into her champagne.

Okay, different tactic.

"Well, I'm glad you could make it. Who is your friend?" I asked pointedly, turning my attention to the brunette.

She glanced up from her champagne. Her eyes were wide open and as vivid green as I had ever seen. Her mouth opened slightly, and that vision was more intoxicating than my whiskey.

"Heidi," she groaned, "what did you do to my face?"

"This is...Em," Heidi said over Em's widened eyes of disapproval.

I wasn't sure what that was all about. She seemed particularly affronted that I was asking about her. I was sure I'd never seen her before. I definitely would have remembered.

"Well, it's nice to meet you. I'm Jensen," I said, trying to smooth over her concerns.

"Uh-huh," Em murmured. She took a long sip of her champagne, as if she were looking for liquid courage.

I couldn't get a read on her. I didn't know if she was actually uncomfortable around me or if she was just nervous. But she seemed like she wasn't sure how she was supposed to be acting right now.

"Head of Wright Construction, Em," Heidi said, nudging her with her hip.

Em shot her a withering stare. "I know who he is."

"I promise, whatever you've heard is a lie," I said with a laugh.

"I didn't say I'd heard anything bad," she countered. She downed the rest of the champagne in one quick drink and then winced. "Seriously...what is it with you Wright brothers?"

"Excuse me?" I asked with a furrowed brow.

"Ignore her," Heidi said. "She's an old friend, and she just needs another glass of champagne." Heidi leaned over and hissed in Em's ear, but I could still hear her say, "Give. Him. A. Chance."

Em sighed, as if resigning herself to the task. But, when she turned back to face me, she did have a half-smile on her face. It seemed a little forced, like she wasn't used to smiling for strangers.

"I'm just..." She held up her champagne glass and motioned to the bar.

"Mind if I join you?" I asked.

"Sure," she said.

We weren't that far from the bar, but even that short distance, I couldn't seem to take my eyes off of her. And she seemed to be looking everywhere but at me. She chanced one look at me, and a blush crept into her cheeks. So, she wasn't completely unaffected by me.

I'd said that I wanted a challenge after all. She was gorgeous and probably had guys hitting on her all the time, but I hadn't expected her not to even give me the time of day. Something about that only made me want to try harder.

Why is she so closed off?

She retrieved another glass of champagne, but I stopped her before letting her walk back to her friends. I was not relinquishing this opportunity.

"I noticed you at the ceremony," I said, my voice low and gravelly.

Her eyes widened as she looked up at me. And, fuck, that face. Those intense green eyes and bright red lips. The way her dark hair tumbled over her features, as if it were used to being unruly and was having trouble with staying tamed. Just like her. Something in her expression, in those sharp cheekbones and angled jawline, said she was wild and reckless. No amount of makeup and pretty clothes could remove the girl underneath.

"Yes. That was…" She trailed off. Her eyes darted to my mouth, as if she were distracted. Then, she sighed this short breathy thing that went straight to my dick. "I noticed."

"Are you in town, visiting?" I prompted.

She slowly shook her head and then glanced away from me, as if she needed a breather. "Look, whatever this is, it's not going to work."

I arched an eyebrow. "And what do you think this is?"

"Honestly, I don't know."

"I'm just talking to you," I said.

"I'm not fooled by that notion, Jensen."

The way she dragged out my name was the sexiest thing I'd ever heard. I was going to have to make her say it over and over again.

But I was so distracted by the way her mouth moved around the syllables of my name, I hadn't processed what she had said. She wasn't fooled by me. I wasn't trying to fool her. I thought my intentions were perfectly clear now that we were standing together. So very close together.

I wasn't even sure she realized that she had drawn closer toward me, the longer we talked. But, as I stared down at her, we were mere inches apart. I could feel the heat of her body, and it was turning my brain fuzzy.

Why didn't she want this? Her body was saying something else entirely. I could think of only one explanation.

"Do you have a boyfriend?"

She stepped back from me, as if my question were insulting. "I don't need a reason to say no to you."

She tried to brush past me, but I reached out and grabbed her hand. She didn't need a reason. Of course not. But her refusal made no sense with the way her body was responding to me.

"I know you don't need a reason. But it feels like you have one," I said, instinctively pulling her toward to me.

"Yes, I have a reason. And, when you figure it out, you'll no longer be interested in me."

"I highly doubt that," I said with blustering confidence.

"I swore off the Wright family a long time ago. So, you'll have better luck somewhere else."

She extracted her hand from mine, gave me one last sad smile, and then retreated back to Heidi and Julia. Both girls were frantically waving their hands, trying to figure out what had happened. And that was exactly what I wanted to know.

Jensen

I had just struck out.

Majorly struck out.

I was sure that I'd had girls who weren't interested in me before but certainly not any like this.

I couldn't remember having this sort of visceral reaction to anyone in a long-ass time. But even women I had been mildly interested in were eager to get to know me.

Biblically.

Yet Em seemed unfazed. She wanted me. I could tell that from looking into her bright green eyes. She definitely wanted me. Still, she'd held back. And I had no idea why.

What could she know about the Wright family that would cause this reaction?

Sure, we had more baggage than most families, but nothing that made sense in this situation. Well…okay, that was a lie. There were plenty of reasons for her to stay away from me. My reputation with women, for one. And my ex-wife, for another. But she couldn't have known anything else beyond that.

Her reaction flabbergasted me.

She didn't seem the type to play hard to get either. She had actually walked away and not looked back.

Mostly, I wasn't used to getting rejected.

Actually, I couldn't think of a time when I had been rejected. Not that it mattered. First time for everything. But it only made me want her more. I wanted to go back over there, pull her aside, and kiss the breath out of her. I wished that I knew where it had all gone wrong.

Seriously, what the fuck?

With an unfamiliar feeling of rejection, I retreated back to where I'd stashed my whiskey. I poured myself another glass as I contemplated my next move.

She obviously knew me, but I didn't know how. Nothing popped into my head. I had no clue how I could know her. And, now, I wanted to get to know her. It was an interesting woman who could turn me down...no matter how egotistical that made me. Just a healthy dose of self-confidence.

Morgan stumbled over to me a few minutes later as I was contemplating the dilemma.

"Fuck!" she said. "Gimme that."

She took my glass of whiskey and downed it like a shot. I glared at her and poured another glass. I was going to need that.

"Trouble with Landon?" I asked, passing her a glass.

"With Miranda, of course." She eagerly grabbed for the glass and took a large gulp.

"What happened this time?"

"Get this," she said with a shake of her head. She glanced back over to where she had just abandoned Landon. "Miranda was pissed because Landon's ex-girlfriend is here!"

"Why would she care if his ex was here? He's married to her, for Christ's sake."

"Well, that's Miranda." Morgan shrugged.

"Yes, it is," I grumbled. I took another sip of my drink. "She drives me batshit crazy. I don't know why they're together."

"Your guess is as good as mine."

I nodded, but my eyes had locked back on Em, who was laughing at something Heidi or Julia had said. They each grabbed her hand and practically dragged her out to the dance floor. She shook her head, but they just gave her pleading looks and started dancing to the hip-hop music that Sutton had requested for the night. It was as if she thought we were in a club or something, not a wedding.

Heidi was dancing all over Em while Em just stood there. She was saying something to Heidi and Julia, but they ignored her. And, after a few minutes, Em relaxed, and they were all dancing like they were having the time of their lives. Or they had just had an exorbitant amount of alcohol. Either way, I loved watching her move.

Once she got into it, it was intoxicating. The way her hips slid from side to side. The way she tilted her head back and laughed unabashedly with her friends. The way she lifted her arms over her head and sank low and then came back up to her full height. The way she tossed her hair and swung her hips in mouthwatering circles. It was hypnotic.

I stood there for two dances before she finally dared to glance over at me. Her eyes lit up when she saw that I was watching, and then she blushed furiously. She turned away from my look, but a minute later, she was back to staring at me. She was giving me a come-hither look, and it was killing me not to go over there and move with her on the dance floor. I wanted to oblige that look, but I didn't want to be turned away again either. I was dying for her to ask. Not just with her body, but also with her eyes and her smile and her mouth.

She turned back to her friends, but her eyes kept coming back to mine. Over and over again. It was as if we were the only two people in the room. Everything else tumbled away, and she was dancing just for me.

Yes, I was watching.

Yes, she wanted me to.

She wet her lips and then did a little dance next to her friends. My dick pulsed as I thought about all the things I could do with those hips and all the promises I would keep with those lips. I had to straighten myself out, because thinking about fucking her while watching her dance was making my dick respond all too temptingly. I adjusted my pants and then finished my whiskey. She slanted her eyes back to mine and then discreetly tilted her head to the left.

I sighed.

Finally. Let's play ball.

She spoke hurriedly to her friends on the dance floor and then pointed toward the restroom. They said something back to her, but I could see the secret smiles on their faces. They knew where she was going and what she was doing.

Em meandered away from the dance floor. She glanced over her shoulder only once to see if I was following, and I was. When she realized I had interpreted her gesture, she smiled and then tried to smother it. We meandered into the darkness, past the restroom, far enough away from the crowds.

When she turned back to face me, her cheeks were pink from dancing and being here in this moment. "You were watching me."

"Is that a crime?" I asked.

"Suppose not. Why were you watching me?"

"Because you're the most beautiful girl in the room, and I like the way you move."

"Jensen, this could *never* happen."

"You mentioned that," I said, sliding another step toward her.

Her back pressed up against the exposed brick wall.

"Do you know who I am?" she pleaded.

"Em. And that's all I need to know."

I trailed a loose lock of her dark hair between my fingers. Her eyes were open and raw, showing me all the thoughts roaming through her head. She wanted me. I wasn't wrong in that regard. She might have rebuffed me, but she hadn't been able to walk away.

"Fuck," she whispered.

Her hand ran down the front of my suit, and I leaned into her.

"Yes," I agreed. "You tell me to go away yet ask me to come here. What exactly do you want?"

Even though she wanted me, her head was warring with her body. Tension and desire mingled in the space between us. I could move in and take her lips with my own. I wanted to. But I didn't want to take. I wanted her to offer. Like she had offered to come back here with me.

"I don't know. This is a bad idea," she whispered.

"Seems like a good idea to me."

She released a breath. "I've had a lot to drink."

"Me, too," I said, taking a step closer.

"And, now, I really want to kiss you."

I chuckled. I liked her blunt honesty a lot more when it was directed toward me positively rather than negatively.

She practically glowed at my laugh, and her eyes darted down to my lips. "But we can't."

"Can't?"

She shook her head a miniscule amount and then tugged me a little closer. "Nope."

"You want to kiss me," I said, stepping into her personal space and glancing down at her lips. "But you can't. Or won't?"

"Oh, I will," she breathed. "But I shouldn't."

Then, she dragged me against her, and her lips landed on mine with a tenacity that was enthralling. Our lips touched, and the world ceased.

I ran my hands around her waist and pulled her flush against my body. My tongue licked along her lips, begging for entrance. She opened up to me at once, and our tongues met as we flat-out made out in the back of the building.

And she was a fucking amazing kisser. I could do this all day. Even though my dick was telling me to move faster, my brain was saying that this was incredible. Her body against mine. Her lips on mine. Her heartbeat ratcheting up to meet mine in tempo.

It was a life-shifting kiss. One of those that came only once in a lifetime. The kind that you didn't want to mean more. You just wanted it to be a lust-induced kiss in the dark, but you couldn't even fool yourself. This one was everything.

I didn't know how long we stayed there, kissing. It could have been hours or days. My brain could not function beyond that moment.

But, eventually, she was pulling away, stepping back, shaking her head. And I had no idea what any of those motions meant.

Hadn't she just had the same kiss I had?

She touched her lips. They were swollen and red. "Jensen...I...we..."

"Em," I whispered, reaching out for her.

But she slipped through my fingers and disappeared into the night. I tried to follow after her, but one minute, she was there, and the next minute, she was gone.

My own fucking Cinderella. Great.

Seven

Jensen

My head pounded the next morning as my phone blared on the nightstand. I grabbed it and pressed Accept without looking at who it was. *Fuck, how much had I had to drink last night?*

"Hello?" I said.

"Hello, Mr. Wright," my receptionist Margaret said. "I hope this is a good time. I just got the paperwork in that you need to look over, and you told me to contact you as soon as it arrived."

"Yes. Thank you," I said as I tried to crawl out of bed.

Work. Of course, it's work.

I listened for a few minutes more as Margaret continued to discuss the paperwork.

I stumbled into the bathroom and downed a pair of Tylenol. I appreciated Margaret's enthusiasm for the merger, but I knew I wouldn't be able to concentrate on the logistics of the paperwork until I got rid of this headache.

"Do you need me to come into the office today to go over this with you, sir?" she asked.

"No, thank you, Margaret. I'll look at it in my home office and get back with you about it on Monday."

She hesitated on the other line. "I think they're going to want an answer today, sir."

"They've kept me on the line for five days about this. And I'll have to fly there to finish off the negotiations with Tarman. We have another day to wait. Plus, if I can lower their offer, we'll all have bigger bonuses this Christmas."

"Make them wait all you like then, sir."

"Thank you, Margaret," I said.

I hung up and then looked at myself in the mirror. I'd had way too much to drink last night. With a wince, I hopped into a scalding hot shower to try not to think about Em any longer. I'd tortured myself enough with it last night. Patrick, Austin, Morgan, and I had finished another bottle of whiskey while I was thinking.

By the time I completed my daily routine, I felt like a new man. Still a fucking confused man, but more like myself at least.

I checked the time as I changed into a pair of jeans and a button-up. It was still early. The alarm I had set for this morning hadn't even gone off yet. I could probably still get in at least an hour of work before I needed to meet everyone for church—Sunday morning tradition for as long as I could remember.

With the added time on my schedule, my office beckoned. I walked into the first-floor office and took a seat at my mahogany desk. The sun was just rising through the giant floor-to-ceiling windows overlooking the swimming pool that was closed for the season. I booted up my iMac and drowned myself in legalese that I would just have to go over again with my lawyer. My eyes felt like sandpaper, and my throat was raw from all the alcohol and the sleepless night.

I thought my body would at least be used to not getting any sleep. Insomnia usually did that to someone. I couldn't remember the last time I'd had a full night's sleep. It was one of the reasons the company was flourishing. If you never had to sleep, then you could do double the amount of work.

My thoughts were so focused on the project at hand, I didn't even notice Landon standing in my doorway until he cleared his throat.

"Bad time?" Landon asked with a wry grin.

I finished typing up the memo I'd been working on and then stood from my desk. "Of course not. Just got bogged down in work."

"On Sunday, Jensen?" Landon said with a shake of his head. He entered the office and crashed back into one of the leather seats in front of the desk.

"Every day. Someone has to run the company. Not everyone gets to play golf on the weekends."

Landon laughed. "Every day. Not just the weekends."

"How's your back anyway?" I walked around to the front of the desk, leaned back against it, and crossed my arms.

The light left Landon's face. "It's fine. Better anyway. The physical therapist thinks I shouldn't be pushing it as much as I have this year, but none of the Wrights know how to slow down."

That's for damn sure.

"As long as you're taking care of it, then you'll be fine. People can have a professional golf career forever."

"Yeah, I'm on it." Landon shifted and stood. "Actually, I came over here so early because Miranda and I are going to head out."

"What?" I asked in confusion. "I thought you were staying through the holidays."

Landon grimaced. "Miranda wants to go back to Florida until Christmas. We'll be back."

"You're staying for church today though, right?" I prompted.

"I...no," he said.

I sighed heavily. "Not even for Mom?"

"I know," he said softly. "I want to, but Miranda..."

I wanted to make some wisecrack about Landon being whipped, but it didn't seem to be the time. Something was going on with him and Miranda. Their relationship was looking all too familiar. He knew better than this.

"Speaking of Miranda, I heard she freaked out last night."

Landon blew out a grateful breath at the change of subject. "Yeah, bro, my ex-girlfriend Emery Robinson was there. You remember her?"

My body stilled, and everything narrowed down to that name. "Emery Robinson," I whispered.

"Yeah. You know, my high school girlfriend. I didn't even recognize her, and Miranda was pissed that she hadn't been informed she'd be there."

"You didn't recognize her?" I whispered as horror and realization began to dawn on me.

"Nope. How fucked up is that?"

I ran a hand back through my short hair and closed my eyes. "Fuck."

"What?" Landon asked in confusion.

I just shook my head. This could not be happening. Em—my mysterious Em, my fucking Cinderella—was Emery Robinson. Of course, she would recognize me. But I hadn't seen her in...God, ten years. No wonder she had ran away from me. I'd just tried to pick up my brother's ex-girlfriend.

"Jensen, what's up?"

I couldn't tell him. There was no way I could tell him that I'd had the best kiss of my life with Emery Robinson. I hadn't known it was her. And I knew Landon too well to just drop that on him.

"Nothing. Hangover headache," I lied. "Tell me more about Emery. I remember her...only vaguely."

Understatement of the century. I remembered the taste of her lips and the feel of her skin and the way she kissed *very* well. Intimately. Everything else that came to mind about Emery was like a bridge over water on a foggy night. I knew it was there, but I couldn't see it.

"We dated in high school for two years, but we broke up on graduation. The last time I saw her was our five-year high school reunion, and we didn't talk then, and I had no idea she'd be at Sutton's wedding. I guess Heidi invited her." He shook his head. "I mean, I didn't even recognize her!" he repeated.

"How could you not have recognized her?"

"When we dated, she was the captain of the soccer team, who liked to skateboard on the weekends," Landon said in his defense. "Even at prom, she wore her hair up and no makeup. I don't know what she's been up to in the past decade. We're not even Facebook friends."

"And Miranda was pissed?"

Landon shrugged. "I don't know why. I'm not interested in the girl I dated in high school, who I haven't seen in years. I married Miranda."

Oh, I knew why Miranda was pissed off. Emery looked hot as fuck. Whatever she had looked like and acted like in high school, she was a woman now. One I would very much like to get intimately acquainted with. Too bad I would probably never see or talk to her again.

"Is that the real reason you're leaving this morning?"

Landon groaned and glanced back toward the door. "I don't know, man. Probably. She's super jealous of all my exes."

I opened my mouth to say something to Landon about last night with Emery. It wasn't that I wanted to keep it a secret, but what would really come of telling him? I wasn't the dating type. I was the fuck-'em-and-leave-'em type. Even if I had done more than make out with Emery, it would have just been a hot-as-fuck one-night stand. It wouldn't have fucking mattered who had dated whom a decade ago.

"Are you sure you can't stay for church?" I asked instead.

At that exact moment, the front door crashed open. Landon sighed heavily and seemed to retreat into himself at the very thought of the person at the door.

"Miranda?" I hazarded a guess.

"The one and only," he agreed. "I should probably head out."

"Landon! Let's go! We have to get on the road!" Miranda yelled from the foyer.

Landon's eyes traveled through the open doorway. "I should probably go. I certainly don't want to stand between the two of you in another confrontation."

"Morgan's the instigator; I assure you."

Landon glanced back at me and rolled his eyes. "You don't fool as many people as you think you do."

I sure hoped I did in that moment.

I held my hand out to my brother. Landon clasped it tight.

"I just want you to be happy. Tell me Miranda makes you happy."

"Landon!" she shrieked. Her heels clomped across the hardwood floor, drawing ever nearer, like a dragon ready to breathe flames.

"You're a good brother," Landon said with a smile and shook my hand.

Miranda stomped into the room. "Would you hurry up, or would you rather me leave you behind so that you could be with your ex-girlfriend instead?"

Landon winced. "Come on, Miranda. I've told you a hundred times that I didn't even know she was going to be here."

"Well, I'm sure you'll know when we're back for Christmas so that you can sneak away and see her," she accused.

"Seriously, she's just back from college for a few days, visiting a friend. She'll be gone before we get back. Just calm down," Landon said with a sigh.

"Whatever. Just don't make me late for the flight," she said, turning on her heel and storming away.

"I'll see you in a couple of weeks," Landon said.

We hugged, and then he hurried down the hall toward his tyrant wife. And, while I was sad to see my brother go, I feared even more for the things he hadn't said. One day, I would figure out the disaster that Miranda had created in our family but not today. Today, I had to go to church.

Eight

Emery

"**I** cannot believe you're making me do this," I said to Kimber as we stood outside of our mother, Autumn's, house.

It was the house we'd grown up in. Small and squat with red clay bricks and dark roofing. Like everything in Lubbock, it had a monstrous fence for the entire backyard. A tree her mother had planted when she moved in towered over the property. The house was in one of those timeless parts of town. Nothing had changed, not even the people. They'd just settled here like dust.

"You were never going to come over here unless I made you," Kimber said.

She mashed the old, smashed-in doorbell, and I could hear it hollering through the house, announcing our presence.

"Don't act like you know me."

Kimber snorted. "Okay. Done," she said with a sarcastic bite.

The door popped open, and my mother's face appeared in the doorway. She was gorgeous. Even at her age, she was still a knockout. It was a bit unfair to think that Kimber had gotten all of my mother's beauty-queen looks, and I had only gotten her snarky wit and unbearable attitude.

"Well, look what the cat dragged in," she said.

"Funny, Mom. I've never heard that one before," I said with a grin.

"You're not too old to have your ass paddled, young lady."

Kimber nudged me forward, and I laughed. My mother had never paddled me in my life. Believe it or not, Kimber was the troublemaker.

The three of us wandered into the living room, and my mother closed the door behind us. Everything was exactly how it had always been—same brown fabric furniture with our initials scrawled into the wooden paneling on the side, my great-grandmother's china cabinet full to the brim with my mother's Precious Moments collection, and a sea of pictures on the mantel. At least some of those were new, the pictures with Noah and Lilyanne as additions.

But not a trace of my father. He had been swept clean out of the house since he walked out on my mom when I was a kid. Only a forgotten old military medal and a box of photographs in the attic crawl space remained.

We all took seats around the living room, suffocating from our past.

"If I'm not too old for a paddling, that means you're not too old either, Mom," I told her, searching for levity.

"Oh, I know, honey." Then, she winked at me. "You know, I've been talking to Harry Stevenson across the way, and he used to be a police officer."

"Oh God, Mom!" I said, covering my ears.

My mother cackled with glee at my embarrassment. "Now, where is my granddaughter? You can't make me feel old by popping out babies, Kimber Leigh," she said, patting my sister's very pregnant belly, "and then not bring them around when you come visit."

"Lilyanne is with Noah. We're going to meet up with them at the church."

"I suppose that will be fine," Autumn said with a sigh of dejection. "How am I supposed to spoil her rotten?"

"You're doing just fine at that," Kimber said.

My mother's eyes returned to me, assessing me in that uncanny way only she could do, and then she smiled softly. Light wrinkles crinkled around her eyes. Happy wrinkles. The ones I adored.

"I've missed you, Emery," my mother said. "But, girl, what have you been eating in Austin? Is anyone feeding you? You're skin and bones."

I glanced over at Kimber, whose eyes were wide with amusement.

Out of Kimber's closet, I'd chosen a plain black dress for church this morning. She couldn't wear it and had insisted that I should since we all knew I didn't have church-appropriate attire in the bags I'd brought from Austin.

"I'm eating fine. And...I left Austin," I blurted out. "I dropped out of the program."

"Oh. I was really looking forward to having another doctor in the family," Autumn said with a mischievous grin.

"Ah, if only I had been guaranteed Noah's salary."

"If only we all were," Kimber agreed.

"Are you sad about it? You don't seem sad," my mother asked.

Strangely, I wasn't. I thought I should have been. But, even though I'd just dedicated three years to this endeavor, *sad* was not the word. I was relieved.

"Nope. I think it's the right choice. Just have to get a job and clean out my apartment. I know someone who will sublet it for next semester. At least that's covered."

"Maybe you'll change your mind," my mother said with a nonchalant shrug. "Let me just put on my Sunday best, and then we can go."

As soon as my mom exited the room, I breathed out heavily.

Kimber swatted at my knee. "It was not that bad," she whispered.

"You're right. It wasn't. Probably because you're here."

"You're so dramatic. She's happy you're home."

"Yeah," I said, looking around the room again. "Maybe so."

"Okay, all ready to go," Autumn said, strolling back into the room. She was in a red dress with a black shawl, and she was wearing her signature red lipstick. "Think Harry Stevenson will be able to resist me?"

I groaned as I stood. "If we talk about your sex life one more time, I will vomit on your floor."

"We could talk about yours," my mother said.

"Let's not," I said with a sigh.

She followed Kimber out to her enormous SUV and took the front seat. Kimber pulled out of the driveway and headed toward the church down the street.

"I heard that you saw the Wright family yesterday," Autumn said.

"Good news does travel fast," I said dryly.

At the mention of the Wright family, my head spun...but not from Landon. It was because of Jensen. Seeing Landon had been...awkward, like seeing an old friend from high school you'd rather avoid. But Jensen...that was a different story. I hated to admit how much he had affected me. So much for swearing off men. It had been a total of one day, and already, I'd made out with Jensen fucking Wright.

"If you had told me that you were in town, I wouldn't have had to hear it from Barbara," my mother said. She peered at me in the backseat, and I blankly looked back at her. "Tina was there, too. She said you looked very pretty, and all the boys were staring at you."

Sometimes, I forgot that, my mother knew *everyone*. Born and raised and never left. She was a total extrovert and made instant friends with everyone she met. Another thing I had not inherited.

"Heidi did my hair and makeup. Only reason anyone looked at me all night. You know, Landon didn't even recognize me."

"What?" Kimber gasped. "You didn't tell me that."

"So, funny story, Landon didn't recognize me, and then his *wife* showed up and flipped her shit."

"Language, Emery," my mother said.

I rolled my eyes. Yeah, I did need to watch my language since we were about to walk into a church.

Kimber drove into the parking lot that was already more than half full. I knew Kimber and Noah only still went to this church because my mother had been going since she was a kid. Otherwise, they would find one a bit more…contemporary.

Lubbock was the kind of city that had a church on every street corner. Huge whitewashed buildings and old brick edifices dotted the brick-lined roads downtown. Giant pickup trucks with metal Texas Tech decals on the bumpers filled the parking lots. Jeans and cowboy boots were acceptable attire. The preachers were just as likely to give a sermon as spout political drivel. And, every week, there was a fifteen-minute interlude, mid sermon, for people to shake hands and greet their friends who lived down the street from them. In a town where crosses on walls in the living room were an interior design statement, church was practically mandatory.

We piled out of Kimber's SUV and meandered over to the entrance. I left my mother behind as she chatted with every Tom, Dick, and Harry—*gross!*—who stood in the entranceway. I trailed Kimber past the ladies handing out pamphlets, and I took one with a half-smile before going into the sanctuary.

The ceiling was mile high with stained glass windows over the chancel. The choir was already seated off to the right, and the pastor's wife was playing the piano nearby. A large wooden pulpit was rigged with a microphone, and there was a semicircle of cushioned prayer benches to be used for communion.

This wasn't exactly where I'd thought I'd be this early in the morning after drinking a couple bottles of champagne last night with Heidi. Mercifully, I didn't have a hangover. I'd had a bottle of Gatorade and some Tylenol before bed, and Kimber had babied me in the morning. But that still didn't mean I was prepared for this.

"Kimber," Noah said.

He waved from his spot near the front of the room. Lilyanne was seated in the pew, tapping away on her iPad.

We moved up the aisle, and Kimber kissed the top of Lily's head. "Hey, baby girl. Are you excited to see Grandma Autumn?"

"It's not autumn, Mommy," Lilyanne said, looking up very seriously. "It's winter."

"Actually," I interjected, "the winter solstice isn't until the twenty-first. So, it still *is* autumn."

"But it's cold," Lily said.

"Sound logic."

Noah cracked up and scooted Lilyanne down so that we could take our seats on the end of the row.

"So, tell me about seeing Landon," Kimber said, elbowing me in the side.

"Shh, Kim, we shouldn't gossip in church."

Kimber rolled her eyes. "It's not gossip if it comes from the source. Aren't you all about firsthand accounts in history?"

"Meh. Let's not talk about history right now. I've thought of next to nothing else for nine years. I need a break."

"A break like Landon Wright?" she whispered.

"Uh, no. Landon is married, remember?"

"Oh, right," Kimber said, sounding disappointed. "Well, there are a lot of other hot guys in town."

Noah's head swiveled around so fast, and Kimber's cheeks turned pink.

"What was that?" he asked.

"Oh, shush, you!" she said, flustered.

Kimber and Noah were a year older than Austin, the middle brother, so they never had a Wright in their grade. Though they knew the family, of course. Everyone knew the Wrights.

"I'm just asking if you are looking for some fun while you're here," Kimber said with a wink.

"Speaking of hook-ups in church?" I said, crossing myself in mock horror.

Kimber laughed and shook her head. "You're horrible."

"Lilyanne!" my mother said.

She burst onto the scene, as if she owned the place. But Lily adored her. She jumped from her seat, iPad abandoned, and threw herself into Autumn's arms. She twirled Lily around and then placed her on the ground before claiming the seat beside her.

"She sure loves your little girl," I said.

"She does. I couldn't have asked for a better grandma," Kimber agreed.

"Who would have guessed?"

"Everyone," Kimber said. Then she grinned. "Look who just walked in the building."

I swiveled in my seat just in time to watch the entire Wright family stride into the building. My eyes first latched on to Jensen in a crisp black suit, white button-up, and burgundy tie. He looked…sexy as hell. In fact, I would not mind so much seeing what was underneath that suit. My cheeks burned with the thoughts running through my head. I was in church, for Christ's sake.

My eyes darted down the line of people—Austin, Morgan, Sutton, and Maverick. *Huh, I guess not all the Wrights were here.* I couldn't help but feel grateful that Landon wasn't here with his wife. Then, I didn't feel as bad about checking out Jensen.

As Jensen passed my row, he turned all his attention to me. A smile dimpled his cheeks, and I stopped breathing. *Fuck, I had made out with that face.*

Then, he and the rest of his family took their seats in the front row. I distantly remembered that they came to church every Sunday after their mother died. They did it to honor her memory since she had been such a devoted churchgoer. It was pretty amazing that they still did it. Even the morning after Sutton's wedding.

Maybe I had judged them all a bit too harshly after Landon.

Maybe it wasn't the worst thing to fantasize about those dimples.

Maybe…just not in church.

Nine

Emery

I'd say that the service was interesting, but I was a horrible person and didn't pay attention. Not that I was *not* religious. Not exactly. But, when the most eligible bachelor in the city was sitting three rows in front of you and you knew he'd wanted nothing more than to get into your pants the night before, it was a bit hard to concentrate.

Especially at the halfway mark when everyone was allowed to get up to greet their neighbors, and he turned to look right at me. I probably should go up to him to apologize for running away yesterday and just fucking explain who I was. I still couldn't believe that I hadn't just told him.

How hard was it to say I dated your brother?

Apparently, really difficult. Really, really difficult. Especially with his tongue down my throat.

I'd known what Heidi was doing by only giving him my nickname, Em. Emery was not common at all, and the light bulb would have registered immediately. Still, I hadn't corrected her, and I hadn't told him why I'd run away. Because I hadn't wanted to walk away. Maybe a part of me was still thinking about that unattainable, hot college guy that Heidi and I had dreamed about in high school.

Now, he was an even hotter billionaire CEO who was looking a whole hell of a lot more attainable.

If only I hadn't dated his brother.

My mother, of all people, saved me from humiliating myself in front of Jensen. She latched on to my arm and dragged me over to Betty, a woman I used to work for at the Buddy Holly Center when I was in high school. They had an opening after their latest hire quit, and she was more than excited to have me back on staff.

So, at least something positive came out of the whole church experience.

When the service ended, my mother milled around, chatting with all her friends. I knew that we wouldn't be going anywhere for a while unless I hitched a ride with Noah. And, by the look on Kimber's face, she was already getting ready to tell me off for considering it.

I stood and stretched, all the while wondering whether or not I should just wait for everyone outside…or if I should say something to Jensen.

Before I could decide on what to do, Jensen left his family behind in the front row and then walked casually over to where I was leaning against the edge of the pew.

"Hey. Surprised to find you here," he said with that same charming smile.

God, did he have another smile? Oh my God, I had made out with those lips.

"Hey. Yeah," I said back, glancing away.

Smooth.

Let's just take awkward to a whole new level.

"I didn't realize your family went to church here," he said.

His eyes wandered past me to Kimber, Noah, and Lilyanne and then traveled to my mother.

"Yeah. My mom has been going here since...forever."

"Right. I just didn't put two and two together." He smiled. "Well, I really just came over to apologize about last night."

My eyebrow quirked, and I shot him a dubious look. "What exactly are you apologizing for?"

Last I checked, that kiss was the hottest thing I'd ever experienced, and he had no need to apologize.

"Everything apparently," he said. "I realized that my advances must have been...unwanted. I think I might have pushed you and made you feel...uncomfortable, which was not my intention."

Ha! Uncomfortable was not the right word. I'd felt like my body had a different brain. One that was screaming *yes* when I knew *no* was the right answer.

"You didn't push your luck. It's fine," I said with a wave of my hand.

What I wanted to say was, *Kiss me again. God, please, kiss me again. I won't run this time.*

And the look in his eye said he knew.

"I assume you've figured out who I am."

"Emery Robinson," he drawled. "Yes, I know who you are."

"And see, *now*, you're not interested," I said before tacking on a shaky laugh.

"Oh," he said, his eyes intense and commanding, "but I am."

My mouth popped open into a tiny little O of surprise. *Jensen knew I'd dated Landon, and he was still interested in me? No way. He must be mistaken.*

His eyes dropped to my mouth, and he swallowed. We both seemed to be having the same damning thoughts.

He took a step toward me, entering my personal space, and leaned in near my ear. "Perhaps we should take this conversation outside. I try to avoid impure thoughts in church."

A small gasp escaped my lips, and then I covered my mouth with my hand. My eyes slid from his to survey the church as I was slammed back into reality.

Jensen Wright was having dirty thoughts about me in church.

Oh, hell yes!

"Okay," I found myself saying.

He even seemed surprised that I had agreed. Last night, I'd dashed away from him and into oblivion. Found Heidi and disappeared entirely. Now, I was saying yes to talking to him again.

"Okay then."

"Hey, Kimber," I said, turning to face my sister.

Her eyes were as wide as plates when she looked at me.

"I'm...I'm just going to go outside, all right?"

"Sure," she said.

"Just, um, come find me when Mom is done."

"Will do. But...if you get another ride home, that's okay, too," Kimber said boldly.

I rounded my eyes in exasperation, but Kimber just stifled a laugh behind her hand. Between Kimber and Heidi, they were determined to set me up by Christmas. As if I hadn't just gotten out of a sort of three-year relationship with Mitch. God, just thinking about that made my head hurt. *What a huge mistake.*

"Good to go," I said, snatching up my cell phone.

Kimber had my wallet in her purse since I hated carrying one.

"That's it?" he asked.

"What? Oh, my phone? Yeah. Purses are annoying."

He laughed and cocked his head to the side. "Interesting. Why do you think that? I thought most women loved purses."

I fell into step beside him. "Yeah, well, I'm not most women. I think they're pretty, but why would I want to lug something around full of junk that I probably won't need, only to hurt myself by carrying the weight around?"

"Fair point," he said with an amused smile on his face.

We passed through the narthex and went out into the Texas sunshine. I stripped off my cardigan since the weather was in the seventies. It never stopped amazing me, how bizarre the weather patterns were here. But I would take it if I got to wear a short-sleeved dress in December.

"This is a little strange," I said.

"Why?"

I chewed on my lip and shrugged. "I don't know...because I dated your brother?"

Jensen shifted his feet and then stared down at me like I was his next meal. "That was a long time ago, right?"

"Yeah," I admitted. "You're right. It was forever ago."

"And you're away at school right now?"

I narrowed my eyes, wondering where he had gotten his information. Not that I wanted to tell him that I'd just quit pursuing my degree. Only my mother, Kimber, and Heidi knew that.

"*Away* is kind of a loose phrase for someone who hasn't lived in Lubbock in almost ten years," I said nonchalantly.

"That's true, I suppose. It's not like many people move back once they've seen the big wide world," he said with a grin.

"Yeah. There's a reason for that."

"What would that be?" he asked, genuinely curious.

But he had to know. Lubbock was suffocating. Big enough to have an airport, small enough for the airport to have to reroute you everywhere you really wanted to go. It had improved in every way since I left in high school. Better restaurants, better shopping, better amenities. But it was still Lubbock—dry, dusty, and flat as hell.

"Because not everyone has a private jet that can fly them wherever they want," I said. Then, I covered my mouth in horror. "Oh God, you know what? That was really rude. Definitely rude. I don't even know if you have a private jet."

"I do," he said with blatant amusement as I tried to cover up my mishap.

"Okay. Well, even if you didn't…still rude."

"Do you want to go out with me?" Jensen asked point-blank.

"What?" I gasped. "I was just rude to you. Why would you want to?"

"You're refreshing. You don't have to apologize to me. I've been in your presence for fifteen minutes, and I'm already certain that I want to continue to do so."

His eyes slid to my lips with the unsaid words hanging between us.

I'd like another one of those kisses. Please, and thank you.

"But…but you don't even know me," I said. I had no idea why I was arguing with him.

"That's true. However, I would very much like to get to know you, if you'd let me, Emery."

I was pretty sure that it was the way he said my name that made me realize he was serious.

It made no sense to me. I couldn't be like the other girls he had dated. I remembered a tall blonde girlfriend he'd had in college who was around the house when I dated Landon. Smart, beautiful, legs for days with a body that belonged in a Victoria's Secret ad and a smile that belonged on a Crest commercial. She was the kind of girl someone like Jensen Wright picked up. Not me.

Yet, in some strange twist of the universe, this was happening. To me!

I wanted to ask why. Perhaps the glamorous look from last night had won him over, but today, I was once again makeup-free. My hair still held the curls from last night, so they looked all right. But I still didn't understand it.

I was an average girl, and he was a gorgeous Texas billionaire. He could have anyone he wanted, but he'd picked me.

"All right," I said finally.

"Great. Let me get your number."

He handed me his phone, so I could add my number into his cell. Then, I texted myself from his phone.

"I was thinking tomorrow night. Does that work for you?"

"Tomorrow?" I squeaked.

"Fine, you've convinced me," he said with a grin. "How about tonight?"

"Tonight?"

"We could just go now," he suggested. "I don't have a free day, but I can rearrange."

My mouth was slightly hanging open in disbelief. "You want to see me right now?"

"I am seeing you right now." He passed me back my phone. "And I like what I see."

I laughed at the comment and felt a blush creeping up my neck. "Well, I think maybe tonight would be good. Where do you want to go?"

"I have an idea," he said with a grin. "Bring a big coat, and wear something comfortable."

My brows furrowed. "You don't strike me as a wear-something-comfortable sort of date."

"It's the suit, isn't it?" he asked.

"I suppose so."

"I have a question. How do you like sleeping?"

"What does that even mean?" I asked with a laugh. "I love sleeping. Doesn't everyone? Though I didn't get much of it in grad school."

"Okay, good. Don't plan on getting any tonight," he told me.

"That's awfully presumptuous," I said softly, averting my eyes again. The blush was full-blown now.

He pressed his finger under my chin and tilted my head up to look at him. His eyes were warm and inviting. I suddenly felt as if I could drown in them. My body responded to his touch like a struck match, and I was sure he knew it.

"Big coat and something comfortable. We'll see if I'm presumptuous tonight." He smiled and looked like he wanted to kiss me again. "I can't wait until then."

Then, he released me and disappeared into the parking lot.

My body was humming. I couldn't believe what had just happened. I had a date with Jensen Wright tonight. And he had already promised that I would be out all night. Even though my logical brain was saying not to lose my heart to someone like him, my body was screaming to lose everything else.

Emery

"I should call and cancel," I told Heidi a few hours later. She was crashed back on the guest bed at Kimber's and staring at me with raised eyebrows. "Why the hell would you do that?"

"Because he's Landon's brother!"

"So?" she asked, exasperated. "He's smoking hot! You've already made out with his face. You should so fuck him."

I rolled my eyes and flung a sweater at her face. "Shut up! We're not going to have sex."

"Sure. Then, why are you wearing that?"

I was standing in a skimpy black lace bra and a thong that I'd thankfully brought with me from Austin, and it looked sexy on my curvy frame.

"What?" I asked defensively. "I have nothing in my closet. I need to get the rest of my stuff from Austin."

"Yeah, okay," she said sarcastically.

I swung around to face her. "Isn't it just a little...weird?"

"You are the only one making it weird."

"I just think maybe I'd feel better if I talked to Landon."

Heidi snorted. "Now, that's something I never thought I'd hear you say."

"Oh, shut it," I said, flipping her the bird.

"You've talked to Landon twice in over nine years since the breakup, including this weekend! Other than the sad, sappy messages you left on his voice mail in college."

"Don't," I hissed. My cheeks flamed.

I hated to think about the heartbroken girl I'd been when Landon dumped me. But, at eighteen, he had been my first serious boyfriend. I'd gone on to forget all about him with a long line of mistakes. And, now, I was going on a date with his brother.

"Come on, Em. This will be fine. You thought Jensen Wright was sexy as hell since before you had any interest in Landon. Cut loose."

I sighed. Sure, I'd had an unhealthy obsession with Jensen, just like every other girl my age, but I was a totally different person now than I'd been ten years ago—physically and emotionally. Plus, I'd gotten through three years of a PhD program. I could handle one night out with Jensen Wright and not make a fool of myself. Hopefully.

"All right. I won't cancel."

"Excellent. I'd go with this." She plucked a black V-neck sweater off the floor and passed it to me.

I tugged it over my head and paired it with my classic black skinny jeans and boots. Swishing my dark hair over to one side of my head, I held my hands out. "What do you think?"

"I still think a little black dress would be better. Are you sure he said warm and comfortable?"

"Definitely."

The doorbell rang downstairs, and my eyes widened to saucers.

I heard Lilyanne screaming, "I'll get it. I'll get it. I'll get it!"

"He's early," I groaned, glancing at the clock.

"Well, hurry up. Go and intercept the minion, or he's going to be taking Lily," Heidi said.

I snatched my phone off of the nightstand, slid it into my back pocket, and dashed out of the room. I could see Noah and Kimber moving toward the front door, and Heidi was on my heels. With my luck, this would turn into one big family affair. *Ugh!*

"And who are you?" I heard Jensen ask from the front door.

I hopped the last two steps and turned to find him bending down, eye-level with my niece. He had a big smile on his face and a bouquet of gorgeous flowers in white, deep dark reds, and plum purples.

"I'm Lilyanne. Who are you?" she asked.

"So nice to meet you, Lilyanne. My name is Jensen."

"Are those for me?" she asked, stretching her hands out toward the flowers.

He laughed. "They most certainly are. Do you have a vase to put them in? I can show you how to keep them pretty for a long time."

Lilyanne squealed and clutched the flowers to her chest. "Mommy! Daddy!" she shrieked. "I have flowers!"

"How nice," Kimber said.

"I think I have a boyfriend!"

Everyone laughed at that comment. But Lilyanne just twirled around in a circle and dashed to her parents.

Noah scooped her up in his arms. "You're a little young for a boyfriend, I think. Right?"

"Yep," Kimber agreed. "Much too young."

Lilyanne stuck out her bottom lip and hugged her flowers.

"Let's go with Mom to find something to put them in," Noah said, carrying her out of the room.

Jensen stood from where he'd been crouching, and his eyes found me across the distance of the living room. His eyes seared into me like a brand. I immediately felt flushed. I watched him peruse my outfit, starting at the tips of my toes and agonizingly dragging his eyes up to my face. My cheeks burned like a torch as a smile bloomed on his face, dimpling his cheeks, and it reminded me that not only was he drop-dead gorgeous, but he was also somehow *amazing* with kids.

Fuck, what am I getting myself into?

Heidi nudged me forward into the charged space and then disappeared into the kitchen.

"Hey," I said, feeling the weight of our distance and moving toward him like a magnet. *How did he have this kind of effect on me? Did all women feel like their bodies were on fire when Jensen Wright settled his gaze on them?*

"Hey, Emery," he said, taking another step toward me so that we were nearly touching.

He held out his empty hand and brushed my arm. My skin crackled, and I had to control my emotions not to show it.

"I had flowers for you."

I cleared my throat and smiled up into his deep dark eyes. "That's okay. You just made Lily's day. She's going to be talking about you forever now."

"Ah, good. She's adorable. How old is she? Four?"

I nodded and used the opportunity to glance back at Lily, who I could just see in the kitchen. "Yeah."

"That's a great age."

"She's the best," I agreed. I swiveled back to face him and was met with a molten gaze that brought back all of the dirty thoughts I'd had in church earlier today. Yeah, there was no way I could end this date tonight. Not with him looking like *that*.

A heavy black Arc'teryx jacket molded to his body over a T-shirt. Dark jeans ran down his powerful thighs, revealing dark boots that were definitely worn and loved. I was a lost cause.

"I know I'm early," he said. "I just saw that a cold front would be moving through tonight. That was not in the plan, especially with how the wind is now."

"Only in Texas," I said with a laugh. "The weather is crazy unpredictable. With my luck, we'll have a dust storm blow through."

"Let's hope not."

"I'll just get my coat." I dashed to the closet and grabbed my winter coat, sliding it over my sweater.

Heidi waved at me from the kitchen and mouthed, *Have fun*. I winked at her and then returned to Jensen.

"Ready."

Jensen raised his hand at my family, who were staring at the pair of us from the kitchen. I hurried out the door in embarrassment and put getting my own place on the ever-growing list of things that I needed to do. He pulled the door closed behind us and veered me toward a lifted black truck. It was huge and masculine and looked like I was going to need a step up to ride it. Just like Jensen.

I shook my head to get my mind out of the gutter and let Jensen open the door for me. I brushed past him. The contact sent shivers up my arm that I knew I couldn't blame on the weather. I sank into the passenger side, and then Jensen shut my door and climbed into the driver's side. I checked out the kick-ass interior and reworked my Jensen framework around this truck. I definitely hadn't pictured him for a big-truck guy. For some reason, I'd assumed he'd have a shiny little sports car. I really needed to get over my prejudices about this guy.

Jensen backed out of Kimber's driveway, and then we started heading toward town.

His eyes peeked over at me in interest, like I was a puzzle he wanted to put together. "So, what are you in school for?"

Okay, play it cool. I wasn't hiding why I was here, but I just hadn't really talked about it with anyone outside of my family and Heidi. And we'd been friends long enough that she knew which questions not to ask.

"Um...PhD in history at UT Austin."

Both eyebrows rose at that, and I realized that I liked surprising him.

"A PhD? That's incredible."

"Thanks," I said. Even though I knew that I had made the right decision in leaving, I knew earning my PhD had made me stand out and given me focus. Without it, I didn't really know who I was or what I was doing.

"What kind of history?"

"Oh. European female figures with some interest in European monarchy mistresses. Well, I was writing my dissertation on Madame de Pompadour, who was the renowned mistress of King Louis XV of France."

"Mistresses," he said with a shake of his head. "There's a lot of research on that?"

"A surprising amount honestly," I told him.

"Interesting. I always wanted to go back and get another degree," he admitted.

"Pretty hard to do while you're running your own business, I would guess."

He nodded, resting his hand on the gearshift between us. I got distracted by his long, masculine fingers and the way they wrapped around the head of the stick. *Wow, he had big hands.*

My eyes shot back up to his as my thoughts strayed all over again. Damn, it hadn't been that long since I'd gotten laid. I felt like a dog in heat.

Jensen didn't say anything about the look on my face, but I could tell in the barely suppressed grin and cocky tilt of his head that he knew I'd been checking him out. "That would be the main reason. Just too busy to go back to school."

"Aren't you in charge though? Why would you need another degree?" I asked, keeping to safer territories.

"I wouldn't." His face went disturbingly blank for a second. His bright and shining eyes turned flat and empty. His smile disappeared.

It was like all the joy had been sucked out of the air from that one little question. And I didn't even know why.

I chewed on my lip and faced front again just as we pulled off of the main road and into a parking lot. With my mind swirling with possibilities as to why that had upset him, I hadn't put much thought into where we were going to eat or what we were going to do on this date. I'd been too preoccupied by the warm clothing aspect.

But, now that we were standing outside of Torchy's Tacos, I burst out laughing. "You're taking me for tacos?" I asked when I met him by the bed of the truck.

All the seriousness of the last bit of our conversation had disappeared, and no tension remained in his shoulders.

"What? Do you not like tacos?" He apprehensively assessed me. "Tacos are a deal-breaker."

I gently shoved him as we angled toward the front of the restaurant. "Of course I like tacos. Do people not like tacos?"

He shrugged. "Traitors maybe."

"You're ridiculous," I said with a laugh. "I just didn't expect…tacos."

"What were you expecting?"

His body angled toward me, and once again, I felt that crushing inescapable force vibrate between us. There was just something that made it so that I couldn't seem to get my bearings with him.

"I don't know. I guess I'm just realizing that you're not what I thought."

"Good. You aren't what I was expecting either."

"Oh, yeah? What were you expecting?"

"After meeting you yesterday? A girlie girl who likes makeup and hair and designer clothes."

I couldn't seem to help myself at that image and abruptly laughed out loud.

"Yes, well, I realize that's not who you are."

"Not even close." I straightened but kept my smile firmly in place.

He leaned forward, so our bodies were nearly touching and brushed a lock of hair off my face. My head tilted up, and I stared into those deep eyes, hanging on to every word with bated breath.

"Let's suspend all preconceived notions about each other then. What do you think?"

I nodded. "I'd like that."

Eleven

Jensen

Emery wasn't what I'd expected.

I knew that I had just told her to put preconceived notions behind us, but she was turning me on my head. I had thought she was just a hot piece of ass. Patrick wasn't lying when he'd said I got a look in my eye when I was chasing women.

But Emery didn't seem to be the kind of girl who just fucked around. She was smart. Another quality I was not used to in the women I dated. She was clearly driven and seemed to have her shit together. It was actually refreshing.

I hadn't really known what to expect, walking into this. When I'd seen her at church, I just couldn't help myself. Landon had said she was going to be here for only a few days. *What would he care about me going on a date with his ex?* It wasn't like we were going to get married or anything. No, I'd definitely sworn that off after Vanessa.

But, if this was a quick trip for her, then it wouldn't be any different than hooking up with someone I met when I was away on business. We just happened to meet in Lubbock and not when she was in Austin.

Emery's phone buzzed noisily while we waited in line at Torchy's. Her laugh was effortless, and I enjoyed the flush that followed. Whoever had just messaged her certainly made my night easier.

I raised my eyebrows as she shoved her phone into the back pocket of her jeans. "What was that about?"

"Heidi," she said, as if that explained it.

Heidi. Right. They had been together at the wedding. I liked Heidi. She was a bossy, hard-working, and energetic woman and an HR nightmare. Not for me, mind you, since I didn't mix business with pleasure, but half of the men on my staff were head over heels for her.

"Heidi's great. I don't know what we would do without her. Though you'd never guess that from talking to her about it. How long have you known each other?"

We scooted forward in line, and she edged closer to me. I was glad that I'd gone for casual. I did enough fancy dinners to know when a girl was into it. As soon as she'd said that she didn't carry a purse, I knew a fifty-dollar steak wasn't going to do the trick. Plus, even though this never happened, I really did prefer this. Tacos were my favorite.

"That sounds like Heidi. Always the hard worker who acts as if she couldn't care less," she said, flipping her hair off her shoulder. "We've been best friends basically forever."

"Well, she's lucky then."

She shook her head and nudged me. "Nah, I'm the lucky one. She keeps me on the straight and narrow." She mischievously grinned up at me. "Well...mostly."

I decided right then and there that I liked that look and would do a whole lot to make her keep looking at me like that.

"No one wants to be too straight and narrow." I leaned down and whispered into her ear, "I color outside of the lines."

She burst out laughing just as we reached the front of the line, and I held out my hand so that she could order first. I left her to fill up her drink and then grinned at the woman behind the counter.

A few minutes later, we had our tacos in a bag, and I hefted them up to eye-level. "Ready?"

She tilted her head in confusion. "Tacos on the go?"

"We have places to be," I told her.

Her eyes flickered between me and the bag of tacos. I couldn't read what was going on behind those eyes. *Is she enjoying this, or am I going too far?* I did have things planned for the night, but they could change if she wasn't interested. She looked adventurous, and I wanted to see if I was right.

"All right," she said after a minute, "lead the way."

We moved back out to my truck, and I passed her the bag of tacos after she hoisted herself up into the passenger seat. I didn't always drive my truck either, but where we were going, it was always better to have four-wheel drive.

I sped us out of town, and Emery handed me my tacos. She suspiciously eyed me while we ate.

"Where the hell are you taking me?" she asked halfway through her second taco.

"You haven't guessed?"

She seemed to consider it. "I mean...I know what's out this way, but I have no idea why you would be taking me into the middle of nowhere on a first date."

"Lubbock, by definition, *is* the middle of nowhere."

"That is a fair point," she agreed.

Her leg was bouncing in place, and I could see she was curious but trying not to be.

"You don't like surprises?"

She shrugged and then grimaced. Then, she shook her head. "I mean...sometimes. Like, surprise, my sister is

85

pregnant, that's awesome. But I'm kind of horrible at this waiting thing. I was that kid who would sneak into my mom's closet and peek at my Christmas presents. I called Oklahoma before they announced scholarship letters and convinced the person in administration to tell me whether or not I'd made it."

I couldn't help it; I laughed. She sounded just like me. If someone had planned something like this for me, I would be losing my mind, having to know what was going on.

"Don't laugh at me," she said, swatting at my sleeve. "I'm impatient."

"I don't fault you. I am the same way."

"So…where are we going?"

"It's a surprise."

Then, she slumped back down. "Ugh! Okay. I'll wait."

Luckily, she didn't have to wait for long. Before she knew it, we pulled into the small town of Ransom Canyon. It was only about twenty minutes outside of Lubbock and generally considered a sort of suburb of Lubbock. Not that Lubbock actually had suburbs. It was just one of the closest towns.

"Ransom Canyon?" Emery asked, staring at the flat lake that took up the center of the canyon.

Unknown to most people, west Texas had a series of canyons that studded the land, like holes in Swiss cheese. Palo Duro Canyon, an hour and a half north of town and just outside of Amarillo, was the second largest canyon, after the Grand Canyon, in the United States. It was one of the many things that made this side of Texas interesting if you knew where to look.

"Have you seen their Christmas lights before?"

"Nope. I've been here a million times before. We used to go to the lake as kids. I've spent many a summer weekends on boats here. But I didn't know about the Christmas lights. When did they start to do that?"

"A couple of years ago. They even have a radio station tuned in so that you can listen to Christmas music as you circle the neighborhood and the lake."

"Festive." Her tone instantly changed. She had gone from skeptical to excited. She leaned forward in her seat, wondering where we were going to start first. "Are we going to see them all?"

"Of course," I told her. Even though I'd had something else in mind, I was not going to miss a minute of that smile.

I switched the station over to AM radio and drove around town. It was a small area of only about a thousand people, but the people who had chosen to move out on the lake rather than live in town generally had considerable wealth. The mansions were decked out in Christmas lights, which had all likely been done by the same company. It was like the modern version of *How the Grinch Stole Christmas* when the two Whos were fighting over who had the best lights. That was the entire town.

Our drive was punctuated by Emery's oohs and aahs and the occasional, "Slow down; you're going too fast."

I had to say, that was something I'd never heard before.

Emery lit up brighter than any of the houses that we'd passed. Halfway through, she must have begun to relax around me because she started singing along with the Christmas music. She was a little off-key, but I found that it didn't even matter. And, eventually, we were both belting out the chorus to Mariah Carey's "All I Want for Christmas Is You."

Emery was laughing so hard that a few tears rolled down her face. "Oh my God, if I had thought for one second in high school that I would be singing Mariah Carey with Jensen Wright on a real date, I think I would have dropped dead."

"Hey, don't dis Mariah," I said. "She's an icon."

"She can't even *sing* anymore!"

"I'm going to pretend like you didn't say that."

She snorted and then covered her face. "Oh my God, what is my life?"

"Seems pretty awesome," I said with a grin. "Even if you don't like Mariah."

"I do like Mariah!" she cried. "Stop twisting my words, you!"

"I'm not twisting anything."

Her smile was magnetic, and I just wanted to kiss her. I mean…I'd wanted to kiss her all night. But sitting there, in front of the last lit house, with Christmas music playing in the background and her smile radiating joy, there was nowhere else I'd rather be. That thought hit me so suddenly and I didn't even know why.

I put my truck into park, leaned over to her side of the car, and pushed my hand up into her dark hair. She froze, silhouetted by the light display behind her. Her eyes locked with mine, green meeting brown, and her eyes widened with surprise. She breathed out softly, and I could feel her pulse ratchet up at my touch.

This was the girl who had pulled me across the room at Sutton's wedding, like a magnet finding its pair. This was the tension that I'd felt when we first spoke. Here was the world of desire and lust that had clouded both of our minds ever since our first kiss.

My face was only inches from hers. I wanted to take what was mine. I wanted to claim her mouth and then her body right here in the cab of my truck, like we were young, wild, and carefree.

But, instead, I couldn't seem to stop staring at her.

She laughed lightly to try to defuse the tension. But it wasn't possible, and it was a feeble effort.

"Are you going to kiss me?" she whispered boldly.

I didn't need any further prodding. I crushed my lips against hers. It was like striking a match. Our lips moved against each other, desperate with the need to get closer, to have more. She opened her mouth for me, and I brushed my tongue against hers. The groan that emanated from deep in the back of her throat made my dick twitch. Our tongues volleyed for position. She was just as aching for attention as I was.

I heard the click of her belt buckle, and soon, she was pushing her body closer, moving over the divide of my truck. My hands fell to her ass, and I effortlessly hoisted her up and into my seat. She squeaked in shock but didn't break contact. Instead, she straddled me and let her hands wander across my chest.

My hands never left her ass because, damn, did that woman have an ass. She was grinding up against me, and I moved into a full-blown hard-on at her ministrations. She must have realized what she was doing to me because, when she swiveled her hips in place, she moaned against the feel of my dick.

In that moment, I didn't give a shit that we were acting like teenagers, parked outside of a stranger's house, bucking against each other for just an ounce of satisfaction. I was ready to strip her bare and fuck her until she forgot every word to every Christmas song and only remembered my name.

That was, until she rocked back just a little too hard, and a loud honk erupted from the hood of the truck.

Twelve

Emery

I broke away lightning fast, and my head whipped to the side. I stared out at the house we were parked in front of. All the lights were lit, and surely, anyone who was inside had a front-row view to what we had just been doing.

"Fuck! I didn't mean to do that."

"It's fine. You should kiss me again," Jensen said.

He hadn't moved his hands from my ass, and I couldn't deny that I liked it.

Fuck, I had just had the most amazing make-out session in my life and ruined it.

Jensen nipped my lower lip, basically deciding for me. I leaned into his kiss again with a low moan.

Forget common decency. I just wanted Jensen Wright. Right here. Right now.

Then, I heard the sound of a door crashing open. I reared back and found an old woman rushing out of the front door in her nightgown. She had to be in her eighties with her white hair in curlers. She was shaking her fist at the truck as she wandered out into the frigid night.

"Fuck. Fuck. Fuck!" My eyes widened in horror.

No sweet talk from Jensen was going to change my mind this time. There was an old woman *shaking her fist* at us. Comically, I suddenly felt like I was in an old movie, and I was dying of humiliation.

I scrambled off of Jensen's lap and landed with a thud back into the passenger seat. I frantically waved my arms at Jensen. "Come on. We have to get out of here."

He just laughed at me. There wasn't an ounce of shame on his face.

"Jensen," I spat like a curse, "get your cute ass moving."

"All right, all right," he said with a grin. He languidly adjusted his pants, which was a nice distraction from the woman approaching us from her front porch. "So long as you think my ass is cute."

I buried my face in my hands. Not only had we been caught making out by a woman, but I had also just admitted to checking out Jensen's ass. I was out of my damn mind. That had to be the only explanation.

Jensen put the truck into drive and pulled away without another word. He seemed to find the whole thing amusing. I thought he might have even found my own humiliation funnier than the woman rushing out at us. Just my luck.

"I cannot believe that just happened."

"It wasn't that bad," he said, slipping his hand across the seat and taking mine.

I just let out a groan. "What is your definition of *wasn't that bad*?"

"You don't know that woman, and you'll never have to see her again."

"Not with my luck!"

Jensen reassuringly trailed his thumb down my knuckles. "Emery, look at me."

My gaze shifted to his from where I was bent over. "What?"

"Don't be embarrassed. I thought it was sexy as hell."

"Getting caught?" I asked.

He tilted his head and arched an eyebrow. "The way you rode me," he said in a husky deep voice.

I blushed at his words, but that got me to sit up. I shouldn't be so embarrassed. We weren't kids anymore. I was an adult... sort of. I wasn't that great at adulting. I didn't even really know what was considered adulting. But, if it involved riding Jensen like a bucking bronco, then I'd be on board with trying to be more of an adult.

"You liked that?" I asked, finally finding my voice.

"I'd like to do more than let you ride me in my truck," he admitted.

He took a left and then headed back up the canyon. His eyes slid to mine in the darkness, and the intensity of them shot heat straight between my thighs. I squeezed them together in anticipation.

"I'd love to get you to make those moaning noises all night."

I choked on my own saliva at those words. My mouth dropped open.

"I wouldn't mind *this* either," he said, untwining our hands to rub his thumb across my bottom lip.

"Oh, dear God," I whispered.

My tongue darted out and caressed his thumb, and we both shivered.

"Is that what you want?"

"For you to fuck me?" I countered.

He grinned, dimpling his cheeks and sending me swooning all over again. "I'd like nothing more than to fuck you, Emery."

My head nodded in agreement, as if without my body even realizing it. Because, hell yes, I wanted to get fucked by Jensen Wright.

Normally, I wouldn't talk about sex like that. It was Heidi who had messaged me at Torchy's to ask if we were fucking already. I hadn't thought for a split second that it was even a possibility that we were going to get hot and heavy. I had thought that maybe he'd kiss me on my doorstep when he dropped me off.

I wasn't naive. I'd gone through my one-night-stand phase in college. I'd meaninglessly dated a guy in college who I fucked every day until I realized I hated that he smoked. I'd dated my own PhD advisor for going on three years. We never commented on our sex life. We'd had long debates about seventeenth century monarchs, drunk French wine over philosophical commentaries, and made love in the dark under the covers on days when he didn't have to teach in the morning. But none of those relationships or pseudo relationships had ever had a guy who wanted to talk about what he wanted to do to me. To count the ways that he wanted to fuck me and then follow through.

Jensen Wright wanted to fuck me.

He wanted to use my mouth and body all night.

And I was perfectly fine with letting him.

A couple of minutes later, we pulled up to a one-story cabin overlooking the canyon and the flat lake in the middle. It wasn't as enormous as some of the ones inside the canyon walls, but it held its own. At least what I could see of it.

"Whose house is this?" I asked as Jensen pulled into the driveway.

He cut the engine, and he looked over at me, almost apologetically. "Mine."

"Oh," I said as realization dawned on me.

He had planned this. That much was clear. He had wanted to bring me back here for sex the whole time. Part of me wanted to be flattered, but I suddenly had a bad taste in my mouth, and I felt frozen in my seat.

"I originally planned to bring you here," he said. At my appalled face, he shook his head. "Not like that. I planned to use the fire pit and make s'mores. I have the supplies in the back. I figured it'd be about fifty degrees, and if the weather permitted, we could night hike. Hence the warm clothes..." He trailed off when I didn't move.

My brain was trying to catch up to his statement. I turned around and found a paper Sprouts bag in the back, and marshmallows were on the top. Okay, so I had overreacted. He hadn't brought me out here just to fuck me. He wasn't using me.

God, why had I automatically thought the worst of him? I was sure it was just latent prejudice against the Wright family. Not to mention, my not-so-stellar luck with guys.

"We could still do that," he offered. "Though it has dropped down to twenty with a wind chill of eleven. So...we might freeze."

"You turned the car off, so I'm already freezing," I told him. My hands were shaking. I'd stupidly forgotten my gloves. I stuffed them into the pockets of my jacket.

"Let's get you inside and warm you up then."

I hopped out of the truck and followed him to the front door. He had the bag of groceries in his arm and unlocked the door with his other hand. He kicked the door open with his foot and let me in first. I still felt cautious after my suspicions returned to me. I had just been having the best time with Jensen, and I didn't want to think things like that.

Having sex with him on the first date to get his hot body out of my system might be the best thing I could ever do. There was no future here. I didn't even want to date right now. And it didn't matter how much fun we'd had while Christmas caroling. Jensen Wright was Landon Wright's older brother. And Landon wouldn't just disappear if this continued.

So, I might as well have my fun now.

"Brr," Jensen said. He flipped on the lights, and the cabin was illuminated. "I'm going to build a fire. If you want to look in that crate right there, there's a bunch of blankets. Make yourself at home while I get some firewood."

I took a few tentative steps inside as Jensen got to work. The cabin was even more spectacular on the inside with high vaulted ceilings and dark wood beams bisecting the room. The hardwood floors were a dark glossy finish, and a bricked fireplace took up half of one wall in the living room. It had clearly been professionally decorated, and it was the first time tonight that I remembered that Jensen owned and ran Wright Construction and had more money than God.

The wooden crate was behind the brown leather couch, and I fished out a half-dozen blankets. I still wasn't sure if that was going to be enough to keep me warm in the meantime, but it was a start.

I burrowed into the blankets, trying to warm up my extremities. Jensen appeared with a bag of twigs and an armful of firewood. The kindling took a while to ignite, but once it started going, he was able to add logs to it pretty easily. Jensen cut the overhead light and let the flames bathe the living room in a soft glow and easy warmth.

"Why don't you come get closer to the fire?" he suggested.

A sheepskin rug lay in front of the fireplace. I couldn't tell if it was real or fake, and I shuddered. "Did that thing used to be alive?"

"Synthetic," he told me. "Just as warm."

I relaxed, grabbed the blankets, and carried them over to the rug. Jensen grabbed a pair of red pillows from the couch and tossed them to me. Then, he disappeared into the kitchen. After the sound of a loud pop, he came out a few minutes later with a tray in his hands.

He offered me a glass of red wine with a smile. "I hope you like red."

"Red or champagne." I took a sip and nearly groaned again. This was the good stuff.

"And since we didn't get to do s'mores"—he placed the tray off to the side, pointing at the bars of Hershey's chocolate, graham crackers, and marshmallows in bowls atop it—"I thought this would have to do."

"This had better be a dessert wine," I joked.

He grinned and took the seat next to me, throwing a blanket over his lap. I reached for a marshmallow and popped it into my mouth. Jensen's eyes caught on my lips, and I almost forgot that I was still holding a full glass of wine. I took a good long sip to steel my nerves, and then I placed the glass to the side.

"If I didn't know better, I'd think you were seducing me," I teased.

"I think I made my intentions pretty clear in the truck." His hand slid up the leg of my jeans under the blanket and then across the top of my thigh.

My breath hitched, and for the first time, I realized that I was nervous. Not of the situation. This seemed magical. But of Jensen. I'd spent much of my life thinking he was entirely out of my league, and even when I despised their family, I never thought I was above them but certainly not on level footing either.

"But," he said, stopping his hand and then moving back to my knee, "I would be okay if you just wanted a nice fire, some good wine, and deconstructed s'mores. I could get you home at a semi decent hour even."

I swallowed all the apprehension I'd been feeling.

Who said I couldn't be on a level playing field with a Wright? Just because they had money and prestige didn't mean shit. Jensen wanted me, and I definitely fucking wanted him. Stopping myself from having the hottest rebound of my life sounded ludicrous.

"What happened to, *don't plan on getting any sleep tonight?*" I whispered huskily. I leaned forward, sliding his hand back up my leg.

My own hands moved to the hem of his T-shirt and ran along the exposed skin just north of his jeans. He inhaled deeply at my bold move. Whatever hesitation I'd had from my discomfort or the sudden change of plans disappeared at that touch.

He shoved one of his hands up into my hair and kissed me like a dying man begging for his last breath. Our bodies were perfectly in sync. One moving against the other in harmony, unbroken by any of the million little thoughts that had flitted through my mind before coming to this moment. There was only me and Jensen. And I couldn't think of anything else I wanted or needed.

Heat suffused us from the warmth of the roaring fire in the grate and the friction we were creating with our bodies. Jensen's mouth on mine pulled the pin on a grenade, and as his hands dragged my shirt over my head and slipped me out of my jeans, the tension exploded between us.

I forgot that I had once been cold and just marveled in everything that was Jensen Wright. I kissed my way down every inch of his six-pack abs. Then, I unbuckled his belt and shoved his pants to his ankles. He bulged out of his boxer briefs, and I licked my lips. I was one of those freaks of nature who loved giving blow jobs. I loved making a man squirm underneath my ministrations. And Jensen certainly didn't object when I removed him from his pants and dropped my mouth over the head of his dick.

I licked all around the head and then down the shaft. His hand buried itself into my hair as I took him fully in my mouth. And his gasp made it all worth it. I bobbed up and down on his dick like I was deep-throating a Popsicle. His eyes were hazy and unfocused as I worked my magic. I could feel him getting close, and he grunted.

"Emery," he murmured to warn me. Proper etiquette and all.

But I had no intentions of stopping.

I sucked him off until hot liquid filled my mouth, and he was shuddering in ecstasy. I pulled back from his cock, braced myself, and then swallowed his cum like a champ. His smile was infectious.

"Holy fuck, woman," he growled.

He didn't even wait for a response. He pushed me back onto the fur rug, opened my legs wide, and buried his face between them. I cried out as he lapped at my clit while his fingers dug into my inner thighs. My back rose off the rug as trembles ran through my body. He slowly inched one hand down to the lips of my pussy and tenderly stroked my opening.

"Oh God," I cried out when he inserted two fingers at once inside me.

He didn't pump in and out like I'd thought he would, but instead, he strummed the inside of me like he was playing a guitar. My body responded like a harmony.

I tried to close my legs as pleasure hit me from head to toe, but he just forced my legs further apart. Then, he reached out with his free hand and tweaked my nipple. I nearly came right there. My nipples were unbelievably sensitive. And, since I responded so well, he left his hand there, playing with my nipple, until I cried out, and my orgasm hit me full-on.

My legs seemed to have a mind of their own, shaking like I'd just run a marathon.

"I take it back," he said, kissing up my orgasm-flushed stomach and then to my nipples. He lavished each one with his tongue as I writhed beneath him. "I like your screams as you come better than your groans as you ride me. I wonder if I would like your screams as you rode me the best."

"Do you want to find out?" I breathed suggestively.

99

"I want to find all the ways to make you scream." He nipped at my nipple, and I cried out all over again. "Fuck, woman. Fuck."

I could feel his dick against my leg, already hard again. I lazily stroked my hand up and down his cock, and it was his turn to twitch at the movement.

"Please," I pleaded.

"Oh, I do like when you ask nicely," he said with a grin.

"Then, let me try again," I said, bringing his lips down to mine. "Please, oh, please, Jensen Wright, fuck me. Fuck me right now."

He located a condom in his jacket pocket and slid it on before positioning himself at my opening. He positioned himself on his forearms so that he could kiss my lips one more time. My hands rested on his biceps.

God, I want this. I want him.

"I'd like to give you what you want, Miss Robinson," Jensen said, teasing his dick against my pussy. "I might have to hear you ask one more time."

I hooked my legs around his back and tried to tug him forward. I even lifted my hips off the ground, but he easily held me at bay.

"I want you inside me. All of you. Until you have me screaming again from your cock and not just your mouth."

"Fuck," he whispered and then slid inside me.

I rocked my head back and moaned at the feel of him stretching and filling me. It was perfect. Utter bliss. This was even better than I'd thought it would be. He started moving in and out of me, and I used my leverage to meet his practiced thrusts. He was controlled and methodical, and I was aching for more.

He was devilishly grinning at me, as if he knew how much I wanted him to fuck me senseless. But he held back as he worked me into an uncontrollable frenzy. Until I was right on the brink of the biggest orgasm of my life. Until I was ready to beg him to let me release.

"Jensen, God, please. Harder."

He picked me up off the rug, and let our naked bodies be silhouetted by the firelight. He held me up in his arms with his hands on my hips. Then, he moved me up and down on his dick as hard and as rough as I had just pleaded with him for. My tits bounced in his face, and his cock drove into me. And, just as our slicked bodies were hitting the peak, I screamed out his name into the cold night air. He grunted and came inside me a few thrusts later.

We both sat perfectly still, collapsing in on each other.

"Wow," I whispered. "Holy fucking wow."

"You can say that again."

"We're…we're going to need to do that again."

"A few times."

Jensen was right. As we spent the rest of the night in each other's arms, we found that he did like my screams best when I rode him.

Thirteen

Jensen

I came to, holding a beautiful, naked woman in my arms. My eyes jolted awake, as I was unable to believe the turn of events. Not because I'd had the most amazing sex of my life. Or that the person I'd had it with was Emery Robinson. Or even that I was enjoying having her in my arms the next morning.

It was because I had slept.

I had *really* slept.

My eyes darted to the red alarm clock on the nightstand next to the bed we had migrated into at some ungodly hour last night. But, right now, it read nine o'clock.

Nine o'clock.

I had slept for seven blissful hours. I didn't even care that I was late for work for the first time in my life or that I probably had a thousand emails and just as many texts and calls to find out if I was alive. I hadn't slept seven straight hours since my father died nearly a decade ago.

"Mmm," Emery groaned, rolling over to face me.

In the light of day, she was even more gorgeous than lit by candlelight, and I hadn't thought that was possible. I'd been a fool to think she was beautiful as she could get coated in makeup with her hair done. Here she was with traces of last night's mascara on her eyelashes and her hair down and messy in a freshly fucked way, and I was done. I was...totally fucked.

"What time is it?" she asked.

"Nine."

"That early?" She stretched her arm out.

"Mmhmm," I said, suddenly realizing how utterly fucked I was. Utterly and completely fucked. I needed to get out of here and stop this now.

I couldn't have had fucking incredible sex and slept through a whole night with a woman who was so wrong for me on every level. Attachments were overrated, and I had prided myself on being emotionally unavailable. I needed to find that in me now.

Emery Robinson had belonged to Landon. She was living in Austin. She'd grown up here. And I could think of a hundred other strikes against her.

I flung the covers off my naked body and moved to get out of bed. Emery reached for me with her delicate little fingers, and I careened away from her. I avoided her gaze. I didn't want to see if she was hurt. I wasn't an asshole. I just... couldn't do this. I couldn't feel anything for her.

I searched in the closet for clean clothes. Ours were still strewed across the living room.

"I'll just...get your things, so we can go," I said, stomping out of the room before she could say anything.

I found my cell phone first and glanced at the influx of messages. I texted my secretary, Margaret, to let her know I would be coming in late. Something had come up unexpectedly.

My phone dinged with a message from Vanessa, and I nearly threw the thing across the room. Just what I wanted to deal with my ex-wife after the night that I had and the morning that only reminded me why this was all a bad idea. Instead, I returned the message, because I knew she would hound me if I didn't, but I made sure that my impatience was blatantly clear.

I ignored everything else and scooped up Emery's clothes from the floor.

She was sitting up with the charcoal-gray sheet wrapped around her body. She seemed off-balance, as if last night had been a dream and she was waking up and realizing it hadn't happened. She had been so comfortable with her body last night that it seemed a damn shame that she was covering it up.

"Just late for work," I told her. "We have to get going."

"Right. Of course," she said.

She took her clothes out of my hand, and I gave her privacy to change. The notion was absurd, but between being late for work, how content I had felt the moment I woke up, and the text from my bitch of an ex, this morning itself felt absurd.

Emery appeared a minute later, dressed in the clothes she'd worn last night, with her dark hair up in a high ponytail. "All ready."

"Great."

We hustled back into my truck. The drive across town was quiet, punctuated only by the Christmas songs that were still playing on the radio. I didn't have it in me to turn it off even though they reminded me of our night together. I pulled up in front of her sister's house twenty minutes later.

She smiled weakly at me. "Have fun at work," she choked out.

I wanted to kick myself. But I'd known that this wasn't a smart idea. I didn't date girls in town—whether or not they were here for a weekend—for a damn good reason. It made things…complicated. And complicated was not something I could afford outside of the boardroom.

"Thanks. Have fun with your sister."

"My sister," she repeated numbly. "Okay. Well, um...bye."

She hopped out of the truck, gave me a half-wave, and then darted for the confines of the house. She didn't look back before disappearing into the house, and I had the distinct feeling that I had just made her feel cheap.

"Shit," I whispered in the still-freezing air.

I hurried back to my house, took a much-needed shower, and then changed into a crisp black Tom Ford suit that I'd had custom-made at Malouf's in town. It was like the Nordstrom of Lubbock. Family-owned, the store provided and tailored designer and custom-fit clothes by appointment only. I had a standing appointment. I looked like a million bucks. I should feel like a million bucks after last night. Instead, I felt like something had gone horribly wrong when it should have been much simpler.

An hour later, I tramped into my office and was ready for lunch since I'd foregone breakfast in my haste to get into work. Margaret was hot on my heels when I entered Wright Construction.

"Good morning, Mr. Wright," she said, shuffling along with a notebook, iPad, and a pad of sticky notes. "Mr. McCoy called this morning, said it was urgent about the merger, sir. You also had a call from Vanessa. Well, two calls, but I let one go to voice mail. Nick Brown left a message about canceling his appointment because he's going out of town. Alex Langley called out sick. Personally, it sounded like he was out late and hungover. Elizabeth Copeland had an important update on the Lakeridge complex, sir. Sounded rather urgent as well."

"Margaret," I said with a sigh as I reached the door to my office.

"Yes, sir?" She was bright-eyed and bushy-tailed this early in the morning.

"I feel a bit under the weather. Cancel all of my appointments for the day and let Mr. McCoy know that I'll handle the merger in the morning."

"But, sir—" she said again.

"Margaret, let me run my company."

"Of course," she said in a daze, handing me the iPad with my daily notes on it. "Also, Morgan is waiting in your office."

I sighed heavily. "Thank you, Margaret. That will be all."

When I entered my office, Morgan was sitting on the top of my desk, fiddling with the Newton's Cradle kinetic pendulum that swished back and forth. Her dark eyes met mine across the room. "Late night?" she asked with a sardonic tone.

"Indeed."

I set the iPad down on my desk and flipped through the list of things for the day. Margaret would cancel all the extraneous items, but I had a lot to catch up on.

"What's with the late start, bro?" She hopped off the desk, landing on her sky-high heels, and grinned down at me.

"I slept in."

Morgan's eyes widened in disbelief. "Yeah, right! You don't sleep. You're a vampire."

I shrugged. I had no response to that because, up until last night, that had been true. "Don't know what to tell you."

"How about who you were fucking when you *slept in* this morning?" she asked with a mischievous light in her eyes.

I stared back at her with a blank expression on my face and then nodded at the iPad.

"Wait…do I even want to know?"

"Probably not," I told her.

That was a lie. Morgan would love the juicy details. She adored gossip. She read all those trash magazines just to laugh at the absurdity of it all.

"Okay, whatever. Landon called this morning," she said.

My head snapped back up to her. "What for?"

She tilted her head. "Miranda, of course. Why? Why do you look so scared?"

I painted my face back into a mask of indifference. "What did Miranda do now?"

"She wants to keep him in Tampa for Christmas," Morgan said with a wave of her hand.

"He's not considering it, is he?" I asked.

She sighed. "I guess he is."

I grabbed my office phone off the desk. "I'll call him right now and set him straight. He can't stay there because of Miranda. It's Christmas, for Christ's sake."

"I know, Jensen. Miranda has it in her head that Emery Robinson is here to win Landon back," Morgan said with a roll of her eyes.

"That seems very unlikely," I said. I made sure to keep the edge out of my voice. "She's leaving in a few days."

"What?" Morgan asked. "No, she's not. Landon said she was staying here for a while."

"He...what?" I asked, my mouth going dry.

"He tried to tell Miranda that she'd be leaving soon to get her off his case. But she just didn't believe him, and it turned out, she had a reason. Emery told Landon at Sutton's wedding that she was staying here indefinitely. But I mean...I don't know why Emery is back in town, but it sure isn't for Landon. He doesn't even live here. Miranda is out of her mind."

I was completely silent. My head was spinning. Landon had said that Emery was leaving only to appease Miranda. I'd never brought it up with Emery because I thought I already had all my cards in order. She was supposed to be leaving in a few days to head back to Austin. She was supposed to be finishing her PhD. She was *not* supposed to stay in town after we fucked all night.

"Shit," I hissed.

"Right? So, you have to call and convince Landon to bring Miranda here for Christmas. Do whatever you have to, all right? I mean…I can even call Emery or whatever and ask her to stay away from Landon if that helps…" Morgan trailed off when I said nothing. "Why have you gone pale."

"Morg," I said, meeting her worried gaze, "I fucked up."

Fourteen

Emery

"And he just threw my clothes at me and then drove me home!" I recounted to Heidi over lunch.

"Bastard!" Heidi said on cue. "What a bastard!"

"Right? I mean...we had sex for hours last night, and then this morning, it was like a light switch had been flipped. Walking into this, I just *knew* it was a bad idea. He totally used me."

"And it sucked, using him back, right?" Heidi asked, digging into her pad thai—our requisite best friend meal—at the downtown Thai Pepper.

"Dude, the sex was phenomenal," I told her for the hundredth time. "The *turning into a jerk in the morning and dumping me at Kimber's, like a dorm-level walk of shame*, not so much."

I twirled my own extra-spicy pad thai noodles on my fork and dug in. I was famished after my late-night sexcapades. I'd only had two tacos, half of a bag of marshmallows, and some Hershey's chocolate in the last eighteen hours, and I was starving.

"Yeah, well, at least you had some fun," Heidi said. "That was good for you after Professor McJerkface."

I snorted into my food and then hacked and coughed to clear my airway. "Professor McJerkface?"

Heidi shrugged and winked at me. "Pretty much."

"Well, it was a good time. But, you know…it was more than that." Thoughtfully, I set my fork down and sipped on my water. "I kind of like him."

"A Wright brother?" Heidi asked with wide eyes. "Aren't you President of the Anti-Wright Family Fan Club?"

"Something like that," I agreed. "But he was different."

"Oh, boy! Here it goes," Heidi said.

"What?" I demanded.

"You're doing that thing."

"What thing?"

"You know," Heidi said. "The whole *the guy is a jerk, but he's different with me.* News flash, Robinson, he's not different. He just wanted to fuck you."

I flinched. "Thanks for that cheery message."

"Gah, I'm sorry. I just had a weird night, and I worry about you. What happened with Landon was bad enough."

"You were the one pushing me into Jensen's arms."

"Yeah, but that was before you got all doe-eyed and decided he was different. I like Jensen just fine. He's a great boss. He cares about his employees. He knows what he's doing, and he makes us all a lot of money. But I can't pretend that he's this perfect person either. I've heard that he sleeps around when he's at business meetings out of town."

"Ugh! I don't want to think about it. We've all done stupid things. I don't want to judge him. Maybe he's just a manwhore, and that's what last night was about. But you should have warned me!"

"I thought you'd fuck around with him as a nice rebound, Em. I didn't think it'd be anything."

"Well, it's not," I said instantly. "It's definitely not. Remember the whole dropped me off at Kim's like he was taking out the trash? Because I'm pretty sure no matter how different he was with me that asshole sure shone through."

"Well, it's not," I said instantly. "It's definitely not. Remember the whole *dropped me off at Kim's like he was taking out the trash*? Because I'm pretty sure, no matter how different he was with me, that asshole sure shone through."

"Good. That's good. I don't want to see you get hurt again."

"I'm not going to get hurt. Now, what was this about a weird night?" I asked her.

She brushed her hand in front of her face and laughed. "Nothing honestly. I just had a strange phone call, and I ended up talking to the person all night. It was unexpected."

My eyebrows rose in question, but Heidi was already moving on to another topic.

"Do you want to go shopping with me and Julia sometime this week?"

"Two weeks before Christmas. Your favorite time to shop."

"All the crowds and sales and screaming—it makes for a great horror flick."

"Sure, I'm in. I can never resist a good bit of horror."

Right then, my phone pinged noisily.

"Fuck," I groaned, digging it out of my pocket.

I'd forgotten to turn the ringer off this morning. I'd taken a good long shower and an even longer nap once I got home and left the ringer on, so I could get Heidi's text when she got out of her morning meeting.

I clicked the button, and my screen lit up. I had a text message from Jensen. My stomach dropped, and I glanced up at Heidi.

"Let me guess…lover boy?"

"Yeah."

I swiped to open and read the message.

> *Emery, are you free this afternoon? I canceled my meetings for the day and wanted to see if you would be interested in getting coffee. I know this little place over by campus; it's my favorite—Death by Chocolate. I don't know if you've ever been since it's pretty new. I could meet you. Say two o'clock?*

"What does he have to say?"

I passed the phone over to Heidi. "I'm way more confused now."

"He wants to meet you at Kimber's bakery?" Heidi asked with a chuckle.

"I'm sure he doesn't know that she owns it."

"True, but damn. I wonder what happened in his head. Besides the fact that canceling meetings is so not like him. I've never heard of him willfully canceling a meeting. He must have realized how much he fucked up."

"Maybe."

"Or he wants round two."

I snatched my phone out of Heidi's hand. "There's no way."

"Well, are you going to meet him?"

"Did curiosity kill the cat?" I asked her.

"Yeah, but it had nine lives and shit."

———

Death by Chocolate was the love child of my sister's bachelors in food science and her achievements in culinary school. The sugary-sweet smell was what I always associated with Kimber. When we were younger, I used to jokingly sing the Bagel Bites commercial jingle to her with new words about all the baking she did.

"*Cupcakes in the morning, cookies in the evening, chocolate at suppertime. When Kimber's in the kitchen, you can eat baked goods anytime*," I hummed to myself as the bell dinged overhead.

It was a quaint and totally adorable coffee shop and bakery. The floors were black-and-white tiles, and the walls were iced in mint glaze. The countertops were powdered-sugar white granite, and the cabinetry was a buttery lemon bar. Each table was a different-flavored French macaron with cushioned fruit-tart chairs. Elaborate wedding cakes in glass boxes decorated the room. The best part was the bar filled with row after row of sweets hiding behind glass, just waiting to be enjoyed.

"Can I help you?" a girl asked. She wore a Death by Chocolate apron and looked to be a Tech student.

"I'll take a snickerdoodle cookie and two of the strawberry macarons, please."

"And a slice of death by chocolate cake," Jensen said from behind me.

I nearly jumped out of my skin and whirled around. "Jesus, you scared me."

"I didn't mean to sneak up on you. I thought you'd have heard the bell chime," he said.

My eyes traveled the length of him, and I enjoyed every single moment, as if I were looking at my last sunrise. He had on a midnight-black suit that had to have been custom-fitted for his body. His button-up was white and crisp with a herringbone texture that had always been my favorite, and his Texas Tech Red Raiders red tie. And, even though he was dressed as sharp as ever, it was his eyes that caught me. Dark as Kimber's famous chocolate cake and looking at me like most of the customers did when the cake was presented to them.

"It's fine," I said, turning my back on him.

Because it didn't matter how hot he looked or how much he looked like he was ready to devour me again, he had reminded me all too well why I had sworn off the Wright family.

"Anything else for you two?" the woman asked. She placed our treats on the counter.

"I'll take a cup of coffee," I said.

"Make that two."

I pulled out my wallet to pay. I did not want him to think this was a date.

He just shooed me aside. "I've got it."

"I can pay for my own things," I said irritably.

"I know you can, but I invited you here. So, I'm paying." His face was stern, and I realized he had switched into business mode or something. Because he was not brokering any arguments.

I raised my hands in defeat and grabbed my plate of sweets. "I'll get us a table."

A table was open in the back corner, and I plopped down into the open seat that faced the rest of the store. I was maddeningly curious about what Jensen wanted to talk about mere hours after ditching me. Part of me wanted to have a plan for whatever was going to come out of his mouth, but I felt woefully unprepared.

Jensen set our coffees along with his slice of cake on the table. I added cream and sugar while I avoided eye contact.

"Emery," he began, "I…"

I glanced up at him over the rim of my coffee. I blew on it a little and then took a sip. "What?"

"I think I've made a horrible mistake."

"And what would that be?"

"Going on a date with you," he answered.

I was out of my seat before I could even process what had been said. "Well, that's just…that's wonderful, Jensen."

"Emery, sit down. Come on, just sit."

"And why should I?" I set my mug of coffee down but didn't sit. "We had an awesome time last night, and then poof, you turned into an asshole. Then, you invited me here, only to tell me you regret last night?"

"Emery, please," he said. His body was still, perfectly in control. He didn't even glance around at the people who were looking at me funny. "Let me explain."

I sank back into my seat. "Explain what?"

"I thought you were getting your PhD. I thought you said you were still at school in Austin, studying history and European mistresses. That's what you told me. That's what I thought. But you're not doing that," he accused.

My blood ran cold. "What do you mean?"

"You're staying in town, aren't you?" he asked. The idea seemed to distress him.

"How could you possibly know that? I've told only a handful of people, and even my mom doesn't believe me," I told him.

"Because you told Landon," he said with raised eyebrows.

"You talked to Landon?" I gasped. "About me?"

"Not…exactly."

"You didn't tell him what happened, did you?" I asked with wild, wide eyes.

"Look, I didn't talk to him. Morgan did. His wife is still pissed that you're here. Morgan didn't know about what happened with us. So, no, he doesn't know. And I'd like to keep it that way."

"You said…*didn't* know. Morgan didn't know, but she does now?"

Jensen shifted uncomfortably. "It was kind of an accident."

"Oh, for the love of…" I cried, trailing off. "You don't want Landon to find out about your big mistake, but you told Morgan? Are you out of your mind?"

"Starting to feel like it," he grumbled.

"Great. You brought me all the way here just to tell me what a big mistake I was and that Landon is probably going to find out." I grabbed my snickerdoodle cookie and took a giant bite out of it. Then, I gave him a thumbs-up and mockingly nodded my head.

"It's not like that. It's more a matter of principle, Emery. I had a great time, but I don't date girls in town. And, if I had known you were staying, I never would have asked you out."

I swallowed back the choked words that wanted to come out at that statement. I was wrong. Jensen Wright was not different. He was just like every other guy on the planet. He'd used me for sex, and then he'd ditched me. And, even worse, he was making it a point to cement that knowledge with me in person.

"I guessed that when you dropped me off this morning. You didn't need to come here to tell me that to my face," I told him with venom in my voice. I pushed the plate of macarons toward him. "Have a macaron. They're my sister's favorite. She owns this bakery. She'd want you to have one."

I stood and walked away from Jensen.

"Emery," he called.

And then I heard him curse loudly. He jogged to keep up with me as I walked to my Forester waiting on the street.

He grabbed my elbow and tried to pull me to a stop. "Emery. Hey, stop."

"Why?" I asked. "We had one night together. What am I to you?"

"I don't know!" he said, frazzled. "I don't know, all right? It's like some goddamn self-preservation kicked in, and I had to stop this before it got out of hand."

"How could it *possibly* get out of hand?" I demanded.

"Because being with you breaks all the rules!"

"Rules are meant to be broken."

"Not these rules."

I shrugged. "I have rules, too. I swore, I'd never look at another person from the Wright family. I decided Wright *isn't* right," I said, mocking the Wright Construction motto. "Yet here we are."

Then, suddenly, Jensen's fingers pushed up into my loose ponytail. His palms cupped my cheeks. His dark eyes gazed down into mine, and I didn't move a muscle to stop him. The energy felt charged, heating the air between us and dragging me into his downward spiral. I could see our breaths mingling in the frigid air. His lips met mine, soft and tender, searching to make sure this was allowed. I was frozen for a second before I met his touch. He pulled me against him, crushing our mouths together. And it didn't seem to matter in this moment that we were in broad daylight on one of the busiest streets in Lubbock.

I couldn't get enough of his mouth, his body. The feel of him through the layers of clothing. The taste of him. He was everywhere.

Slowly, my brain came back to my body, and I shoved him away from me.

"How dare you!" I spat. "You cannot send me mixed signals like this, Jensen. Either you want more or you don't. I won't play games with you. I'm tired of being jerked around by men who think that they can do whatever they want."

"Emery, that's not—"

"Save it," I said, raising my hand to silence him. "I've heard enough."

Fifteen

Emery

I leaned back against the giant glasses sculpture outside of the Buddy Holly Center. They were iconic to the legend who had been born here and gone on to such fame. I'd worked here on and off throughout most of high school, and being back felt just as surreal as everything else that had been happening in my life. I felt like I was reliving high school, only with a different Wright brother.

Betty hit the curb in her old red Buick LaCrosse and then parked in front of the center. She waved at me from the driver's side. I could only laugh. She had always been out there.

"Hi, Emery, dear. How are you?" Betty said. She hurried over to where I was standing and then gestured for me to follow her.

"Doing all right. How about yourself?" I asked.

Betty jingled the keys and then hit the door with her hip to let us inside. "I'm just fine. This way. Oh, you know the way."

I did, but I didn't say anything.

"I'm dreadfully sorry that we're closed today. We had to do some maintenance and decided to just shut down during the holidays."

"Maintenance?" I asked.

"Replace the floors, new roof—that sort of thing. Wright Construction offered to do the whole thing at a discount since we're a historic museum. Isn't that wonderful?" Better asked. She finally reached her office and let me inside.

"Just wonderful," I agreed, unable to escape the Wrights for even one day.

"That Jensen Wright came over to tell me himself."

"That was nice of him," I said through gritted teeth.

"Here we are," Betty said. "Thank you for being able to meet with me today. I'm going to Florida to visit my grandbabies for Christmas, and I won't be back until after the New Year. It would have delayed everything for you."

"This is great. I just appreciate you coming in early for me. Who is going to be here to let people in for the construction crew?" I took the stack of paperwork from Betty and hastily filled out the sections to get my job back and be on payroll.

"We have a few people who will be here for the holidays. They have keys and can alternate days. But we're closed up from Christmas to New Years."

"Well, if you need someone, just let me know. I will be around."

"I'm sure they would love to work you into the schedule. Let me get you a copy of the key while we're at it," she said.

A few minutes later, I had successfully filled out the paperwork, gotten ahold of the keys to the Center, and was on the schedule for the construction crew. That also meant I was going to be getting some money in for the holidays.

I left Betty, feeling more accomplished. Even though this wasn't my dream job, it was at least *a* job. Something tangible to hold me in Lubbock that wasn't just family and old memories.

When I hopped back into my Forester, I realized that had taken a lot longer than I'd thought. It had only felt like a few minutes, being inside there, but I was definitely going to be late for my shopping date with Heidi and Julia. They seemed intent on me going, and I did need a pick-me-up.

I had been trying not to think about Jensen and what had happened. But I was just so confused and upset, something I didn't really like admitting. I hated him thinking that what we had done was a mistake. I wanted more of his kisses. I wanted more of the guy who had unapologetically sang Mariah Carey with me. And, even worse, I knew that he was right. I hadn't thought this was a real thing to begin with. I'd wanted to get a piece of him without thinking about what would come next. I wanted to think it was better this way, but it didn't feel like that. I was hoping retail therapy would help.

Malouf's was swamped for the holidays, and it wouldn't have been my first choice. Mostly because I couldn't afford anything in the store. Everything was designer and custom-made. Kate Spade, Kendra Scott, Tom Ford. Oh, my! But Heidi and Julia each had well-paying Wright Construction jobs, and I was sure I could find *something*. Maybe on the sale rack.

I hurried across the parking lot to get out of the frigid, windy weather. Screw Lubbock and its freezing air the day after it was seventy. I barreled through the front door and found Heidi talking animatedly to Julia, who was holding up a black dress with a plunging neckline.

"I'm here. I made it. Sorry I'm late," I said to the girls.

"Em! Just in time," Heidi said. "Tell Julia that she would look smoking hot in this dress."

"It's black. I like it." That had been my motto since junior high. My closet was filled up with black jeans, black sweaters, black tank tops, and black sneakers. All black everything.

"I knew you would say that," Heidi said with a grin.

Contemplatively, Julia held the dress at arm's length. Black was a good choice with her hair that had all the burgundy undertones that she'd highlighted. Plus, it was slimming, which was good for everyone, except for Heidi, who was built like a Barbie doll. And, while Heidi had the enviable prom-queen looks, Julia just had something about her. Between her mahogany hair and studded ears and tattoos peeking out from under her edgy leather-detailed dress, she was the mysterious girl you didn't bring home to Mom. I liked her for that. Kind of felt like she and I could gang up on Heidi together…and maybe even win. But probably not.

"It's so not me, but I'll try it on."

"Nothing in this store is ever me either," I told Julia. "But, if you don't try on everything Heidi wants you to wear, then you won't make it out of here alive."

"Damn straight," Heidi said with a sharp nod of her head. "Now, let me play dress-up!"

We wandered around the store together with Heidi randomly throwing things into our arms. Julia and I exchanged looks full of sympathy for each other. I had something hot pink in my pile. Julia had a pastel. Heidi herself had all the best pieces that only worked on someone who was five foot nine or above.

The manager came over and procured dressing rooms for all of us, offering us assistance if we needed different sizes. I shimmied into the hot-pink dress first just to get it over with, and Heidi hysterically laughed at me until I went back into the dressing room for something else.

"Okay, I know it's a touchy subject," Heidi called over the dressing room wall, "but can we talk about Jensen?"

I stepped out of the dressing room and crossed my arms until she came out of her room. "No."

"What about Jensen?" Julia asked.

She appeared in a stunning olive-green dress that complemented her style perfectly. I was sure it would be a winner.

"Can I tell?" Heidi asked.

"Fine, but I'm not trying on that weird patterned thing you gave me," I told her.

"Ugh! Fine! I'm just trying to brighten up your wardrobe."

"You've been trying for twenty years. It's not going to work."

She laughed and flipped me off. "Anyway, Emery went on a date with Jensen."

"Oh, wow! Was it hot?" Julia asked.

"So hot," Heidi said.

"Heidi, can you not?" I demanded.

"Sorry!" she squeaked. "Anyway, he was a total ass to her afterward, and then he was an even bigger ass by asking her to coffee to tell her the whole thing was a mistake."

"That sucks. Sorry, Emery," Julia said.

"It's fine," I told them. "Really, it was one date. And then… another kiss that meant nothing. He kissed me after telling me how much of a mistake us our date was because he doesn't date in town and how it never should have happened because I moved back home. Oh! And he fucking told Morgan. Now, Landon is totally going to find out."

"And Landon doesn't know you went on a date with his brother?" Julia asked.

I shook my head. "I'd like to keep it that way."

Okay, so I wasn't fine. I was still frustrated. Even more so because Jensen hadn't left me alone. He'd messaged me a handful of times to try to talk to me again. I couldn't figure out why he thought I would see him again. After our last conversation and how it had ended, I didn't think that was a good idea.

"Yeah, but he's still messaging you," Heidi said.

"Then, he must like you," Julia said. "Maybe he's just… bad at communication."

"Just what I want in a guy. A bad communicator."

"That's not what I meant," Julia said. "I mean, what if he is scared of how he feels for you? You said he didn't date in town. Maybe it just freaked him out when he realized that you were going to live here, and he said things all wrong."

I slid my gaze over to Julia. "Jensen Wright does not say things wrong. He is a businessman. He says what he means and takes what he wants. I feel that I have to take him at face value."

"That seems fair," Julia said. "But the real question is it worth always having that what-if with him?"

I shrugged. That I didn't know. It was too much to think about.

"Just go into it with your eyes wide open," Heidi said. "You know he has baggage and shit. He's a Wright. He's filthy rich and sleeps with supermodels and all that. You know his deal. If you can live with him flying to New York every holiday, then who am I to stop you from having some fun? I just want you to be happy."

"Also, that dress is fucking hot," Julia said to change the subject.

I glanced at my dress in the trifold mirror and smiled. It did look fucking hot. Actually, it was perfect. It was a skintight black dress with a lace front neckline that went down to almost my navel and had an open back. Paired with some stiletto heels out of Kimber's closet, and I could even pass for a girlie girl.

"You need it," Heidi said at once. "I mean, you really, really need it."

I checked the price tag, and my eyes doubled in size. "It's three hundred dollars. I don't need it that bad."

"Oh, but you do! And…I haven't gotten you a Christmas present yet. So, that can be my present!" Heidi said.

"Psht! Are you insane? I'm not letting you get me a three-hundred-dollar dress for Christmas."

"Why not?"

"Because I could never repay you for a present like that. Anyway, where would I even wear this? I live in jeans and T-shirts. I would get no use out of it."

"Actually," Heidi said with innocent eyes.

"Oh no," I said with a sigh. "You're about to tell me the real reason we're shopping, aren't you?"

"There's a Christmas party I want you to come to with me and Julia on Friday night. And I thought we could all get our dresses for the party here!"

My eyes slid to Julia. "Where's the party? I know she won't tell me."

"Uh…"

"Come on, Em. It's just one party."

"Yeah, and it was just one wedding. Look how well that worked out for me," I told her.

"I think it worked out pretty well. You're not thinking about Professor McJerkface, and you had a lot of sex."

Julia snort-laughed and then covered her mouth. "Professor McJerkface?"

"It's a long story," I told her.

"Okay, picture this," Heidi said. "You wear that dress. I do your hair and makeup. You borrow Kimber's stilettos, the really fancy Louboutins that crush your pinkie toes. But how can you resist the red-lacquered backs?" It was as if she were reading my mind. "You walk into the party. All eyes fall on you. You're like fucking Cinderella for a moment. And then, poof, your Prince Charming shows up, and voilà, the night has endless possibilities."

"Oh God," I said in horror. "You're talking about your office Christmas party."

Heidi bit her bottom lip. "Um…yes."

"And, when you say *endless possibilities*, you mean, I trip over my feet in front of Jensen, and he's the same jerk he was and laughs at me or something."

"Don't be ridiculous."

"Yeah, really, I don't think Jensen would ever laugh at someone like that," Julia added. "Plus, it won't suck because, it's open bar, and we can all get wasted on champagne."

"Oh, I like you," I told her.

"See, Em?! Please, please, please," Heidi said.

"I'll think about it."

"Yes!" Heidi said, as if I had relented.

"While we're at it," Julia said, her cheeks turning a soft shade of pink, "want to find me something that sexy? There's a Wright brother I wouldn't mind looking at me twice in something like that."

"Landon?" Heidi asked at the same time as I said, "Austin?"

I glanced over at Heidi with an arched eyebrow. "Landon doesn't even *work* for Wright Construction."

"Process of elimination," she said quickly. "So, Austin?"

"I think he's scared of me because I work in HR. But he's not technically my boss; Jensen is. I don't think we could get in trouble. And I'm head of HR anyway."

"Oh, I can find you something," Heidi said. "Each of my girls with a Wright brother will be my New Year's resolution."

"You kill me," I said with a shake of my head. "I'm not letting you buy the dress."

I changed out of the dress and shimmied into a few of the other outfits. But none of them came close to the other one. I hung the dress back up, and Heidi snatched it back. We went back and forth until I finally gave up. In the end, I got the dress. And, secretly…I couldn't wait to see Jensen's face when he saw me in it.

Sixteen

Jensen

Patrick hadn't stopped laughing at me for a solid ten minutes. If I were a violent man, I would have put my fist through his face a long while ago. Instead, I just waited patiently for him to chill the fuck out. Austin would be here in about twenty minutes, and Patrick needed to get his shit together before then.

It was bad enough that Morgan knew about what had happened with Emery. I didn't want Austin to know anything. Morgan and I, at least, were on the same page. We always had been; it didn't matter that she was seven years younger than me. For a long time, everyone had thought she and Landon were twins, but they couldn't have been further apart as far as personalities went. And, sometimes, I thought it was scary how much she and I were on the same wavelength.

So, at least I knew she wasn't going to run to Landon to try to make things right. I just had to figure out what I was going to do. Because texting Emery all week and getting radio silence had clearly not been working out well for me.

And I should have just left her alone. That was what I'd said I wanted even if it was a lie. It just wasn't smart to bring her into all of my baggage. Yet I couldn't stop thinking about her. And texting her. And I was considering showing up at her sister's house with a boom box and waiting until she came outside.

No, I probably wouldn't do that last one. That only worked in the movies.

"Tell me again that the girl from the wedding is Landon's ex-girlfriend. It's funnier every time you say it," Patrick said.

I just stared back at him with a look of deep disinterest. "How about we skip that part?"

"Okay, okay," Patrick said. He straightened up and wiped a tear from his eye. "I'm just imagining you striking out now. I've seen you pick up more girls than most famous athletes."

"I didn't strike out," I told him through gritted teeth.

"Yeah, y'all fucked, and then she straight fucked with your head. What were you thinking, man?"

"I was thinking that things were too complicated with Emery already," I told him honestly. I leaned back against the door to my office with a weary expression. Things *were* too complicated. Much too complicated. Yet part of me didn't give two fucks. We'd had an amazing night, and then I'd slept through the night. Both things were nothing short of a miracle in my world.

"Complicated?" Patrick asked. He poured out two shots of top-shelf bourbon. The liquid made a *glub, glub, glub* sound as it flowed out of the crystal decanter. "Shit's not complicated, Jensen. You like her. That's why you're freaking out."

"That would be a problem," I told him.

Patrick shook his head and passed me a shot. He held his up in the air. "The problem is with your head, man. Get in good while you can. You don't know if things will go south, and stressing about it will only ruin it. Enjoy it while it lasts."

We each tipped back the shot of bourbon, and Patrick stood from the desk. He grinned with a boyish look. He never thought too hard or long on his own problems. It was why he and Austin were still bachelors and hadn't had serious girlfriends since college.

I hated to tell him that I *did* know that things would go south. It was a guarantee with me considering my past. I hated thinking that I liked Emery because I didn't want to hurt her. And, if she actually got to know me, it would be inevitable.

"Y'all ready?" Morgan asked, appearing from around the corner of my office.

She was decked out in a shimmery red cocktail dress with her dark hair curled, nearly reaching to her waist. Her eyes shot to Patrick. We were both sporting the standard-issue tuxedo. Her look said one thing and one thing only. And I wished she and Patrick would fuck it out or move on already.

Not that I was one to talk right at this moment.

"Yeah. Austin?" I asked.

Austin walked into the office a second later, carrying another bottle of bourbon. It was half-empty, and in his eyes, I could see that he was already drunk. All-too familiar at this point. As much as I needled him about it, I did fucking worry about him becoming the alcoholic that our father had been.

"Good to go, bro," Austin said. He held up the bottle, as if in a toast.

"Let's get upstairs then," I told them.

We all walked out of my office and down the hall to the elevator that led to the top floor of the Wright Construction building. It was a massive high-rise downtown that overlooked the Texas Tech campus. The restaurant at the top had a panoramic view of the skyline and some of the best food in town. We held business dinners up here and hosted parties, and every year, it was the spot for the annual Wright Construction office Christmas party.

Already, the room was full of the corporate staff who worked in the business below. People were dressed in their best cocktail attire, leaving behind their business suits for dress clothes. It was like seeing the office come to life once every year. Even Mick in accounting had dressed up, and he was acting like he was having a good time. He was the most curmudgeonly old man I'd ever encountered.

The line at the bar was the biggest attraction, and soon, the buffet would open up. We had the food catered every year as a thank-you that went with the year-end bonuses.

I shook hands and said my fair share of hellos as we moved through the crowd, heading toward the DJ that was currently playing Christmas music. It was my mission to make sure I knew each person on the team. Ever since my father had died and I'd taken over the company, my life had been almost entirely about work. The few exceptions to still lived in New York and hadn't exactly worked out as I'd expected. Work was always reliable.

As I greeted people, my eyes sought out one person. Heidi. She was Emery's best friend. She would know what to make of the whole situation. And, though I had never had a conversation with Heidi that wasn't about work, considering the array of men falling at her feet, I thought maybe she would understand where I was coming from on this one.

But I never found her.

And then I was quickly ushered up to the DJ and handed a microphone.

Here goes nothing.

"Ladies and gentlemen, may I have your attention?" I said.

Slowly, the voices died down, and faces turned to stare up at me at the front of the room. My eyes roamed the room, trying to pick out Heidi in the crowd.

"I don't want to take up too much of your time. I just wanted to say thank you so much for all that you do for this company. Every single person in this room is integral to the development and continual progress of Wright Construction."

A few people in the back clapped, and then everyone joined in, applauding their own accomplishments.

"Additionally, I wanted to make you all aware that, as of next week, Wright Construction will merge with the Tarman Corporation headquartered in Austin."

There were loud whispers all around as everyone tried to figure out what that would mean for them.

"Wright Construction is purchasing the company to continue to grow and expand in and out of Texas."

I was about to say something else when a figure appeared at the back of the room. It was as if a spotlight were being held over Emery's body, revealing her to me. She looked stunning in a tightfitting black dress. And, for a moment, I was completely frozen in place. All thoughts of letting her leave for her own good disappeared. I was *not* going to let that woman walk away from me.

I could feel her eyes on me from across the room. She smirked like she fucking knew what she was doing to me. And it only made me want her more.

"Jensen," Morgan muttered, nudging me.

"Um…yes. Right. More details regarding that will follow," I said into the microphone. I'd completely lost my train of thought. "Now, more booze! Enjoy!"

I handed the microphone back to the DJ and turned to go find Emery, but Morgan blocked my way.

"More booze? Enjoy?" she asked in dismay. "What the hell is wrong with you?"

"Something else is on my mind."

"Jensen, you didn't even tell them that we weren't downsizing here. You didn't tell them what the merger meant or that we'd be getting new employees from Tarman."

"Then, you tell them, Morgan," I told her.

My eyes drifted over her head to try to find Emery again, but she was gone. It was as if she had come to me like a vision in that moment and had since disappeared.

"What?" Morgan asked, staggered. "You want *me* to address the crowd?"

"You're a Wright, are you not? You know just as much about the merger as I do."

"But, Jensen…" she whispered.

I smiled and bumped her shoulder. "I have faith in you."

"Wait, where are you going?" she asked as I moved away from her.

"To make another mistake," I told her before melting into the crowd.

Seventeen

Emery

O kay, so I'd made my grand appearance.

I'd felt like Drew Barrymore in *Ever After*, whispering to myself, "Just breathe," when I entered the room. I'd caught Jensen's eye. He'd stared at me, momentarily in shock. I'd basked in the glow of that attention. And then I'd promptly and completely lost my nerve, disappearing into the crowd by the bar with Heidi.

What am I even doing here?

He'd pushed me away. Twice.

It was no matter that he'd been texting me all week. His text messages had been nonsensical. Half-trying to convince me that leaving me was for the best and half-trying to convince me to give him another chance. I didn't know which half he wanted me to believe. So, I just hadn't responded. I was still hurt from the conversation we'd had at Death by Chocolate. I should have just stayed home. Actually, I should have probably already left.

What am I trying to prove by being here? That I can get his attention? Check.

I knew that I couldn't ignore him if he approached me. That was why I had moved out of the spotlight as soon as I had. I might have had the strength to push him away that day after our date, but after a week of his messages, I was too curious to step back now. I wanted to know why he had been acting like this and whether or not the guy I'd had that first date with still existed somewhere in there.

A hand on my elbow made me jump. I whirled around and came face-to-face with Jensen Wright himself.

"Oh," I said, feeling like an idiot.

"Oh?" he asked.

And then I just stared at him because seeing him across the room had not done him justice. I never thought I would be the kind of girl who swooned at a guy in a tuxedo, but hot damn. Jensen Wright wore a tux like a second skin. It molded to him, and all the long, straight lines did things to his body that just weren't possible in other clothing. Or maybe I was biased.

"It's you," I finally managed to get out.

"You do realize that this is an office party, right?" he asked. He arched an eyebrow, as if asking, *What the hell are you doing here?*

"I might have heard that somewhere." I sank into my hip and let him get a good look at the black dress I'd gotten earlier this week.

"Last I checked, you didn't work for me, Miss Robinson."

"True," I agreed, fluttering my eyelashes. "Are you going to kick me out?"

"I might let you stay…if you tell me what you're doing here."

I swallowed. I had no answer to that one. I'd come at Heidi's request, but I knew that wasn't the answer he was looking for, and it wasn't even half of the real reason.

"I came to listen to your inspirational speech. More booze, Mr. Wright. Very motivational."

He laughed unabashedly. It was deep and masculine and sincere.

"Thank you. Probably not my best speech, but I got a little distracted."

"Oh, yeah?" I asked innocently. "What distracted you?"

"A beautiful woman walked in the door."

"Oh," I said with a shrug. "You must get distracted a lot then."

Jensen ran his hand down my bare arm and firmly shook his head once. "Never."

Where he touched me on my arm seemed to be radiating with heat. In fact, my entire body was aching to get closer to him. To let him run his hands all over my body again. Being with him was supposed to be something light and fun. I wasn't supposed to want more. I'd thought I could get him out of my system. Yet here I was, at his office Christmas party. It was now crystal clear that I was not going to get Jensen Wright out of my system with a one-night stand. But I was sure that I wouldn't mind trying it again and again until it worked out.

"I think I should escort you out, Emery," Jensen said, drawing me nearer to himself.

"Right now?" I asked, confused.

"Yes. Would you like to see my office on the way out?"

My mouth opened slightly, and I watched the way his gaze drift to my lips.

Was he thinking about how I'd sucked him? Was he thinking about much more?

It was all there in his eyes, and I was sure it was reflected in mine.

"I'd love to."

Jensen and I walked out of the party without a backward glance. I thought for sure that someone would stop us as we exited the top-floor restaurant. But it seemed that everyone was too engrossed in the end of Morgan's speech, the open bar, and the buffet. No one paid us any mind as we disappeared into the elevator and to the darkened floor below.

The elevator doors opened, and Jensen took my hand to guide me down to his office. We reached the end of the hall, and Jensen flicked the switch to turn on the lights. It was a massive corner office with a giant mahogany desk taking up the center of the room and an all-glass wall facing campus. It was modern and sleek and undeniably powerful. I could feel the energy from the room. It was the same power and control that I felt from Jensen.

He stood directly behind me and ran his hands down my arms. His mouth came down to my shoulder and placed a soft, possessive kiss there. "You've been ignoring me," he muttered.

I shivered at his touch. It was amazing, how moving from a crowded party and into his office had given him so much authority. We were on his turf. This was his domain. And he knew it.

"You told me you made a horrible mistake," I whispered into the room.

"Emery." His hands moved to my waist and trailed down the curves of my body.

The back of my dress was open, and I could feel the heat coming off of him through his tux.

"You have principles, Jensen," I teased.

That was what he had said. Though I still had no idea what it meant. It seemed to be an odd rule that he refused to date girls in town.

He spun me around, and I nearly stumbled into him. I wasn't used to Kimber's Louboutin high heels, and Jensen made me feel off-balance. Like I was teetering between fantasy and reality.

"Fuck principles," he said.

Shock registered on my face before I hastily concealed it. "Why? Why would you say that about the very principles that pushed me away?"

Jensen cupped my chin and forced me to look up at him. I hadn't even realized that I'd been staring down at his bowtie, trying to hide my emotions. But they were plain on my face. Confusion, desire, hope, disbelief.

My shoulders were up, as if to guard me from the oncoming disappointment. I could see it coming.

"Because I had the best night with you, the best *sex* with you," he added, pushing me back into his desk and making my imagination spiral away with all the things we could do on it, "and I slept seven whole hours with you in my arms. I'm an insomniac, and I cannot tell you the last time I slept that long. I said those things because I like you, and I didn't know how to react to that."

"So, you pushed me away?"

"I did, and I'm not proud of it." His lips nearly brushed mine when he said, "But I can't get you out of my head. You've taken over my thoughts, my daydreams, my every last desire, and I haven't slept since that night."

"How do I know you're not just going to change your mind again?" I whispered. Though I was sure my voice betrayed the fact that I had already made up my mind. I would do unspeakable things with him and not think twice.

"You don't, but I'm willing to see where this goes if you are."

I nodded. "Yes."

"Good. One question, how much do you like this dress?" he asked, speculatively eyeing it.

"It's a Christmas present actually."

"God bless whoever gave it to you," he said with a grin, "but I'd like it on the floor."

I released a deep throaty laugh and reached for the side zipper. The dress slid down my body, all the way to my hips, and then it dropped into a heap on the floor. Since the dress was backless, I had to go braless. Now, I was dressed in nothing but a black lace thong and Louboutin heels.

I slowly stepped out of the dress and kicked it out of the way. *Thanks for the present, Heidi!*

"That's better," he said.

His hands slid behind my legs and lifted me off the ground. I squeaked at the sudden movement as he roughly placed me on the edge of his desk. He swept his hand over the top of it, letting half of the contents clatter to the ground, leaving a space for my body. He laid me back on the desk and raised my legs.

I tried to kick off the shoes, but he stopped me.

"Oh no," he said. "If you're going to wear designer shoes around me, then it'd be a shame not to fuck you in them."

The way he observed me made my core clench, and I could feel my body responding to him…and he hadn't even kissed me yet.

Then, I forgot all about the damn shoes as he kissed his way, achingly slow and tender, up my right leg. He reached the upper limit of my inner thigh, and I was writhing under him, practically begging for more. But he didn't give me what I wanted. Instead, he moved to my other leg and started kissing all the way up that leg. It was torture of the best variety. And different than the last time we had been together.

We might have been at his house, but we had been on equal footing there. Here, he had the power, and I was his to guide. And, for once in my life, I let myself be ravaged. I didn't care what would come after this and how we would move forward. I let him tease me until I could hardly take it anymore. His hands splayed my legs further apart, and then he blew hot against my damp underwear.

"Please," I whimpered.

He hooked his fingers under my thong and slipped it off my body. I was completely naked now, save for the high heels.

He propped my feet up on the desk and stared down at me, as if he were taking a picture for safekeeping.

Then, his hands went to the button of his tuxedo pants. He slipped the zipper down to the base and then dropped his pants. His dick was bulging under his boxer briefs, and I ached to run my hand down it, to take it in my mouth, and to hear him make all those delicious noises all over again. But I could see in his eyes that he had other things on his mind.

He palmed his cock in his hand, found a condom, and slipped it on. Then, he strode back toward me. I hadn't moved a muscle the whole time. My breathing was shallow as I imagined what was to come. But I couldn't have prepared myself.

Without comment, he slid into me to the hilt in one thrust. I was practically dripping on his desk, but I still gasped in shock as he stretched me to the fullest.

My body felt alive.

Alive and euphoric.

He gripped my hips so tight that he left little indents in the skin, and I worried there might be bruising tomorrow. Yet I didn't care one bit. Just a sexy-as-fuck mark to show that he had claimed me. And claimed me, he did.

He pulled out of me and then slammed back in harder than the last time. My body rocked back toward the end of his desk, but he held on, rocking into me over and over again. Keeping up a jarring, uneven, intensely erotic pace that I couldn't hope to match. So, I let him take complete control and tried to keep from screaming so loud that the people one story up could hear me.

We didn't last like last time. We didn't stand a chance. We were both heated up from our time apart and desperate for another round. I wasn't trying to take my time, and he had no intentions of allowing it. It was clear that rough, hard, and fast were the only options in this scenario.

My mind disconnected from my body as I came violently and blissfully. I soared away into the abyss of pleasure. Relegating myself to base emotions only. Allowing myself to relish in how perfect every moment had been. To feel so extravagantly, so intentionally, and so unabatedly that all else fell away.

I realized Jensen was resting forward over me as I came back to myself. My legs were trembling like a newborn lamb, and a light sheen of sweat caressed my skin. Jensen's eyes glimmered with passion and elation. I knew that he could go again soon, but for now, there was only immense satisfaction.

He slid out of me and offered me the bathroom attached to his office. When I finished cleaning up, I came back to see that Jensen looked immaculate again. His tux was perfectly in place, and if I hadn't just seen the raw and wild man beneath, I'd never have known that he'd just fucked my brains out.

"Do you have to go back to the party?" I asked, unable to keep the caution out of my voice. I reached for my dress and slid it back on, securing the zipper in place.

"I seem to be otherwise occupied," he said.

He drew me into him, and for the first time all night, he planted an affectionate kiss on my lips. I fell into it, wanting nothing less than a thousand more of them.

"I like that," I said.

"I think I'm going to have to take you out now."

"Oh? Tacos?" I only half-joked.

"Probably something nicer than tacos after the week I've put you through," he said.

"You don't have to do that. I don't need a fancy dinner as an apology. I liked our first date," I told him truthfully. "It felt...real."

He smiled down at me and captured another kiss. "It was."

Eighteen

Emery

"Emery!" Kimber yelled.

"Just a second," I called back. I was putting the finishing touches on my hair, trying to make it do what Heidi had gotten it to do and failing miserably. I put the curling wand down and shrugged. It was better to go just as myself than to try to be someone I wasn't. And a girl who fixed her hair on the regular was definitely not me.

"Emery, now!" Kimber screamed.

My eyebrows rose, and I hurried out of the bathroom. "What is it? What's going on?"

I found Kimber curled in the fetal position on the floor of her bedroom. She was breathing deeply and winced in pain.

"Oh my God!" I cried. "Are you having contractions? Are you in labor?"

"I don't"—she cried out and then clenched down, as if bracing herself—"know. It could just be Braxton Hicks contractions."

"You're speaking another language to me," I said. I hurried to her side and helped her back up onto the bed. "I don't know what that means. What can I do? Where's Lily?"

"Nothing. Just—oh God!" she said, clenching up again. "Just stay here a minute. Lily is playing in her room."

"Okay. Should I check on her? Should I just stand here?"

"Em, really not the time. Just hold my"—she viciously squeezed down on my hand—"hand."

"Got it. Hand-holding."

"Braxton Hicks contractions are just prep for actual labor. They usually go away all on their own, but if they don't, then I'll have to go to the hospital."

"Should I call Noah?" I asked.

She nodded her head. "You'd better, just in case. I know he'd want to be here."

I dialed Noah's number and filled him in on what was going on. He promised he'd be on his way in a matter of minutes. When I hung up, Kimber was in the middle of another contraction. I didn't know anything about Braxton Hicks contractions, but she looked like she was in a lot of pain. Even if she wasn't going into labor, I wanted her to be seen by a doctor. Noah should be able to tell if something was wrong, but I'd be happier if we got her to the hospital.

Noah arrived from the medical center in record time. He took a quick look at his wife. "Looks like things are progressing quickly. Better safe than sorry, my love."

"Get the bag," Kimber said with a sigh. "I hoped that she'd wait until after Christmas. This is early."

"She's as stubborn as her mother. Comes and goes whenever she wants without consulting anyone at all," I joked.

Kimber gave me a grim smile. "Can you watch Lilyanne for us? I hate to ask. I know that you have a date tonight."

"Of course I can watch Lily. Don't even think twice about it. Just make sure everything is all right with you and know that I have things under control here."

Kimber kissed my cheek. "You're a lifesaver."

"Text me if you need me!" I called as I watched them go.

I traipsed back into my room and dialed Jensen's number. I knew he'd been planning our official date for a few days. He'd had a lot of business to catch up on, and I hadn't seen him, except at church on Sunday morning. But we'd talked every night, and I thought it was progress, on our way to something normal.

"Hey, Emery," he said when he answered the phone. "I was just about to leave my house."

"Actually…"

"Oh no, are you canceling?"

"Not on purpose," I assured him. "My sister went into labor, or maybe pseudo labor, and they're heading to the hospital. I promised her I'd watch my niece. So, I guess we'll have to cancel."

"Hmm," he said. "How about I come over there and help you babysit?"

"You…what? You want to help watch Lily?" I asked, confused.

"I'd still like to see you, and I like kids."

"But it's not our fancy dinner date…"

"Yes. But I haven't seen you in days, and I'm not giving up the opportunity. Unless you don't want me to be around your niece?"

"No, it's not that. I'd love for you to come over. I bet Lilyanne would, too."

"Great. Then, it's a date."

I pocketed my cell phone and hurried to Lily's room. She was still playing peacefully when I entered. Kimber didn't want Lily to know anything was wrong until they were sure she was in labor. She was certain that it would keep Lily up all night. So, it was up to me to entertain the munchkin until I had more substantial news.

"Hey, Lily Bug," I said. "What are you up to?"

"Playing with Barbies." She had a collection of them in various stages of dress on the floor.

"Well, I just wanted to let you know that your mommy and daddy went to the doctor for a checkup, and I get to watch you tonight."

"Is my new baby sister coming?" she asked with big excited eyes.

"Not yet. Just a checkup, but that means you get to hang out with Auntie Em tonight. You know what that means?"

Lily jumped up to her feet. "Ice cream and sprinkles and Disney movies!"

"That's right, missy!"

I lifted her into my arms and carried her downstairs. We raided the freezer. I knew where Noah tried to hide all the good flavors of ice cream, and we took out every last carton to decide on what we wanted. I liked to make her a bowl of ice cream about the size of the one in *Home Alone* and then hand her off to my sister. Tonight, I'd have to deal with putting her to sleep, so I knew that a mountain of ice cream might not be the best bet.

I placed a couple of scoops of chocolate ice cream in her bowl and a mix of strawberry, vanilla, and strawberry cheesecake into mine. We fished through the toppings, drizzling chocolate fudge and sprinkles on our desserts, and then we carried our bowls out to the living room.

Lily was busy with perusing the movies when the doorbell rang. "I'll get it!" she cried. "Mommy, Daddy, is my new sister here?"

I laughed and followed her to the front door. "You know it's not time yet. I have another surprise for you instead."

Turning the doorknob, I opened it to reveal Jensen standing at the front door. My breath caught at the sight of him in jeans and a casual button-up. It had only been a few days, but I'd missed seeing that grin.

"My boyfriend!" Lily cried.

Jensen laughed. "Hey, Lilyanne. I heard you had a pretty awesome babysitter and thought I would drop by to hang out, too. How does that sound?"

"Yes! Where are my flowers?" Lilyanne asked.

I snorted. "Oh, boy!"

"Guess I should have seen that one coming," Jensen said.

I stepped back to let him come in out of the cold. Lilyanne took his hand and guided him into the living room. She babbled the entire time about our ice cream creations and asked him what movie he wanted to watch and if she could paint his nails. I tried to conceal the laugh that was bubbling up, but it was there anyway. Yet Jensen didn't seem in the least bit perturbed by her questions.

"I think I need my own ice cream before we start the movie," Jensen told her.

"I can help!" Lilyanne cried. "I'm great with sprinkles."

"I bet you are." He lifted her up and onto his shoulders, and he carried her into the kitchen.

Lilyanne screamed in pure joy at being so high in the air, and I just followed in awe.

Jensen scooped out his own ice cream and let Lily add the sprinkles. Then, he took the bowl back into the living room with Lily back on his shoulders. He easily dropped her in front of the shelf of Disney movies and then leaned over and pulled me tight against him.

"I missed you," he said. He planted a firm but quick kiss on my lips.

"I missed you, too. Are you sure you don't mind this?"

"Do I look like I mind?"

I shook my head. He definitely didn't.

"Who could pass up a big bowl of ice cream and Disney movies?" he asked.

"I'm certain, no one."

"Found it!" Lilyanne cried.

"Let me guess," I said.

"No! It's a surprise."

"Okay. I won't look," I told her. I took the Blu-ray from her and popped it into the player.

Lilyanne took the spot next to Jensen and instructed me that I had to sit on the other side of her. With Lily in the middle, Jensen draped his arm across the back of the couch and kept his hand on my shoulder. I smiled at him as the opening credits to *Frozen* began. It was only a matter of minutes before the entire thing became a sing-along. By the time "Let It Go" came on, Jensen and I were swinging Lily between us as we all led into the chorus.

We finished *Frozen*, and we were halfway through *Tangled* when Lily began to crash. To my amazement, it was already well past her bedtime. She lay stretched out between us with her head on a pillow in my lap. Her eyes kept fluttering closed as her sugar high dissipated. I waited until she was sound asleep before moving out from under her.

I reached for my phone and saw that I had a text from Kimber.

> *Everything is all right here. It was Braxton Hicks contractions, but they last a long time, so the doctor just wanted to check me out. I've been told I need to rest, but I might die since I haven't even finished Christmas shopping! Be home soon!*

> *As long as you and the baby are okay, that's all that matters. We can shop on Amazon and have all the presents delivered!*

"All right. Everything is okay with Kimber. They're leaving the hospital soon."

"Good. I'm glad that the baby didn't come early," Jensen said. "Want me to take this one up to her room?"

"You don't mind?"

Jensen didn't even reply. He just lifted Lilyanne into his arms like a baby doll and effortlessly carried her up the stairs. I followed, directing him along the way. He gently placed her on her bed and tucked the covers all around her. She let out a satisfied sigh, and Jensen just smiled at her.

Jensen eased the door closed behind us. He took my hand, and we walked back downstairs. I curled into his side on the couch as *Tangled* continued to play in the background.

"You're really great with her," I told him.

"I like kids."

"I like kids who are raised right. Lilyanne is an angel compared to some other kids her age."

"That is true," he agreed. His eyes slid down to me, and he smiled. "She's just full of possibilities. I love that about her. She has so much joy and is full of life. I think she reminds us all that we need to live a little more. Be a bit more carefree."

I nodded. "That's definitely Lily." I sighed and thought about all the things in my life that hadn't been full of joy. All of those things that had led me to this moment. "It's part of the reason I left my PhD program."

"What do you mean? You didn't feel carefree anymore?"

"I didn't have any joy. I just wish I'd figured it out sooner. I wish I hadn't needed to be hit over the head to know the program wasn't right. I mean…I'd already completed my comprehensive exams. I just had to finish my dissertation and defend it to my committee to pass."

"How could you quit if you were so close?" he asked curiously.

I bit my lip and looked away from him. "I really didn't love it. I just think I was doing it because one thread kept pulling me back to it. The stress got out of control. I just couldn't handle it, and I had to get on anxiety medication. Plus, well, I found out my advisor was sleeping with an undergrad."

"Jesus," he said. "What a prick! Did he get fired?"

"I didn't turn him in. I just broke up with him and quit the department."

I wasn't sure I could have shocked him more. Jensen's mouth was actually hanging open.

"You were dating your professor?" he asked.

"Yeah, for almost three years. Welcome to my life," I said with a stiff laugh.

"How long ago did you find out about him cheating on you?" he asked.

His knuckles were white where he had bunched them into fists, and I noticed he looked pissed. No, livid. Like, if he could, he would murder Mitch right then and there for hurting me. Sometimes, I just wanted to murder Mitch for what he had done to me. And, other times, I thought that the whole thing was a big joke. An easy, convenient joke. But I didn't think it was love or even lust anymore.

"I don't know. Two weeks?" I shrugged nonchalantly.

"Fuck. I'm sorry about that. And only two weeks ago? No wonder you didn't want to go on a date." He had released his fists, and his gaze returned to mine. "Is all of this too soon?"

"No," I said immediately. I reached out and ran my hand down his shirt. I didn't want him to think that I was still in love with Mitch or pining over him. "It had been over with Mitch long before I ended it. I just hadn't had the nerve to realize what I really wanted."

"And what do you really want?" he asked, sliding his hand across my back and pulling me toward him.

"Something I'm really passionate about."

"And what is that?"

"I'm really not sure. I think I'd just like time to decide."

"You have all the time in the world."

He brushed his lips against mine. I leaned into him with a sigh. I liked the idea that I had time to figure out what I really wanted in life. Because, besides Jensen kissing me right now, I really didn't know.

"What are you doing next week?" he asked against my mouth.

"Seeing you, I hope."

"I have to be in Austin for a few days to sign some paperwork. How would you like to show me around?"

I tilted my head to the side and looked at him in surprise. "Really? But it's only a few days before Christmas."

"Business calls," he said cynically. "But I'd love to have you with me if you could come."

"I'll have to check my schedule at the Buddy Holly Center, but I should be able to do it. Plus, it might be pretty awesome if we drove out there because I need to get the rest of my stuff from my apartment before someone comes to sublet the place in January."

Jensen smiled a devious smile. "We can definitely stop to get your things while we're there, but, Emery..."

His hands threaded through my hair, and I got lost in his touch and his gentle kisses down my jaw.

"Hmm?"

"We're not driving, love."

Nineteen

Emery

No, we definitely were *not* driving.

I stared at the Wright private jet with equal parts shock and awe. It was a gorgeous, sleek machine that would get us to Austin in just over an hour. And we had it all to ourselves. I'd joked about him having a private jet only a couple of weeks ago, and here I was, about to be on the damn thing. It felt beyond surreal.

"Allow me to get your bags, Ms. Robinson," a man said. He was decked out in a suit and looked proper as fuck.

"Oh, um…okay," I said, relinquishing my bags.

"Thank you, Robbie," Jensen said. He took my hand in his and smiled down at my stunned face. "Why do you seem so surprised? You knew we were flying."

"Sure. Just…crazy." I closed my mouth and tucked my other hand into my back pocket to try to cover my discomfort at the display of wealth. "Is this how you try to impress all the girls?"

"No." He used our linked hands to draw me into his body, and he gazed down at me with intense interest. "Just you."

I didn't believe him, but it didn't matter. I was sure he had used his private plane to woo many girls. But he was mine right now, and I wouldn't cloud our time together by thinking of something like that. I would just enjoy the once-in-a-lifetime experience. Texas was a state that judged distance by hours, not miles. It was a luxury to skip the drive time that I had become so accustomed to.

We walked up the steps and into the luxury cabin. It was outfitted in cream leather with a full wet bar and mounted flat screen TVs. A door was closed in the back, and I could only imagine what it held. I was going to go with either a king-size bed or a Jacuzzi. I laughed at my own wandering thoughts.

Jensen came up behind me and put his arms around my waist. "What is so funny?"

"Nothing."

"Are you sure?" he asked, kissing my earlobe.

"I just suspect that you have a hidden Jacuzzi or something back there," I said with a shrug.

He kissed me again and laughed softly. "Not quite. It's used for business."

"Much more boring."

He drew me into him, and we took a seat on the couch. Robbie returned and offered us drinks before takeoff. Robbie brought me a mimosa and Jensen a Bloody Mary.

I raised my glass to his. "Cheers."

"It's five o'clock somewhere," Jensen said.

He clinked his glass against mine and took a long sip. Then, he rested an arm back across the seat as we taxied down the runway.

"So, what's the big plan for your paperwork thing?" I asked.

"I officially sign the paperback for the Tarman Corporation merger this afternoon. So, we'll have the morning to ourselves today and all day tomorrow."

"Oh, good. I like that. Is there anything you want to see while we are in town?"

"Whatever you want to show me. You're the one who lived there after all."

"True. I have a few things in mind."

"Good. Me, too," he said, dropping his mouth on mine.

We made out through most of the flight. Jensen disappointed me by showing me that the back of the plane was just for business. But I was excited enough being here with him, drinking, and eating gourmet sandwiches a mile up in the air. Soon enough, Robbie announced out descent and we buckled back into our seats.

Our flight landed seamlessly at the Austin-Bergstrom International Airport. Robbie retrieved our bags and placed them in the back of the waiting town car.

I could hardly wrap my mind around the fact that this was the Jensen that I was dating. When we were together, he was not the CEO of Wright Construction. He drove his truck and ate tacos and wore jeans. It lulled me into forgetting about his money, which I appreciated. I didn't find him ostentatious in any way, but I was sure he had to be at times with his business contacts. Appearances were everything.

"Apartment first?" he asked, opening the door to the town car for me.

"I suppose so." I slipped into the backseat, and he took the seat next to me.

I watched the city I had lived in for the past three years zoom by me. Despite having gone to college in Oklahoma, I adored Austin. Maybe not their football team but definitely the town. It had its own vibrancy that was impossible to find many other places. Between the food trucks, hipster living, and overall weirdness, it was a dream local if you could ignore what felt like eternal bumper-to-bumper traffic.

My apartment looked much the same as I'd left it. A mess.

I cringed when I opened the front door. A tornado had come through here for sure. That was the only explanation for what it looked like—besides the fact that I had been neglectful of the one bedroom for close to three years and then torn through it when I moved out.

"Um…maybe you should wait in the car," I said, barring him from entering the room.

"What? Why?"

"Well, because it's a hot mess. And I just need a few minutes…or hours to tidy up."

Jensen arched an eyebrow. "We're not wasting hours here. Why don't we just get the things you need? Then, I can have a cleaning crew come through and box everything else up."

"No way! I can't let you pay to clean my apartment!"

"Fine. Then, let me inside," he countered.

I glared at him. I should not try to negotiate with someone who did it for a living. "All right. Well, don't judge me."

"I'll judge you for the incredible woman that you are, Emery. Not for anything else."

I swooned at his words and let him inside. "You've been warned."

He stepped inside and then laughed. "I spoke too soon."

I smacked him in the chest. "Jerk."

"I'm kidding. I'm kidding. Come on, let's get started."

We spent about forty-five minutes going through my bedroom before I eventually relented. He was right. This was way too much work for one morning. I'd be here for a couple of days, going through my stuff. It would be better if I just packed it all up and shipped it home where I could go through it later. Luckily, the furniture was staying for this semester for the person who would be subletting.

Jensen and I brought out the boxes to the town car and then checked into the suite he'd reserved. I hadn't even seen him pick up his phone to call for someone to come to the loft, but he told me on the way to campus that someone would be there tomorrow.

I might have dated a Wright in high school, but I hadn't had *this*. At that time, their father had been wealthy. But I hadn't understood money then. I hadn't realized what it meant the same way that I did now when I didn't have any. With Jensen, it was clear, the power and prestige that came with that kind of wealth. He made things happen. And he didn't even bat an eyelash.

The town car dropped us off in front of campus, and I was ready to show him around, but I could already feel myself crashing. Early mornings were not my thing.

"Coffee first?" I suggested.

"Definitely."

We traipsed across the street to my favorite local coffee shop. I'd been there about a million times since it was such a short walk from Garrison Hall where the history department was held. The next closest shop was a Starbucks, but in Austin, local was king. Especially when it came to coffee…and tacos.

My heart felt giddy as we approached the building with sleek black tables on the outside, already half-abandoned since school was out. Only a few people were still hanging out. We breezed in through the front door, and I breathed in the scent of the coffee brewing. I could already taste my favorite latte on my tongue.

Then, it all turned to ash.

My feet stopped moving.

Jensen took two steps ahead of me before realizing I had stopped entirely.

But I couldn't look away from what was in front of my face.

It hadn't occurred to me at all that Mitch might be here.

"What's wrong?" Jensen asked. He took one giant stride to appear before me. "Hey, tell me what's going on."

"Emery," Mitch said over Jensen's shoulder.

Jensen whipped around and took stock of the man standing before him. Mitch was about average height with slicked back long blond hair. He wore a black suit jacket with jeans. I had always thought he looked so sharp, and knowing the intelligence under the persona was even more appealing. But, seeing him now next to Jensen, I realized that Mitch looked cheap and grungy.

Cool professor, he might be.

Sexy CEO of a Fortune 500, he was not.

Jensen seemed to put the pieces together almost instantly. He bristled with barely concealed anger and tried to shield me from Mitch. "Let's just go somewhere else."

"It's okay," I said, finding my voice. I put my hand on his sleeve. "This is my favorite coffee shop."

"Are you sure?" he asked.

I nodded, and Jensen instantly backed off. But he was still tense and looked ready to pounce if Mitch came any closer.

"I'm so glad you're back. I knew you would be," Mitch said with a confident smile.

He took a couple of more steps and then tried to pull me in for a hug. I stumbled backward in shock and revulsion.

How could he think I would want to touch him after what he had done?

Before I even had a chance to speak, Jensen crushed his hand on Mitch's shoulder to keep him from getting near me again. He was boiling over.

"Don't lay a hand on her," Jensen growled. He gave a little shove and then released Mitch.

Mitch looked him over, as if he hadn't noticed him. Jensen stretched even taller and broader than normal. He was all testosterone and aggression. Mitch had his classic sly grin in place. He was assessing the situation but not to size Jensen up…just to belittle him with his eyes.

"Always nice to meet a friend of Emery's," Mitch said, sliding a hand back through his hair. "I'm her dissertation adviser, Dr. Mitch Campbell." As if Jensen hadn't just pushed him away from me, he held out his hand.

Jensen coldly stared down at it. "I know who you are."

"And you're not my dissertation adviser," I cut in. "I quit the program."

Mitch laughed and waved his hand like he was brandishing a magic wand that could make it all better. "You were just upset that day. I told the department to dismiss the withdrawal paperwork, and I had you reinstated. I knew you'd want to finish up. You only have another year."

My jaw nearly hit the floor when the words tumbled out of his mouth. "You did *what?*"

"The department seemed confused that you would up and leave out of nowhere. As was I, Emery," Mitch said. "I don't know what you think happened or what you think you were doing by leaving, but it's over now. You don't have to be so irrational about it all. I've fixed it for you."

"What I *think* happened?" I sneered.

"Gaslighting," Jensen said under his breath. "Priceless."

"I don't even have time to listen to this," I said with fury in my voice. "I know what happened. I know what you did to me. And I *am* leaving the program. I cannot believe you went behind my back to toss out the paperwork I'd filed."

"Emery," he said, stepping toward me again.

"Stop."

"You heard her," Jensen said. He moved in between us. "The last thing you want to do right now is make a scene. The last thing you want is for me to take this up with the president or the provost. I happen to be on a first-name basis with both."

"Are you threatening me?" Mitch asked.

"Depends on whether or not you walk out of here right now."

"Who is this guy, Emery?"

"He's my…" I began and then trailed off.

What was Jensen?

"Boyfriend," Jensen filled in.

My eyebrows rose dramatically. *Boyfriend? Whoa! Whoa! Where had that come from?* My mouth was open slightly, and I wanted to say something, but I didn't know what to say. Not that I didn't like the phrase rolling off his tongue, but I hadn't even known what we were doing. I hadn't known where this was going.

Now, he was claiming me.

Jensen Wright was claiming me.

"Boyfriend," Mitch said. He seemed to weigh his options. He faced me, but I just narrowed my eyes in warning. "Well, that was fast."

"Not fast enough," I muttered.

"Why am I not surprised?" Mitch said, reaching for his trendy leather messenger bag. "You always did like to be a kept woman."

I winced at his assessment as he brushed past Jensen and out the door. Shots had been fired. And I'd let him have the last word. *Ass.*

"Emery…"

"Let's just get some coffee," I whispered. My head was spinning. Between the confrontation with Mitch and Jensen claiming he was my boyfriend, I needed a second to think.

"I didn't mean to spring that on you," he said. He sounded sheepish.

I glanced up at him and saw that he actually did look sheepish.

"I meant for the whole thing to be romantic. To take you out to dinner and ask you over candlelight if you'd be my girlfriend. Then, it just kind of slipped out."

"Oh," I said softly. "Wow."

"I know it's fast and that I have a lot to tell you, but I just want you to be mine." He reached out and brushed a stray strand of hair out of my face. "I can't get you out of my head, and I don't want you out. So, do you want to be my girlfriend?"

I laughed abruptly, and then it suddenly poured out of me. This was so formal. So controlled. So purposeful.

"What?" Jensen asked. His body became guarded, as if preparing for the fallout.

"You really aren't like any other guy, are you?"

He arched an eyebrow in question.

"Most guys are too busy trying to keep girls dangling on the line, but you just come right out and say you want a relationship."

"I'm a businessman. I say what I want, I negotiate for it, and then I take it. I don't want to lead you on."

"I like that."

He beamed.

"And I like that you said you were my boyfriend."

"Good," he said, drawing me in for a kiss. "Does that make you my girlfriend?"

"I guess it does."

Twenty

Jensen

I left Emery at the university to handle the remainder of her school issues. I hadn't wanted to abandon her when that prick was nearby, but she'd promised she would be fine. She'd claimed that Mitch was more bark than he was bite. After getting a good look at him, I had to agree. Though it didn't make me feel any better.

Time and time again, I had claimed that I wasn't a violent man. I'd been tested on that twice before.

One time, I'd failed.

One time, I'd succeeded.

This time, I had come so close to losing it and beating the ever-loving shit out of the skeezy, conniving bastard. My hands had fisted, aching to blacken his eyes and rearrange his face.

But I knew that wasn't what Emery wanted. Also, I had a company to think about, and assault charges never looked good in the media. In the end though, threatening him with administration interference had been enough to send him packing. Couldn't even stand up to me like a man. Even without knowing who I was, he had known, if I put some weight behind it, I could get him fired for what he had done to Emery and the handful of other girls he'd seduced in his time as a professor. With my blood boiling as it was, I had half a mind to make the call.

Luckily for him, I had a business meeting that I had to get to. I would have to deal with him later.

I stormed into the Tarman Corporation headquarters like a thundercloud.

A bunch of hurried receptionists teetered out of my way with a squeaked, "Hello, Mr. Wright."

All I had to do was shake hands, sign some paperwork, and then dismantle the Austin-based corporation I'd been trying to get my hands on for years. They were Wright Construction's biggest competitor, and now was the time for it to all get finalized. As our motto said, *What's Wright Is Right*.

"Gentlemen, lady," I said with a brief acknowledgment to Abigail Tarman, the only woman in the room, "let's begin."

I settled in for the long haul. I knew they wouldn't let this go easily. The owner was the son of my father's biggest adversary. We were about the same age and had attended Texas Tech at the same time. Then, we had each thought we would outgrow our respective father's ambitions. We'd both be architects and reshape the industry. It hadn't worked out that way. It had been way more fucked up than that.

"Marc," I said, holding my hand out to the current Mr. Tarman himself.

"Jensen," he said blandly.

He shook my hand, and we each squeezed tighter than we had to.

"Shall we?" Marc asked, gesturing to the long rectangular table in the center of the room.

"I believe we shall."

I stalked to the front of the room and took my seat across from Marc. The negotiations had been over weeks ago, but I knew that he wouldn't let me off this easily. I had been slowly eroding his company over the course of the last five years. I'd have loved to see it burn to the ground already, but it was better this way. Sweeter.

———

It was hours before I officially signed. I had known Marc would take me through the wringer, and I hadn't been disappointed. But I signed the last piece of paper with a flourish. Watching Marc hand over the company to me was perfection. I passed the paperwork to my lawyer to review one last time and then to file.

"Good doing business with you," I said with a smirk.

"I wish I could say the same to you," Marc said with barely concealed animosity.

"Now, now, Marcus," his younger sister, Abigail, said. "Would you care to join us for dinner, Jensen?"

"I have to decline. But thank you, Abby."

"Jensen, come on. I insist. We've known each other too long for it to all end this way."

My eyes cut to Marc's. "I have my…girlfriend with me."

Marc seemed to perk up with both shock and confusion at that statement. "Girlfriend? That's a new one."

"Marcus," Abigail snapped. "Your girlfriend is welcome to come, Jensen. I can't wait to meet her."

"All right. Let me let her know. She's at the hotel."

"Why don't we just pick her up on the way?" Abigail suggested.

Marc looked like it was quite literally the last thing he wanted to do. I couldn't agree more. But, if it made Marc uncomfortable, then I was in for it.

I took out my phone and clicked over to Messages, only to realize I'd missed two in the midst of the negotiations. I gritted my teeth.

Vanessa. Goddamn woman had the worst fucking timing.

> *Don't do this.*

> *You don't have to sign that paperwork today. Your father wouldn't have wanted this.*

I clenched my jaw, willing myself not to show any emotions in front of the Tarmans. They fed on it. Vanessa bringing up my father was a low blow, and she knew it.

I responded shortly.

> *Signed, sealed, delivered.*

Then, I erased her messages and pulled up Emery's number, letting her know that I would be picking her up at the hotel for dinner with the Tarmans.

> *We're going to dinner with the people who owned the company you just purchased? What should I wear?*

> *Something sexy as hell. See you in fifteen.*

I retreated to the lobby with Marc and Abigail. Marc was on his phone in deep conversation with someone who he probably cared very little about. Any excuse not to have to talk to me any longer. And I was grateful.

Abigail could field the tension like a professional.

"Who is the new girl, Jensen?" she asked.

"She's recently moved to town. Was a PhD student here at UT before coming back to Lubbock."

Abigail's eyebrows rose. She knew my policy as well as anyone. "An in-town girl? Why, you never fail to surprise me."

I shrugged. "She's worth it."

"And does she know?"

My eyes shot to her hazel ones. They were searching and curious. Abigail knew too much about me and my family. I suddenly had a bad feeling about bringing Emery to this dinner.

"She doesn't," Abigail said as a matter of fact. "God help you with Marc here."

I ignored Abigail's comment and slid into the limousine that the Tarmans had waiting. It was a bit ostentatious for the circumstances, but I had just paid them a small fortune for the company. They could afford it for now.

We pulled up in front of the hotel a short while later, and Emery was standing there, dressed to kill. I didn't know how she had managed it in the short time I'd given her, but she was in a stunning red cocktail dress and pumps. Her hair was swept off her face, and she had on cherry-red lipstick. A color that had me thinking a million dirty thoughts at once. Like what that color would taste like. And how nice it would look around my dick.

I stepped out of the back to open the door for her, and she practically glowed when she saw me.

"A limo?" she asked.

"A bit much?"

"Or just enough," she countered.

"You seem like you're in a better mood than when I left you."

"Well, I got all that nasty business resolved, and now, I'm with you again."

I slid my arm around her waist and placed a deep kiss on her lips. She leaned into me, both of us forgetting all about her red lipstick. She laughed when she leaned back and smudged a spot off my mouth.

"Come on, Jensen," Abigail called from the door.

"We have to talk," I whispered into Emery's ear as she moved to pass me into the limo. Her eyes shot to mine in confusion. "I just have to...tell you some things. Ignore Marc."

"I don't understand."

"I know. I'm sorry. I'll explain."

Emery slid into the limo, and I cursed, wishing I'd had more time to clarify everything. I just hoped Marc could keep a lid on his anger for a whole dinner without ruining it for everyone.

Emery was already introducing herself to Abigail and Marc as I hopped back into the limo, and it zoomed away.

"Ah," Marc said, looking Emery up and down, "you don't seem the type."

Emery's lips pursed. "What does that mean?"

"Nothing," Abigail interjected. "Ignore my brother. He's in a foul mood."

I knew that Emery was frustrated when her eyes slid to me. I hated that look. She was wary and had her guard up again. I didn't want to blindside her, but I had to say something about Marc.

"I just mean that you're the girl of the weekend, right?" Marc asked. His eyes were mirthless. He seemed happy to taunt her, even before we made it to the restaurant.

"Marc!" Abigail cried.

"Just let it be, Marc," I growled.

"What exactly does that mean?" Emery asked.

He chose to respond only to her, "You know...the fling he has when he's out of town. You must realize that you're it."

"I'll have you know," she spat, "I know all about his reputation, and I don't appreciate your insinuation that I'm that kind of girl. Jensen and I are together. This isn't a one-time thing. And who the hell are you to even say something like that to me?"

I nearly choked on my own laughter at Marc's bewildered face.

"Just an old family friend," Marc said. "Tell me everything about yourself. How did you manage to catch Jensen's eye and keep it? I thought only one person was capable of that."

Emery frowned as she mulled over what Marc had said, and I realized it was an absolutely horrid idea to have brought her along. Marc was a snake, and I had just released her into the viper's den.

"Blow jobs," she said quite calmly.

Marc sputtered and then started laughing. "You surprise me."

I couldn't help myself; I laughed with him. *Man, this girl. She is...perfect.*

"Also, I'm completely irresistible," Emery continued.

"I have no doubt," Marc agreed. His eyes swept up her bare legs and then back to her face. "No doubt at all."

I possessively wrapped an arm around her tense shoulders and leaned her back into me. As far away from Marc as possible. He shot me a look full of questions that I was all too aware of. I just wanted to enjoy this night, and somehow, I'd been left with this.

We all piled out of the limousine when it pulled up to the restaurant entrance. Abigail dragged Marc inside for their table, but Emery drew me aside before we entered the room.

"What the hell is going on?" she demanded.

I sighed and ran my hand back through my hair. "A lot."

"I can see that, Jensen. Who are these people? Why did you tell me to ignore Marc?"

"Marc is an old family friend. Sort of. He and Abigail are Tarmans, who, up until a few minutes ago, were the Wrights' biggest rivals."

"You were friends with your rivals?"

"Money talks to money," I explained.

"Okay," she said uncertainly. "But all of that other stuff?"

"I have a reputation."

"I know."

I hated that she knew. I hated that she seemed to fear my reputation. I could see it in her eyes. I could see it in the set of her shoulders and the stiffness of her body. I wanted to make it go away.

"But I'm not doing that anymore. That's why I brought you. That's why I asked you to be my girlfriend."

"So…you wouldn't be tempted to shop around?" she asked as quiet as a mouse. "God, I'm sorry. I shouldn't have asked that."

I held up my hand. "It's a fair question, considering my background, but no," I said through gritted teeth, "I would never do that. I am a one-woman kind of man."

"One woman being me…or that other girl Marc mentioned?"

I closed my eyes and breathed out through my nose. *Goddamn it, Marc.*

"The woman he was talking about is my ex-wife, Vanessa."

Emery flinched at the name, and I didn't blame her.

"Oh."

"However, she is *not* the woman for me. If she were, I never would have divorced her."

"Okay."

I reached out and cupped her cheeks. I hated this far-away, distant look on her face. The one that she used when she was bracing herself. The last thing I wanted was for her to be afraid of me. Afraid of what I would do to her. I would never be Mitch. That fucking bastard. I would never hurt her like that.

"Emery, I want you and only you. I would never cheat on you. Never, ever."

"How could you know that?"

I hated seeing her so hurt and vulnerable. Seeing what Mitch had done to her. But, at the same time, I was glad she was showing those vulnerabilities to me so that I could prove to her how I felt.

"Because Vanessa cheated on me, and I divorced her for it."

And that wasn't even the half of it.

Emery made a small, almost inaudible gasp. "Oh God."

"It was nasty, and I'd never put another human being through something like that."

"It feels insurmountable."

"It was," I admitted. "And I'm not perfect by any means, Emery. I have trust issues. After what Vanessa did, I never thought that I would be open to another person again, but you're different. I want to open up to you. It's all going to take time."

"No," she said, waving her hand. "I was just cheated on. I'm the one with major trust issues. I just freaked out, and then Marc—"

"Marc is a jackass."

"I've realized."

"Look, I don't want you to doubt me. This is the reason I reacted the way I did the first night we were together. I have enough baggage as it is. Though I may not be a hundred percent since the divorce, I know that I'm better when I'm with you. You make me a better man."

She beamed. The tension and chaos of just that brief interaction with Marc Tarman evaporated. Just like that, she was my Emery again. And I knew, right then and there...I was lost.

Twenty-One

Emery

I braced myself for impact and followed Jensen through the restaurant.

What he had just revealed about his past explained so much about his behavior. It was as if I had been chipping away at the ice and I was finally finding the man beneath. When I'd decided to hate all the Wrights a long time ago, I had never once imagined that there would be so much more to who Jensen was or that he had been hurt like I had. He was so charming and gorgeous and everything.

How could someone do something like that to him?

And why did he even bother with Marc? Why go to dinner with someone he thought was a jackass and after just buying his corporation?

Seemed insane to me, but I wouldn't abandon Jensen, leaving him to deal with Marc alone.

"Sorry about that," I said when I took my seat.

"Of course," Marc said, staring at me with his all-knowing sharp gaze. "I took the liberty of ordering you a vodka tonic. You do like vodka tonics, don't you?"

His eyes slipped to Jensen's, and I noticed the slight tension in his jaw. This was going to be a problem.

"I'm more of a champagne drinker myself." I shrugged. "Or tequila shots. Whatever you're into."

"No vodka tonic? I'm shocked. A girl like you?" Marc leaned back in his chair. "Soon, you're going to tell me you've never modeled with that pretty face."

"Marc," Abigail and Jensen snapped at the same time.

I held my hand up. "Look, it's fine. Whatever you're doing is fine. Take shots at me all you want. I get you might be upset with Jensen, and you're petty enough to try to take it out on me, but I'm not a vodka tonic–drinking, pretty-faced model. I'm not anything you think I am. So, keep hurling insults and layered jabs. I can take it. It's not going to make a damn difference to me."

Marc closed his mouth on whatever he had wanted to say next. Abigail gave me an appraising look, as if I had just passed some unknown test, while Jensen looked like he wanted to kiss me. Instead, my insides were roiling because I had acted so bold. But I couldn't ignore the effectiveness of it.

I flagged down the waitress. "Can you replace that vodka tonic order with a glass of champagne? Veuve Brut preferably."

"Of course."

My point being made now, the rest of the dinner went much smoother. Marc seemed to reel his claws back in, and I found I actually really liked Abigail. She seemed to be a genuine person. I had to assume those were few and far between in this industry.

And, once Marc stopped egging Jensen on, they settled into some kind of routine. Just over dinner, it was obvious that they had known each other for a long time. I had to guess they had even been friends. I knew from experience that only close friends could speak without saying a word and laugh at implied jokes. Jensen and Marc had that levity—underneath all the animosity at least.

Despite how good things had been going the rest of the night, I was glad when dinner ended. We said good-bye to Marc and Abigail and headed back to the hotel. Our fancy suite was waiting for us—something I found extremely strange. I had lived in this city for three years in a shoebox apartment. We could have stayed at my place, despite the disaster, but Jensen had insisted on this. And I enjoyed the luxury of it. Who wouldn't want a Jacuzzi to fit a party of ten and a full living room with a balcony? But it was also…strange.

"Glad I grabbed this dress from my place before we left or else I would have had to miss that really fun time," I said with dry sarcasm, slinging my jacket on the couch.

Jensen ran his hands down my bare arms. He pressed a kiss into my shoulder. "I'm sorry about that. I should have realized it would be a mistake."

"A mistake," I said softly. He was trailing kisses up my neck, and it was hard for me to concentrate. "Are you going to tell me what crawled up Marc's butt?"

Jensen laughed against my neck and then nipped me. "Besides the fact that I just bought his company?"

I swung around to face him. "It was more than that. I'm not blind."

He nodded with a sigh. "You're right. It's a long story. You already know part of it."

"We have all night," I reminded him.

"Indeed we do," he said, his hands landing on my hips and then moving to my ass.

"Tell me about it. I want to know you. I want to understand."

"All right." He took a step back and composed himself.

He gestured for me to take a seat, and I tucked my legs underneath myself on the couch. Jensen took the spot next to me.

"Marc and I have known each other a long time. We were always thinly veiled enemies but hopeful friends. Against his father's wishes, he ended up at Texas Tech because of their architecture program. We were in the program at the same time."

"You went to school for architecture?" I asked in confusion. "I thought you majored in business."

"Yes. My father required I major in business, but I took architecture classes on the side. I believed, as did Marc, that business destroyed the soul, as we had seen it happen with our families. It didn't build anything. It only tore things down. It never made things better. We were visionaries. We wanted more."

"Yet you each run your respective father's business," I whispered.

"I knew I would always have a job at Wright Construction whenever I wanted it. So, post-graduation, I took an internship at an architectural company in New York for a year. Vanessa and I were engaged. My father was furious about the internship, but I had a whole plan. I was going to change the world."

His eyes cut to me, and then he shook his head. He clearly hadn't told this story in a while. "Anyway, long story short, my father died. Left with nothing but his disappointment, I took over the company and moved back to Lubbock. There wasn't another option since Austin was still in college. Landon, as you know, was about to graduate high school. The board needed someone they could trust. They got me. Vanessa stayed in New York. She was…modeling part-time, and things were looking up. We got married that summer. She started modeling full-time, and Marc got my full-time job at the architectural company."

I covered my mouth. I felt like I was watching a train wreck without knowing how to stop it.

"Wright did as much business in New York as I wanted. I could have flown there every weekend to see Vanessa, but I didn't. I was engrossed in work and still grieving."

"But it wasn't enough for Vanessa," I whispered.

His eyes were far away. "Never could have been. Then she ended up in Marc's bed."

I sighed heavily and leaned into him, wrapping my arms around him. "That's not your fault."

"No, it's not. It took many years of therapy to realize that it was entirely her fault. She was the one who found solace with Marc. She was the one who could have stopped the whole thing, but she hadn't. She'd wanted the visionary she had fallen in love with...but I wasn't that man anymore. So, she'd settled for Marc in the meantime. Second best."

"Everyone is second best to you."

Jensen had a sad, lost look on his face. "Thanks."

"So...why is Marc so bitter when he was the one who did wrong?"

"To him, I ruined his life."

"That's ridiculous."

"It is. I understand it from his perspective though. He was always in love or obsessed with Vanessa. Whatever the case was, he finally had her, and then she left him again for me. I got the girl. He ended up having to take over his father's company. And, now, I've taken that, too. He's bitter. But I don't, no, I can't sympathize with him. He might find it convenient to blame me, but he's the bastard who did this."

"And you shouldn't sympathize with him. I didn't, and I didn't even know the circumstances. I'm glad I snapped at him."

"God, you're amazing," Jensen said. "The way you handled dinner, it was brilliant."

His hands were back on my legs and moving up to my hips. He crawled forward over me, and I fell back onto the sofa. A smile teased at my lips. I loved the way he adored me like this. When his eyes were only on me and all those skeletons were shoved back in his closet, he was just a sexy, confident man, unhindered by his past and ready to devour me.

"You think so?" I whispered.

"Know so, love."

He pressed his lips to mine, and I forgot all about our night and deep discussions. I kissed him harder, held him more possessively. I wanted and needed more. This was our first time together since we'd become official, and in the past day, so much had happened to move our relationship forward that I couldn't seem to get enough of him.

We stood up, and I tore his suit jacket off and removed the rest of his layers in a hurry. I cared so little about the expensive designer suit he was wearing, only wanting the birthday suit underneath. My dress was hastily discarded.

He shoved me up against the wall and then fell to his knees to drag my thong off with his teeth.

I groaned and dropped my head back as he kissed and licked his way back up until he was between my legs. My body was on fire. I couldn't fathom how I had ever said no. All I wanted to do was scream *yes* over and over again.

Jensen obliged.

He hooked one leg over his shoulder and then sucked on my clit until I was dripping wet. Only then did he finger-fuck my pussy until I came on his face. My legs were shaking from exertion, but Jensen didn't even hesitate. He stood, hoisted my legs up around his waist, and then thrust into me in one easy swoop. He braced himself against the wall, and bounced me up and down on his dick at a bruising, rough pace that I matched stroke for stroke. It was only minutes before my legs were trembling again, and my entire body exploded.

Jensen lifted me off the wall, and we both tumbled down onto the floor. He pounded into me a few more times with my hands raised over my head. My breath was coming out in pants. I didn't think it was possible that I could come again. But Jensen was so close, and feverish desire in his eyes practically pushed me over the edge a third time. His body sleek and rippled, he came with me, toppling onto me.

We lay there, heaving, for endless seconds before Jensen slid out of me and rolled over onto the floor.

"I can feel my heartbeat," I whispered. "Feel it." I took his hand and pressed it against my lower abdomen.

"You're welcome," he said throatily.

I laughed and then leaned over and kissed him. "Now, he has manners."

"Didn't seem like you minded."

"Not one bit."

"Good. Then, maybe you'll be up for round two?" he asked with an arched eyebrow.

"Oh God," I said with a laugh. "Let me recover first."

He leaned up on his elbow as I stood up to pad to the bathroom. He smacked my ass as I passed him. "How about we use that Jacuzzi for recovery?"

I glanced back at him from under my thick black lashes. "Why do I have a feeling that you'll make that sexual, too, Mr. Wright?"

"Everything about you is sexual, Miss Robinson." He grinned devilishly, flashing me those irresistible dimples. "And I intend to take full advantage of you being naked in my hotel room."

I seductively shook my hips as I walked away. "Guess I'll turn the jets on and get started myself then."

His gaze told me that he was thinking every dirty thought in the book. And I did not regret it one bit when he joined me in the tub and used those jets in all the best ways.

———

We rose late the next day, and I finally got to give Jensen the tour of Austin I'd wanted all along. It wasn't as spectacular as I would have wanted since we were short on time. But he didn't seem to mind when I dragged him back to the hotel, before and after dinner, to use that Jacuzzi again. The feel of those jets combined with his fingers sent me over the edge faster than I'd thought possible. It was even better when he bent me over the side. I could have stayed in that bathtub all day and night.

With all the revelations that had been shared and meeting the people who had been deeply involved in our lives, I felt closer to Jensen than ever. I'd walked into this whole thing, imagining one night of hot sex. Maybe a date after that. Then, our connection had been off the charts. Now, I couldn't get enough of him—physically, mentally, and emotionally. Spending three days with him, almost one hundred percent of the time, had not irritated me once.

If we didn't have to get back to town for work, I would have encouraged him to stay longer. I was reluctant to go home.

Jensen could sense it in me, but I thought he must have felt it, too, because he never commented on it.

After our short plane ride, Jensen drove us back to his place.

I wanted to get back to Kimber and see how she was doing with the pregnancy. She was getting pretty close now. Plus, I definitely needed some Heidi time to fill her in on my weekend. But I also wasn't ready to say good-bye to Jensen yet. I wanted to discover if he had a Jacuzzi as well. I just wanted…to spend more time with him.

As soon as we parked, I hopped out of the car and raced around to his side. He pulled me into his arms and ducked down to give me a firm kiss.

"God, I'm going to miss you," I whispered.

"Don't miss me. Stay here."

I rolled my eyes. "I can't stay here."

"Stay here every night you like. I sleep better when I'm with you."

"We have not been sleeping at night," I countered.

"Exactly."

He slid a hand around my waist and drew me toward the front door. We breached the entrance, my laughter filling the foyer. My gaze was still locked on Jensen's face when he stilled completely. His smile disappeared.

My head snapped to the side, and my stomach dropped. "Landon…"

Twenty-Two

Jensen

"What the fuck is going on?" Landon asked.

Oh, fuck!

Fuck!

"Landon, man"—I casually disentangled myself from Emery as she was hastily doing the same, looking shell-shocked—"you're back."

I'd been meaning to tell Landon about Emery so he wouldn't hear it from someone else first. I had known he was coming back for Christmas. But I'd thought I still had a few days. I'd wanted to make sure things were official with Emery before bringing it up with Landon. Now...he was here.

"Cut the shit, Jensen. Just answer the question. What is happening right here?"

Landon pointed between the two of us, but neither of us said a word. We just stared forward at Landon, as if he might be an apparition that would disappear at any moment.

"I meant to tell you—"

"Tell me what?" His posture was stiff. His eyes kept shifting between the pair of us, as if he were trying to decipher a particularly difficult code. "Are you two...together?"

"Yes," Emily said, regaining her voice, "we're together."

Landon's eyes moved, as if he were watching tennis. "I was only gone a couple of weeks. I don't understand how this could have happened...and why I was never informed that this was fucking happening." He shook his head and then glanced away from us.

"Where's Miranda?" I asked him to try to move the discussion into safer territory. "Did she come in with you?"

"Are you kidding me? After the *fit* she had when she found out that Emery was still here, you think she'd have let me fly back alone?" he ground out.

"So...she's here?" I asked warily. I did not want Emery to be here if Miranda was at my house. That was a recipe for disaster.

"She's out shopping. Fuck, could you imagine if she was here?" Landon ran a hand back through his hair and then glared at me. "Could you fucking imagine? I came back at your request, and you didn't even tell me about Emery? Is this what you wanted?"

"No," I said. It had been my request. I hadn't wanted Landon to miss Christmas with his family. I'd wanted him here because he was my brother, and I loved him. Now, he was pissed off, and I didn't know how to fix this. But I would have to. "I wanted to tell you in advance about Emery so we could talk about this like men and not just get pissed off at each other."

Landon looked like he wanted to tell me to fuck off.

"You know, I should go," Emery said. She took a step back toward the door. "It's been a long weekend."

I turned to face her and wondered what she must be feeling. We'd both been anxious about telling Landon we were dating, because the whole situation felt out of our hands. I didn't want to piss off Landon. He and Emery might have dated almost a decade ago, but it was tricky dealing with someone else's past relationship.

"Are you sure?" I asked.

"Yeah. Um…I should go see my sister. Check in, you know."

"All right. I'll call you later."

"Yeah, sure." She didn't even lean in for a kiss. Just gave a half-wave and then was gone, out the front door, leaving me all alone with my pissed off brother.

"So, you're fucking my ex-girlfriend now?" Landon asked. There was fury in his voice. It was something I hadn't heard from Landon in a long time. Not since Dad had died.

"It's not like that."

"What is it like exactly? Gave up on messing around with every girl you came across when you were out of town and decided to dick around with all those in town, too?"

I ground my teeth and felt the hair rise on the back of my neck. Landon was looking for a fight, but I wouldn't oblige him.

"I don't want to fight with you," I said finally.

"Well, you don't get to make that choice, Jensen. You walked in here with Emery Robinson. We'd dated for two years. You *knew* her when we were in high school, Jensen."

"I didn't know her then, and like you, I didn't even recognize her at first."

"Like me?"

"At the wedding," I bit out.

Landon's face ignited, and he rushed toward me, shoving me backward. "You met her at Sutton's wedding? You've known who she is this whole time and didn't say anything?"

"Yes, all right? Yes. I've known who she was since that next morning. You were the one who told me that she was leaving town after a couple of days."

"That wasn't an invitation to go and fuck her!"

"I didn't take it as one!" I yelled back. "I was going to leave her alone, but then we just kept running into each other. I've fallen for her, Landon. I have."

"For now," Landon said under his breath. "What happens when you're tired of her? We all know you bore easily. You can fool her with whatever you're doing, but I know your reputation."

"Emery does not compare to any other girl I've been with," I growled. "Comparing Emery to any of my flings is an insult to her."

"Or is it just an insult to you?"

There were a million things I could throw back at him—namely, his horrible wife—but I knew that wouldn't get me anywhere. I just needed him to understand.

"I should have told you."

"You said that already."

"I was planning to tell you before Christmas. But I wanted to make sure this was a real thing. I didn't want you to find out this way."

"Whatever, Jensen. Just admit it. It's not that you didn't want me to find out this way. It's that you didn't want me to find out at all. Everyone else in the family can fuck up, and you solve *their* problems, but you can't solve your own." Landon sneered at me and crossed his arms. "You just hide them."

"That's not what I was going to do. I care for Emery. I wanted to make things right. This isn't a joke to me. And why are you so pissed off anyway? You're married." I reminded him. "By the way you're acting, I'd think you still had feelings for Emery."

"Fuck off, Jensen," Landon said. He turned away from me and paced toward the door.

He twitched his hand toward the handle but stopped when I began to speak, "The breakup was ten years ago, Landon. This is all harsh for someone you've barely spoken to since high school."

He whipped around to glare at me. "You don't know anything."

I bit out a laugh, harsh and low. "You went to different colleges. You were going different directions. A lot of couples break up for those reasons."

"If you believe that is what happened, then you don't know Emery."

I tilted my head in confusion. Ten years ago, that was *exactly* what Landon had said about Emery. I remembered it because he had told me after our father's funeral. They'd broken up shortly after that. I hadn't ever suspected there was more to the story.

"And you're smarter than this, Jensen," Landon said. "You know that you don't want to bring her into your mess."

"She already knows."

"Everything?" Landon prodded.

"Not everything," I said slowly. "It's only been a couple weeks. I'm trying to ease her into my life."

"You better tell her, Jensen or I will."

"Don't threaten me, Landon."

"Fuck! You know I won't tell her. Though I should," he said with a glare. "Emery is a good, kind, and genuine person. She's too good for you."

With that, Landon wrenched open the door, leaving me standing there in shock. I stared at his retreating form until he disappeared completely.

How had that all gone so completely fucking wrong?

Twenty-Three

Emery

After checking on my sister, I hurried over to Flips to meet Heidi. Peter was working the bar when I entered. He waved distractedly as he poured out beers for a few guys.

"Heidi here?" I asked.

"Pool table."

"Of course. Should have known."

I grabbed two tequila shots from Peter and then brought them to the back. Heidi was running the table, but it was a slow night, so she wasn't hustling anyone...yet.

"Shot?" I asked.

"God, yes," Heidi said.

We tossed back the alcohol, letting it course through our veins and make our minds all fuzzy. I needed a good fuzzy mind after the day I'd had.

"Good to have you back, baby," she said, winking at me. "Now, tell me all about your Wright brother. Is he the right brother?" Heidi cackled, as if her joke were hilarious.

"How many drinks did you have before this?"

Heidi innocently fluttered her eyelashes at me. "More than one."

"Whore."

"I didn't know you were back yet! And Julia is in Ohio or wherever she's from. Somewhere cold and snowy."

"It's cold and snowy here."

"Yeah, sometimes. But not today!"

"No, not today. But snow is on the forecast for forty-eight of the fifty states next week. Everywhere is cold, except for Florida and Hawaii."

Heidi sighed. "If only. Now, tell me about your sexy weekend. There were sexy times, right?"

"Yes," I conceded. "We ran into my ex-boyfriend, and Jensen bought a million-dollar company from a man who his ex-wife cheated on him with. Then, when we came home, *Landon* was waiting for us at Jensen's house."

Heidi blinked twice and then burst into laughter. She dropped the pool cue onto the table and then doubled over. "Oh my God," she cried. "Oh, phew! Wow!"

"What the hell are you laughing about?"

"Did you not just hear how ridiculous you sounded?" Heidi asked. She swiped at her eyes.

"I just told you what happened!"

"Yeah. Yeah, you did. Wow!"

Heidi chuckled some more, and I couldn't help it; I joined in.

"God, you're such a bitch."

"You love me anyway."

"True," I admitted.

"So…Landon is back in town?" Heidi asked. Her eyes met mine, and then she glanced away immediately.

I narrowed my eyes in confusion at her strange body language. "Yeah. He just got into town with his wife. Not so great timing."

"Did you see Miranda? Was she there?"

"Nah. Lucky for us. Sort of, I guess."

"Yeah. She's a nutjob."

I nodded. "That's true. But Landon got upset when he saw Jensen and I together."

"Landon is a big boy. He's a grown-up and married and living halfway across the country. He shouldn't be upset."

"Yeah," I agreed. "But you didn't see his face when he saw us together. I know I haven't talked to him in forever, but I feel bad for Jensen that we didn't tell him. After all, he's his brother and, we probably should have said something when we realized things were getting serious."

"Serious?"

"I guess we're official now," I told her with a grin.

The idea that Jensen was my boyfriend was too exciting to contain.

Heidi screamed and jumped up and down. "Okay. Well, we definitely need to toast to that."

We hurried over to the bar, and Peter poured us some fancy shots that promised to knock us both on our asses. I tipped back mine and could already feel the ramifications of that drink coming on strong. I excused myself to use the restroom, and when I returned, I told Heidi the full details of my weekend with Jensen. I still felt rotten about leaving Landon and Jensen together like that, but it was good to be with my girlfriend. To not have to worry about it at all.

I was on my third round, and I was unsure of where that put Heidi. If we kept this up, both of us were going to have to cab it back home. I was just debating whether or not to nurse this one for the rest of the night when Heidi perked up in her seat.

"What?" I asked. I was more attuned to my friend's behavior than anyone else I'd ever known.

"Don't hate me."

"Oh God, I already do." I glanced over my shoulder and saw none other than Landon Wright walking into the bar.

He looked the same as I'd left him back with Jensen. Dressed down in a polo and jeans, he just shrugged out of his jacket to reveal his perpetually sun-kissed skin from hours of golfing outdoors in Florida.

"Did you invite him here?" I accused.

"Well, he texted me to find out where you were…and ta-da."

"You're right. I do hate you."

Landon's gaze caught mine from across the room, and his mouth ticked up into a smile. He strode toward us with a purpose that I recognized from my recent, vivid acquaintance with his brother. It was a swagger that I was very familiar with. Strange, considering I didn't really compare Jensen to Landon when we were together. But it felt impossible not to compare Landon to Jensen.

"Hey," he said, slinging his jacket onto the back of the seat next to mine.

"Hi."

"Hey, Landon!" Heidi said with a big grin.

His eyes moved to Heidi's and softened briefly. "Hey, Heidi. Thanks for the info."

"For sure. Why don't you two just…" She trailed off, swallowed, and then darted back to the pool table.

"Do you mind?" Landon asked, gesturing to the empty seat.

I shook my head and concentrated on my drink.

"Emery, I didn't mean to ambush you," he said at once.

"Why not? I kind of ambushed you."

He breathed out heavily. "Not on purpose."

"True."

"I just wanted to apologize."

I turned my head to look at him again. *What was with these Wrights that I always got apologies out of them?* They were the kind of men who probably didn't use the word much.

"*You* want to apologize to *me?*"

"Yeah, I just saw you there…with him…and I kind of blew a gasket."

"I noticed that."

"Which I had no right to do."

I would have freaked out if I had hypothetically found out he was dating Kimber. Jensen and I should have fixed this long before it got here. I knew that. I'd just been too blissful to consider what would happen and where things were going. I hadn't wanted to do anything that could hurt something so fragile. And our relationship was fragile.

"How are you and Jensen?" I asked carefully.

Landon ground his teeth and motioned for Peter to give him a beer. "I needed some time to cool off."

"So, you came to me?" I arched an eyebrow. "Don't think we were ever the cool-off type. I think we argued most of the time."

"Only so we could make up," he said with a grin.

I shrugged, unable to deny it. "You know, Jensen and I didn't mean for it to happen."

"I don't really want to know," he said, holding up a hand. "It might have been ten years, Emery, but it's still weird to me."

"It's weird to me, too."

"Just…be careful," Landon said. He dropped his hand onto my shoulder and looked me deep in the eyes. "I love my brother. But he's an asshole, and he's bad with women. Plus, he has more baggage than the rest of our family combined, and I think one Wright has hurt you enough for a lifetime. I wouldn't want to see you like that again."

I pulled back and let his hand drop off my shoulder. "I know about Jensen's reputation and his past. I know that he hasn't always made the right decisions with women. But that doesn't necessarily mean that he's going to fuck this up, too. If I thought he was playing me, I wouldn't be in his life. This is *me* we're talking about, Landon."

"I know," he whispered. "That's what I'm afraid of."

I sighed and shook my head. "You know what? I've had enough crap for one weekend. I apologized for not telling you about Jensen, but I'm not leaving him because of it. And I'm not being naive about our relationship."

"I just don't think you know him."

"You're right," I conceded. "I don't. I definitely do not know him like you do. How could I? But that doesn't mean I don't care for him and want to get to know him."

"I just don't want to see you get hurt."

I stood from my seat and reached for my drink. "It's about ten years too late for that, Landon."

Landon winced, and I could see that my jab had cut deep. We both knew it. This was why he'd ignored all my messages after graduation. This was why we hadn't really spoken since.

"That's fair. I deserve that," he said.

"Let me take care of myself. I've been doing it long enough without your help. So, why don't we just go and play some pool with Heidi and hang out for a while? I'd love to see Heidi hustle you like old times."

Landon glanced down at his phone. He grimaced, and I had to gather his wife was messaging him.

"Okay, but I don't have that long. Miranda is almost finished shopping. It would be bad for both of our health if she found us in the same place, let alone at a bar."

"She seems a bit…controlling," I ventured as we joined Heidi at the pool table.

"I really do not want to talk about her."

I held my hands up. "Okay."

"What don't we want to talk about?" Heidi asked. Her eyes darted back and forth between me and Landon. She had this little worried tilt to her mouth.

She was seriously confusing me.

Was she…vibing on Landon?

No way. That couldn't be it.

It had to be that she was just concerned about me and Landon being in the same vicinity after everything that had happened with Jensen.

"Miranda," Landon said gently.

"Is she coming here?" Heidi asked, her voice rising an octave.

"God, no."

"We're trying to make sure everyone makes it out of this alive. I mostly want to see you kick Landon's ass in pool. So, hop to. Make this happen for me," I said to Heidi.

Heidi grinned devilishly. Her eyes swept to Landon. "You rack, and I'll break."

"I'd expect nothing less," he said as he got to work.

And, suddenly, the three of us were back in high school. We'd spent countless nights at Heidi's dad's bar playing pool and having a good time. Half of the time, one of Heidi's boyfriends would show up. There was a lot of making out in back booths and trying to convince someone to get us drinks and a whole lot less actual pool.

So, this felt normal and comfortable.

I never thought I'd feel like this around Landon Wright again.

And it was nice.

Twenty-Four

Jensen

One more call couldn't hurt.

I'd told myself that after the last five calls.

But Emery still hadn't picked up.

After Landon had stormed out of my house, I'd called Morgan, and she came over. She hadn't known that Landon was coming in early either. So, she hadn't been able to warn me. Though she thought the whole thing was poetic justice.

I thought she was full of shit. I *had* been planning to tell Landon. That wasn't bullshit, as Morgan kept insinuating. But a part of me had known he would freak out. I'd told myself that I never would have gone after her if I'd known who she was. I'd told myself I never would have touched her if I'd thought she was staying in town. I'd told myself I'd stay away from her when I knew she was here for good.

With Emery, I couldn't seem to keep my promises to myself. And I didn't want to.

I didn't believe in coincidences. If I kept running into her, it was for a reason. Not on accident. And I wasn't about to walk away from someone just because of what might be.

But I hadn't wanted to face Landon. That much was for sure. And it had gone much worse than I had anticipated.

I didn't know what he was doing. I didn't know what Emery was doing. And I just wanted to make this all right.

Landon was wrong about me hiding my problems. I'd fixed one problem this weekend when I bought Tarman Corporation out from under Marc's nose. I could fix this one with Landon a lot quicker if I could just talk to my girlfriend.

Except she wasn't answering her phone.

Morgan gave me a worried look. "Maybe you should just let it go."

I wanted to throw my phone across the room. "I can't just let it go. Landon is out there, pissed off at me. Emery isn't answering my calls. What the fuck am I supposed to do, Morgan?"

"I don't know. You made this mess."

"Well aware of that. Thanks."

"Look, I'm not patronizing you. But you knew this was going to happen. You knew that you would have to tell Landon."

"And I planned to," I told her for what felt like the hundredth time.

"Then, you should have just done it."

"You're right," I said with a sigh. "Do you have Heidi's number?"

Morgan frowned. "I might."

"I need it."

"No."

"Why not?" I asked tersely.

"Emery is not answering your calls for a reason, Jensen. Give her some time. I'm sure that she is freaking out about all of this. No one likes to be ambushed."

"So, I should just let her walk?"

"That's not what I'm saying. I'm saying, give her space. If you were the one freaking out, would you want her to bombard you?"

I closed my eyes and sighed. That was how I had reacted with every other woman post-Vanessa. I hadn't liked to be bothered. I'd wanted my space. I hadn't slept. I'd just worked. That had been my life. I didn't know what it was like anymore.

"Normally, no, but right now, I'm considering going to her house to see if she's there."

Morgan rolled her eyes. "You men, so dramatic."

"What if this were Patrick?" I countered.

"This also has *nothing* to do with me or Patrick. Stop projecting. I cannot believe I'm even having this conversation with you. With Austin, sure. He's the one who fucks everything up. He even fucked up whatever was going on with that girl in HR."

"Julia?" I asked. "They were together?"

Morgan shrugged. "They're not anymore. But I thought you were always the one who had your shit together. Austin always has trouble with women. Landon has Miranda." She scoffed. "Enough said. But your life is put together, even with everything going on with Vanessa. Why are you acting crazy over one girl?"

"I care about her. And I care about Landon. I don't want to see either of them hurt. Not knowing is making me feel insane. I have to go out there and do something."

I reached for my jacket and pocketed the keys to my car.

"What exactly are you going to go do?" Morgan demanded, following me into the garage.

"I don't know. I'll make it up as I go along."

I hurried past the empty space where my black Mercedes always rested and hopped into my truck. Morgan stood, watching, as if she wanted to jump into the passenger seat or talk some sense into me. I noticed the exact moment when she decided it wouldn't matter. She just sighed and looked resigned.

"Will you let me know how it goes?" Morgan asked.

I nodded briskly and then pulled out of the garage. Before I had a second thought, I was already barreling across town. The logical explanation was that Emery was at home. She'd wanted to check on Kimber to make sure everything was all right. They were probably up late, talking, or maybe they had gone to sleep.

Except I didn't believe that.

I didn't know *why*.

But I just had this feeling. A gut instinct.

I wanted to shake it, but I wouldn't until I saw for myself that she was there. I careened down Milwaukee Avenue, out toward her sister's house. Pent-up tension and energy coursed through me. I felt on edge about her lack of response to my messages.

I parked my truck across the street and killed the engine. Shoving my hands in my pockets against the cold, I dashed across the street and up to the front door. I went to ring the doorbell and then shook my head. I couldn't ring the doorbell because Lilyanne could be asleep. That would be a real dick move. I didn't want to wake her up. They probably had a crazy routine to even get her to sleep in the first place. Instead, I knocked on the door and hoped someone was up to hear it.

After about a minute, the door cracked open, and Kimber's face appeared. "Jensen?" she asked in surprise.

"Hey, Kimber. I didn't mean to wake you up."

"Oh, you didn't. It's almost time, and it makes it kind of hard to sleep." She placed her hand on her belly and gave me a genuine smile. "Can I help you?"

"I was just hoping to talk to Emery."

Kimber frowned. "She went out hours ago to meet Heidi. She hasn't come home yet."

"Oh," I said slowly. "I see."

"Have you tried her cell?"

"A couple of times."

"Heidi is a bit of a bad influence. Love the girl to death and back, but they're trouble together. I can't even tell you what they went through in high school."

"I believe it."

"Do you want me to give her a call and see where she is? I didn't even check before she left."

"Uh, no. That's all right."

"Just come on inside. It will only be a minute," Kimber said with a kind smile.

I ducked inside without another protest.

She shuffled over to her phone and then smiled. "I have a text here. Looks like Emery is on her way home. She should be here soon, I guess."

I clenched my jaw and then released it. *Emery was responding to Kimber's messages but not mine? What the fuck?*

Something was wrong here. I could feel it. I could sense it. But I just didn't know what was happening.

"You can stay and wait if you want?" Kimber offered.

"Oh no," I said immediately, backing away. "Uh, no. I'll just check in with her tomorrow. If she's safe, then that's fine by me."

Kimber tilted her head in worry. "Are you sure?"

"Completely," I said.

Then, I exited the house and hurried back to my truck. The reasonable and rational thing to do would be to wait until Emery got home. I wanted to talk to her about Landon—the things that had been said and the things that I suspected about Landon. I needed to clear the air. I needed to figure out why they had broken up and what Landon had meant about me not knowing her.

But maybe tonight really *wasn't* the best night for it. Maybe we should have that conversation when I was in a better headspace.

I shook my head at my own frustrations and then put the truck into gear. I touched the accelerator and hurried down the road. I was almost out of the neighborhood when my eyes cut to the car that was passing me—a black Mercedes.

There was nothing special about it. Nothing to draw my eye at all. It was a plain, standard black Mercedes. It should have been completely unidentifiable. Any number of people could have the same car in this neighborhood where wealth was on display.

But my instincts told me it didn't belong to just anyone.

My instincts told me that it belonged to *me*.

I waited until the car passed me before making my decision. I did a U-turn in the middle of the street and slowly drove back to Emery's house. When I turned onto her street, I cut my lights and parked two houses down the street. My stomach cramped, and tension bottled in my shoulders. My hands were white on the steering wheel. Of all the scenarios I had concocted in my head, *this* had never been one of them.

The Mercedes was parked at Emery's house. The Mercedes that Landon had driven off in earlier that day. He always had access to my cars when he was in town. I'd never cared what he drove or when. Getting a rental when I had a garage full of cars seemed ridiculous. Now, I couldn't believe that he was using my car to come here.

The passenger door opened. My gaze darted to it in surprise. Then, Emery stepped out, and my hands shook in disbelief.

Emery had been with Landon all night?

Kimber had said she was with Heidi. But it was right in front of my face. Landon was stepping out of the driver's side. He sprinted around to Emery's side and wrapped an arm around her waist. She turned her body into his and held on to his shoulder.

I felt like I was going to be sick. I didn't think I could watch any more of this. If I had thought half-hearted that Landon still had feelings for Emery before, it was now confirmed. He'd run out on me to go see my girlfriend. And here they were, together.

They walked arm in arm up to the front door.

As much as I wanted to look away, I couldn't seem to. Landon definitely still had feelings for Emery. And the way Emery was acting—leaning against him, holding on to him, practically gluing herself to his body—showed that not everything was gone from her either.

Emery rested back against the brick wall next to the door that I had walked out of only minutes before. She was staring up at Landon's face, and I didn't even need to hear what they were saying. The picture was clear enough to me.

I put the truck into drive and zoomed away from the sight before me. I couldn't watch any more.

I'd thought that there was nothing that would keep me from Emery.

But I would not compete with Landon.

Not in this lifetime.

Not in any lifetime.

Twenty-Five

Emery

My back was against the brick wall to Kimber's place, and my head felt like I'd blown up a balloon inside it. Landon was hovering. *Little hoverer.* But I should be thankful because I wouldn't have made it to the front door without his help.

Somehow, I'd gone from a three-drink max to, like, ten drinks. I didn't even know how it had happened. At one point, I had been standing, and the next, I had proclaimed to the bar that I was definitely not drunk before suddenly wanting to make out with Heidi. Sure signs that I was a drunky-drunk face.

"Are you going to be okay? You look like you might throw up," Landon said.

"Just go check on Heidi. If she vomits in that Mercedes, Jensen is going to be *sooooo* pissed."

Landon grinned and shook his head. "Man, you're so fucked up."

"This is all. Your. Fault," I said, punctuating each word with a smack to his chest. It might have been some stupid girlie hit, but I felt fierce while doing it.

"Where is your key? Do you still not carry a purse?"

"As if the key would magically appear in a purse," I said, patting down my pockets in a half-assed effort. "It'd be full of other junk I didn't need. I'd never find it."

"You can't find it now, and it's in your pocket."

"Judgy McJudgerson doesn't find pockets acceptable. You only have pockets," I slurred, poking at his pocket and giggling.

"Do not make me look through your pockets for you," Landon said with a sigh. "God, if my wife saw me right now."

"Her head would explode," I crooned. Then, I made the boom sound for an explosion.

"Something like that," he conceded. "So, hurry up, so I can get home and incur her wrath."

I giggled again and then finally dug out the missing key.

Landon plucked it out of my hand and unlocked the door for me. He shoved the door open. "Here you go. Inside with you," he said, helping me blunder inside.

A light flickered on, and Kimber appeared around the corner. She stopped short, her mouth hanging open and her eyes darting between the two of us.

"Hey, Kimmy," I said happily.

"Landon?" Kimber asked softly.

"Hey, Kimber," he said with a short wave.

"That is not the Wright brother I was expecting," she confessed.

Landon's cheeks turned pink, and I giggled at his embarrassment. *Man, I am loaded.*

"Just wanted to make sure she got home safe. Caught her at Flips with Heidi, and they needed a ride home," he told her.

"I see." She crossed her arms over the top of her pregnant belly. "Don't you have a wife to get home to?"

She was using her mom voice, and I wanted to tell her to stop. But Landon seemed to take a cue from her and backed off. I stumbled onto the couch and watched the ceiling spin.

"Good seeing you again, Kimber. Good night," Landon said.

"Good night," she said, closing the door behind him. She turned back to face me with a sigh. "What have you gotten yourself into?"

"Clouds."

"Clouds?"

"They're twirling on the ceiling."

"Oh God, you're so drunk. Why didn't you answer Jensen's calls?"

"He didn't call," I said, trying to sit up. I pulled my phone out of my pocket and tried three times to light up the screen before realizing it was dead. I sheepishly glanced up at her. "Um...it's dead."

Kimber sighed heavily again. "Well, charge it, and give him a call. He was here earlier, looking for you."

"He was?" I asked, sobering up a bit at that revelation. "Why?"

"He wouldn't say, but he seemed concerned. And, since I just saw you with his brother and your ex-boyfriend, I could see his concern."

"Whoa! Wait a second, Kimmy. Reel that mom voice back in. There's so nothing going on with me and Landon. He just apologized to me for blowing up on me when he found out about Jensen. He played pool with Heidi. We had a few drinks. He drove us both home. No big."

"All right. What do I know? Just happily married with no drama in my life."

I giggled. "I love you."

"I love you, too. Now, go. Charge. Now."

I nodded at her and gave her a quick salute. Then, I meandered the way to the stairs like I was walking through a hedge maze, and I more or less crawled up the stairs. I found my charger resting on the nightstand and plugged it in, waiting for the signature *beep, beep* to let me know it was ready to use again.

Then, it beeped and beeped and beeped.

Kimber had *not* been joking. Jensen had definitely texted me. And called. And texted some more.

Holy text messages!

They were very blurry though and kind of all melded together. I didn't know what he was so desperate to tell me, knowing that he'd shown up here after I didn't answer, but I might as well call him. Probably not the *best* idea I'd ever had, considering the amount of alcohol I'd consumed.

Imbibed. Drank. Drunk.

I flopped back onto my bed and stared at the spinny ceiling, contemplating which word was the best. Probably drowned in. Because I felt like I was on a boat adrift in the water, bouncing up and down and up and down on the waves.

Oh God, I was going to be sick.

I sat up in a hurry and tried not to think about vomiting. That was better. Now, I could call Jensen.

I dialed his number and let it ring about a million times before it got to his voice mail.

Then, I tried again. No luck.

I stared down at it in confusion. *Why would he call and message me so many times and then not answer my phone calls?*

I tried one more time and then gave up. I was too drunk for this.

Maybe he'd call me back tomorrow morning. He was probably already asleep or something. And I clearly needed to do the same.

Stripping out of my clothes, I crawled into bed naked and promptly blacked out into oblivion.

———

After puking my guts out all night, I remembered that I had to open the Buddy Holly Center today. I'd switched my schedule around so that I could get away to Austin for the weekend and had given myself the morning shift. I felt like shit and looked even worse. My face was pasty, and my hair was limp. I brushed my teeth three times to get the taste of thrown up out of my mouth.

And then I checked my phone.

Again.

Still nothing from Jensen.

I'd called him in between bouts of vomiting and texted him before I hopped into the shower. I double-checked that I'd contacted him as I put on clothes for the day.

I was royally confused. Beyond confused. And sick as a dog.

Why call and text and show up, only to ignore me when I tried to get in touch with him again? Is he trying to punish me or something for not answering?

That didn't sound like Jensen. That sounded petty.

With a heavy sigh, I grabbed my keys and cell, which was fully charged, and left the house.

The Buddy Holly Center was empty. The construction crew from Wright Construction wouldn't show up for another ten minutes, which meant I had a few extra minutes to try to recuperate and not to throw up again. I didn't have anything left in my stomach. I'd packed a few snacks that would be easy on the stomach, but the thought of doing anything but sipping on water made me feel nauseated.

A knock on the door broke me away from staring aimlessly at my phone, hoping for a text message. I couldn't think that Jensen was sleeping. He didn't sleep unless we were together.

The insomniac would rear its ugly head when we were apart. I couldn't imagine that he was just ignoring me.

I unlocked the door and allowed the crew to come inside. Once they were all inside, I could go back to the office and dick around until someone else came to take over at lunch. We really didn't have to stay the whole time, but some of the artifacts were pretty priceless, and no one liked to leave the place empty. Even if we'd hired the people.

I lay back down on the couch in Betty's office and took another sip of my water. Feeling slightly up to par, I found the number for Jensen's office and pressed Call.

"Mr. Wright's office," his receptionist said. "How can I help you?"

"Hi. Um…this is Emery. I was just wondering if Jensen was in."

"Unfortunately, Mr. Wright is out of the office today, but I would be happy to take a message."

I furrowed my brow. *Jensen isn't at work? That seems…wrong.*

"Do you know when he's going to be back in?" I pressed.

"Mr. Wright is away on business right now."

"Away on business?" I asked in confusion.

"Yes. He had to go to New York at the last minute to take care of some business. I'm not sure when he will be back in the office, but I could get him a message if you like."

New York.

My brain stalled on the word.

What is in New York?

The only thing I could think that was in New York was what he had told me. Vanessa had lived there. He and Vanessa had been together in New York. *Did she still live there? Was he on his way to see her?*

No, that didn't make any sense. He had said that he divorced her for cheating on him. That definitely could not be it.

I was just trying to freak myself out.

Or I was just freaking out, period.

Why wasn't he returning my calls?

What kind of business could he possibly have in New York the week of Christmas right after he had gotten back from purchasing Tarman? And what kind of business would he have where he had to disappear so quickly without telling me...or responding to any of my messages?

By the time lunch rolled around and I was off my shift, I felt like I was going insane. Jensen and I had had an awesome weekend. I'd left him alone with Landon to clear my head. Jensen had called and texted, and then when I'd responded, he'd gone radio silent.

What the hell had Landon said to him?

Before I could second-guess my train of thought, I canceled my standing lunch date with Heidi and swung by Jensen's house. I rang the doorbell and impatiently tapped my toe.

When no one answered, I rang the bell again and again.

Finally, a bleach-blonde appeared at the door. Miranda's gaze dropped to mine, and then she pursed her Barbie pink lips. "What the hell are you doing here?"

Fuck. I hadn't counted for on seeing Miranda. I hadn't even thought about her. I just wanted to talk to Landon about Jensen.

"Um...hi," I said. *This is not going to be fun.* "Is Jensen here?"

"You can't fool me," Miranda said.

She eased the door open more, and I could see she was in some kind of tennis getup. But I didn't know if she had been playing or what because her hair and makeup were still perfect.

"I know why you're really here, and if you get near my husband, I'll file a restraining order."

I held my hands up. "No interest in your husband. Just trying to find Jensen."

Right then, Landon's face appeared. He looked green when he saw that I was talking to Miranda. "Emery? What are you doing here?"

"Came looking for Jensen. I haven't seen him since last night. He's not answering my messages, and his receptionist said that he was away on business."

"Landon!" Miranda cried. "Why the fuck are you talking to her right now? I thought we discussed this before we left Tampa. I would come if you didn't go anywhere near her!"

"Hello? Standing right here," I muttered. "I'm not interested in Landon. I'm dating Jensen."

"I'm not an idiot."

Beg to differ, was what I wanted to throw back at her. But, instead, I just turned back to Landon. "Help? Thoughts? Anything?"

"Landon!" Miranda whined.

"Just give me a minute, honey, okay?" He kissed her forehead as he crossed the threshold. "Just one minute."

"I cannot believe this. You are so going to owe me for this."

"Just one minute. Don't you have a tennis lesson?" he asked.

"Don't you dare try to get rid of me."

"I'll be right back," he said. I could hear the exasperation in his voice as he shut the door in her face. But he looked livid when he turned around. "What the fuck are you doing here, Emery? Miranda is going to murder me in my sleep."

"Jensen is gone and not returning my messages. What did you say to him last night?"

"I don't know. I was pissed last night. Said some dumb things."

"What dumb things?" I demanded.

"It was just me overreacting. I was going to talk to him this morning to try to clear the air, but when I woke up, he was gone."

"What did you say?" I said, my voice low and deadly.

"I might have said you were too good for him."

"Ugh!" I groaned. "Great. I don't know what he's thinking, but he's gone. He went to New York. Why would he be in New York?"

Landon's face dropped, and he was utterly silent. When he glanced away, that was when I knew it was bad.

"What? Tell me!" I said, pushing him.

"Nothing."

"Landon! Is it Vanessa?"

"I know Vanessa has a place in New York, but that doesn't mean he went to see her. He's probably just working. That's all he normally does anyway."

"Landon, *why* would he go see his ex-wife? Why would he do that?" I didn't really want him to answer. I didn't want to consider why Jensen would go see Vanessa in New York after being upset last night. He'd promised he'd never cheat on me, and I had to believe that. I had to latch on to that with everything I was, or I might fall apart entirely.

"It's complicated."

I winced. "Then, make it uncomplicated."

"I can't. You should just…talk to Jensen about this."

"I can't!" I cried in frustration. "He won't return my messages."

"I'm sorry, Emery. I can't talk about it."

"Can't talk about what?"

"Nothing," he said quickly. "Don't jump to any conclusions. It's not Vanessa. This is normal Jensen behavior. He'll come back soon and then all will be back to normal."

I shook my head in disbelief. I couldn't believe what Landon was saying. Things were complicated? Things were always complicated.

But Jensen running away from his problems was not solving anything. Whether this had anything to do with Vanessa or not…Jensen was purposely ignoring me. And that alone infuriated me.

Twenty-Six

Emery

Jensen didn't return a single message for five whole days.

By then, I'd thought of every worst-case scenario—from him being with his ex-wife to his death. My imagination was ripe, but it had no reprieve. I knew that I hadn't done anything wrong. Not a damn thing. And, at this point, he was ignoring me on purpose. We *definitely* needed a good long talk, and maybe he needed a sharp kick in the ass.

By Christmas Eve, I was even agreeing to go to church with my mother of all people just to see if he showed up. That way, we could get all of this out in the open.

Kimber, Noah, and Lilyanne decided to stay in since Kimber was due soon, and the days had gotten harder. She wanted to conserve all of her energy for Christmas morning when she would get to see Lilyanne open her mound of presents from Santa.

So, I drove myself over to my mother's place to pick her up.

"Look what the cat dragged in," my mother said when she answered the door in a chic black dress.

"Ha, Mom. Never heard that one before." It was our normal routine and slightly comforting, considering the week I'd had.

"Well, I *was* going to let Gary Lupton drive me to church, but I suppose you're a worthy substitute."

I cringed. "What about Harry Stevenson?"

"A girl has to have options, Emery."

"Oh God, Mom!"

She cackled and walked out to my Forester. "Don't be such a prude. I know you're seeing Jensen Wright. Everyone knows that he isn't a prude."

I ground my teeth as I turned over the ignition. "I really, really don't want to talk about my love life. Thanks, but no thanks."

"Why do you have to be like this? I thought we were bonding."

"I can't bond with you over who you're having sex with. It grosses me out," I told her as I pulled out of her driveway.

"Well, you refuse to come by and see me. You aren't getting married. You aren't getting your degree anymore. You hate shopping and pedicures and makeovers. What exactly *am* I supposed to bond with you over?"

"Hey, I like pedicures!" I said. "But just because I'm not... Kimber doesn't mean that I don't have my own qualities or whatever."

"I only needle you because I love you. I just want to make sure you're happy. I don't want to see you waste your life away at the Buddy Holly Center again."

"You set me up to work there!" I accused.

"Temporarily. I thought you'd be going back to school."

"Well, I'm not," I said. My mind was still locked on Jensen, and here was my mother, trying to plan my career. As if I wanted to add to the list of things that I had to deal with right now.

"You used to be so full of love for things. Things I hated but you loved them. Soccer and that horrendous skateboard and coaching and tutoring after school and honors society and—"

"Yes, I get it. But, now, I'm adrift, and I need something of my own."

"Exactly."

I rolled my eyes. "I'll figure it out."

My mother put her hand on my arm and sighed. "Maybe you should consider working at the high school. You have the degrees. You'd need to be certified, but I know you could do it."

"High school students?" I shuddered.

"You'd make a difference."

I brushed her hand off my arm.

I didn't want to admit that she was right. I probably could get a job teaching history at the local high school, and maybe I'd even get to help coach the soccer team. I'd played on the intramural team at Oklahoma and at an adult rec league for two years at UT. I just didn't know if that was *it*.

I'd loved teaching when I was in graduate school. That was the best part. The least stressful part honestly. It was the research and papers and endless criticism that had done me in. Some people were made for that and loved it but not me. I could take some critiques, but eventually, my head had exploded, and I'd felt like it was doing more harm than good.

"Just think about it," my mom said as we pulled into the church parking lot.

"Okay," I said, "I'll think about it."

"Good, or else I'd have to start talking about Jensen Wright again."

I groaned and parked in a spot. "You kill me."

217

"I love you, too," she said. Then, she hurried toward a cluster of her friends standing at the entrance.

I scanned the parking lot for Jensen, but it was impossible. The church was huge, and I would never find him out here like that. I killed the ignition and then checked inside the church to see if the Wrights had arrived yet. No luck.

Then, I planted myself at the front of the church with my arms crossed. I felt like I was staking the place out as I waited, but if Jensen was here, then I needed to talk to him. I needed to figure out what the fuck was happening...or end it. Because I was not going to be toyed with.

Just when I had that thought, a bleach-blonde bob appeared before me.

"Ugh! Are you literally following me everywhere?" Miranda asked.

She was in a skintight blue dress that barely hit her at mid thigh and had a low-cut neckline. She looked good in it, but it wouldn't have been my first choice for a relatively conservative church service.

"I go to church here," I responded with a sigh.

"Uh-huh. Oh, I'm sure."

"Miranda," Landon said, hurrying to catch up, "let's just go inside."

"You *knew* she was going to be here."

"We've gone to the same church since we were kids, Miranda. I can't help that."

"And I get no warning?" she asked.

"You don't need a warning," I said, "because there's nothing going on here, and you're worrying for nothing."

"Don't tell me how I feel. Just stay away from us."

Then, she sauntered inside, as if she owned the place, and Landon gave me a sympathetic look before following her. I shook my head at her ridiculousness and then looked to see if the rest of the Wrights were following. I wasn't disappointed.

Little Sutton Wright and her new husband, Maverick, had finally come back from their honeymoon in Cabo. She was a deep olive tan, and his nose was a bit red, but they both looked happy. After them, I saw Morgan and Austin enter. She looked to be scolding him, pointing at his pocket. I narrowed my eyes to try to figure out what she was saying. Then, I noticed the top of a flask peeking out of his pocket.

Oh, eesh!

Then, I couldn't be bothered. Because walking straight toward me was none other than Jensen Wright himself. He looked…unbelievable. I might be mad at him, but he was undeniably attractive. He was in a tailored charcoal suit that fit him like a glove. He had on a red patterned shirt and a dark tie. His cheekbones were sharp, and his eyes were even fiercer. But I could see underneath it. He looked like he'd lost weight… and definitely sleep. There were dark circles under his eyes, like he'd been living off of caffeine and power naps.

He caught my eye, and I stopped breathing for a second. In that second, I just wanted to forget the last week. I wanted everything to be right. I wanted Wright to be right even though it felt so wrong.

But then that moment passed, and I knew what I had to do.

I marched straight over to Jensen and blocked his path before he could get inside. "Where the hell have you been?"

"Language, Emery," he said, his voice clipped.

"Don't do that," I ground out. "Just answer the damn question."

"I've been in New York."

"Why haven't you answered any of my calls or messages?"

"I've been busy," he said simply.

I grabbed his sleeve and pulled him out of the way of the entrance. "I'm missing something here. What the hell happened? Is it because I didn't answer your calls that night?

My phone died, and I didn't see you'd called until I got home. I called you back as soon as I charged it," I rambled on.

"Not *as soon as*."

"What the hell does that mean?" I asked, not following him.

"I really don't want to get into this with you, Emery."

He moved to brush past me, but I latched on to his arm. "Was it Vanessa?"

Jensen turned back to face me with confusion. "What do you mean?"

"Do you still love her? Is that why you were in New York?" I knew I sounded desperate and jealous, but I cared very little at this point. If it was going to end, then I just wanted him to do it.

"You ask me that after last week?"

"Why shouldn't I?" I demanded. He wasn't making any sense.

He took a step toward me, towering over me. "I saw you with Landon. I saw the way you were all over him that night. Landon is still in love with you, and it sure looked like you felt the same."

Landon was in love with me? Ha! That was a riot. And Jensen thought I was still in love with Landon? That was equally laughable.

"That is not what you saw!" I told him.

"Save it, Emery."

Then, he turned and walked into the church, leaving me sputtering in shock. He thought I loved Landon. He thought that I had somehow chosen Landon over him. And I didn't even know how he could think that.

Where had he seen me with Landon? At Flips? I definitely had not been all over him then. I'd never even touched him, except when he'd helped me to the door so that I wouldn't fall over.

I stumbled back a step. *Oh, shit.*

Kimber had said Jensen had come by. Maybe he'd seen Landon help me. Maybe he thought something had been there that wasn't. Because *nothing* was there. And it was preposterous to presume something like that. It was even worse to assume it, not have a conversation about it, and then run.

Twenty-Seven

Jensen

Emery's gaze burned me like a brand throughout the service.

Luckily, the Christmas Eve service was almost entirely comprised of singing, and there was never a point where she could talk to me.

I'd been prepared for her to be here tonight. I'd figured, after the way I'd left things—or hadn't left things—that she would want a confrontation. She was that kind of girl. But she'd made her choice that night, and then I'd made mine when I hopped on that plane and flew to New York.

What I did regret was that things were still tense with Landon. I should have fixed things with him before leaving. He was my brother. He would always be in my life, and if I had to endure his love for Emery, then I should at least let him know that I would stand down. I knew he was married to Miranda. But I always thought that was a temporary thing and that he'd find someone better in the end.

It had been impossible to get near him when I got back this morning. Miranda never left his side, and I couldn't be in her vicinity for more than a few minutes before wanting my eardrums to burst.

But I would fix it tonight.

When the service ended, I reached down for my jacket, and when I stood back up, there was Emery, looking pissed as all hell. She was looking up at me with fire in her eyes, and it was impossible not to stare back. She was…stunning. Breathtaking. My chest tightened when I looked at her.

Avoiding her had seemed like the best option. I'd thought that telling her what I had seen would send her careening away from me. Yet, here she was, gazing up at me, as if she couldn't decide whether she wanted to kiss me or punch me. *What a quandary, this woman.*

"You're an idiot," she snapped.

"Not now," I muttered.

"Yes! Right now. I've waited all week for this. Why wait another minute?"

I could see in her eyes that she was in no way going to let this go. "Fine. Let's do this somewhere else."

"Fine," she spat. "Outside then."

I made my excuses to my family and then followed Emery outside. Emery nodded her head to the left, and we started walking in the bitter cold weather. She was in a warm jacket and scarf, and already, her cheeks and nose were pink from the cold. Temperatures were dropping rapidly, and we were actually expecting a white Christmas.

"All right, we're outside," I said. "What is it that you have to say to me?"

"You're being such an incredible idiot right now."

"You mentioned that."

She glared in my direction. "I can't do this, Jensen."

"Can't do what?" I asked, knowing full well what she meant.

"You don't trust me. You don't value my opinion. You couldn't even bother to talk to me. You ran at the first sign of trouble. Then, when things got tough, you went to see your ex-wife."

"This has nothing to do with Vanessa. You know that."

"How?" she demanded. "How could I know that? Do I know anything at all about what the hell this is about? You're pissed about Landon. Then, you ran to your ex, and you expect me to just not care about that? Look at how you reacted when you just *thought* something had happened with Landon. I have every right to be upset."

"You do," I conceded.

None of what she was saying was wrong. But that didn't mean I was going to stand here and let her yell at me. I knew Landon. I knew what he was feeling and thinking. She must just be blind to it.

"But it doesn't change what I saw or how you feel about Landon or how Landon feels about you."

"Oh my God, give it a rest! I do *not* love Landon, and Landon does *not* love me," she hissed.

"I know what I saw."

"No, you don't. You really don't. You have never given me a chance to explain what you *think* you saw. I can't sit around and let you walk all over my heart, Jensen. I put myself out there after I'd been hurt. And then, at the first sign of trouble, you ditched me. And all of it could have been fixed with one little conversation that you *refused* to have with me."

"If you think that one conversation will magically change everything, then tell me what I saw. Tell me what really happened."

"Look, the night you saw me with Landon was in no way romantic. He came to apologize to me for being a dick when he found us together. Then, Heidi and I got drunk, and he offered both of us a ride home. I was too drunk to walk to the front door, so he helped me. I got inside and immediately called you. The end. That's the whole story."

"And you were all over him because…"

"One, I was not all over him. Two, I was drunk, and I'm not a good drunk. I'm a face-plant-into-the-concrete-and-bust-my-nose-and-get-two-black-eyes kind of drunk. Trust me, I've been there."

I snorted, just imagining her falling over like that.

"That's really all that happened?" I asked.

I suddenly felt panicked, like maybe Landon hadn't been the one who overreacted…that I had been the one to overreact. If what she was saying was true, then I had hurt her this week for no good reason.

"Yes!" she cried, exasperated. "And you would know that if you had bothered to pick up the phone. Go ask Landon. Go ask Heidi! She was in the car that night. If anything, I think that Heidi might be into Landon. Not me! I don't understand what I did to make you not trust me, but I hate this."

"Emery," I said slowly. I was an idiot.

"Save it," she said in frustration, throwing my words back at me.

"You're right," I said automatically.

She gave me a wary look. "I am?"

"Yes. I am an idiot."

"Well, that's very obvious at this point."

"What I'm trying to say is, I was so afraid of losing you that I pushed you away. I made assumptions. It didn't help that Landon had said that, if I didn't know what had really happened in your breakup, then I didn't know you at all."

Her eyes ignited in fury. "He said what?" she cried. "Oh, I'm going to kill him, I swear."

"What I'm saying is that I want a second chance," I said, reaching for her hand. "I don't want to argue with you, and I don't want to run. I was an idiot. A complete idiot."

"I don't know," she whispered, turning her face away from mine. "How do I know that this won't happen again?"

"You don't. But I don't know how else to make this right. We both have pasts. We both have issues. Trust is mine. After what happened in my past, I have a hard time taking anyone at face value. But I'd really like to try to handle everything together. To start over."

She sighed. "Jensen…"

"Give me a chance, Emery. Please."

Snow slowly started to fall around us. She looked up at me through snowy lashes with fluffy flakes tumbling into her dark hair and blanketing her jacket. I knew she was hurting, and I had done almost irreparable damage. But I wanted to make this right…if she would just let me.

"Okay," she said finally. "One chance, Jensen. That's it."

Then, I tilted my face down toward hers, and our lips met, gently and nurturing. It was a kiss I'd missed all week. A kiss I'd remember forever.

"You won't regret it," I whispered against her lips.

She sighed into me and wrapped her arms around my waist. "I hated the last week."

"Me, too. I hated being away from you."

"Why are you such an ass?"

I laughed. "Can't seem to help it."

"God, we're so fucked up."

"Emery?"

"Hmm?"

"What really happened with your breakup with Landon?"

She sighed again, heavier, and took a step back from me. "You really want to know?"

I nodded. "Yes. I would like to be on equal footing. Figure things out together. That way, maybe neither of us will be blindsided again."

"All right." She dropped her head forward, swallowed, and then nodded. "Landon and I had dated nearly two years when he got into Stanford on a golf scholarship, and I got into Oklahoma as a National Merit Scholar, but both of us wanted to stay home and go to Texas Tech, so we could be together. We had this whole plan. Then…as far as I know, your father told him to go to Stanford."

"No way," I argued. "My father wanted nothing more than for all of us to go to Texas Tech, just like him and all our relatives."

She shrugged. "I was there. This is what happened. He thought Landon should be more serious about school and about sports. He wanted Landon to go to Stanford and try to walk onto the football team, which Landon didn't want to do."

"That at least sounds like my father."

"Yeah. Landon was a good football player, but he always preferred golf. He got into a huge argument with your dad one night right before the deadline where we both had to decide where we were going to school. His dad said that he needed to break up with me or something like, if I was so important, then we could make it work long distance. As you know, your dad died shortly after that."

I nodded. That part, I was well aware of.

"Landon felt…responsible for what happened. As if that argument had pushed him over the edge."

"He wasn't and it didn't."

"I knew that; I still know that. But the last thing that he ever said to your dad was something mean, and he couldn't cope. He accepted the full ride to Stanford because that's what your dad had wanted, and I took the Oklahoma spot. Then, Landon was just…gone."

"Gone?"

"Adrift. I tried to bring him back and to help, but he just disappeared those next couple of weeks before graduation. We were still together. I knew he still loved me, but he was broken. So, he broke up with me the day of graduation. He told me that he'd talked it over with his family—with you—and you'd all agreed it was best."

"We never talked about this. He told me that you were going to different colleges, and you'd grown apart."

"Well, I see *now* that you didn't know." She swallowed hard. "But, as you can imagine, as an eighteen-year-old, I was heartbroken. He still loved me. I still loved him. I knew he was only doing this because of what happened to your father. I tried calling him and messaging him and emailing him. No answer. He just disappeared off the face of the planet. I know he got my messages. He never blocked me. He knew how much I was hurting and ignored it. Sound familiar?"

I winced. It did. I'd seen her messages and how desperate she was. I'd put her in the same spot Landon had ten years ago, and I hadn't even known it. And I'd done it for no good reason.

"I'm sorry."

"I know," she whispered. "But, as you can see, history repeating itself wasn't so good on my psyche. Landon made his choice all those years ago. I know he did what he thought was right. I just hated all of you for a long time because of him."

We walked on in the snow in silence for another minute. I didn't know what to say to all of that. I hadn't realized how hurt Landon had been. When he'd disappeared to Stanford, I'd thought he'd been fine. Boy, was I wrong.

"So, since we're being all open and honest now," Emery said, glancing over at me. "Did you see Vanessa when you were in New York?"

"I did," I answered slowly.

I weighed my option. How much could I tell her right now. There were still things that she didn't know. Things that I knew I should tell her. But she looked so tense and ready to run. I worried one more thing would push her over the edge.

I promised myself that I would tell her though when the time was right.

"But I didn't go there to see her, and absolutely nothing happened. I was there for business."

"Landon said it was complicated between the two of you."

"It is. Vanessa is complicated," I confirmed.

She crossed her arms over her chest, as if she were trying to keep her insides from squirming at the thought.

"But it's not like that," I rushed on. "I told you once that I could never be with her after what had happened, and that hasn't changed."

"Then, why did you see her?"

"We're divorced, but not…disentangled. It's complicated."

"Disentangled?"

God, I didn't know how to explain this. "I'm working on the disentangling, part of the reason I went up there. Plus, I was selling off a part of Tarman. I bought the company to dismantle it," I confessed.

She frowned and pursed her lips. She looked like she was considering everything else I had just said and finding it unsatisfactory.

"That's not really an answer," she said finally. "Why did you see her?"

"She still lives in my apartment in New York."

"Why the hell would you let her live there?"

"This is part of the disentangling," I admitted. Soon. I would tell her soon.

"And nothing happened?"

"Emery, no," I said softly.

"I know, I know," she said, shaking her head. "I should trust you in return. If you said it's not like that, then it's not like that."

God, I had fucked up. She was so wary now. It was so clear to me, what an idiot I'd been.

Staring down into her beautiful face as snow slowly fell from the sky, I knew.

I'd tried to run.

I'd tried to hide.

I'd tried to say fuck it all.

But there was no turning back.

Emery Robinson was it for me.

And I would do anything to keep her.

"I'm sorry," I finally said, pulling her to a stop again. I ran my hands down her arms. "I knew, even while I was doing it, that what I was doing was wrong. I just...fuck, I was just so angry. I felt like I was going through the same shit again. But, this time, I would not just be hurting the woman I love but my brother, too."

"Love?" she whispered. Her mouth opened slightly in shock. "You love me?"

"Oh, Emery," I said, threading my fingers through her hair and pushing it behind her ear. I stepped toward her, feeling all my walls crumbling down. "Of course I love you."

Twenty-Eight

Emery

Having Jensen Wright love me was like walking in the sun. But, while I played in the sunlight, I feared the darkness.

I wouldn't forget the week Jensen and I'd spent apart. The shadow that he cast when the sun disappeared. I wasn't crazy enough to believe that love would conquer everything, and I wasn't naive enough to think that running was out of the question for him. He had proven that he would do it, and now, he had to prove to me that he wouldn't.

Things hadn't been perfect since I agreed to give him a chance. I was guarding my time and my heart, wary of what was to come. I'd seen him on Christmas after his time with his family and had been mostly welcomed, Miranda aside. Landon had been uncomfortable around the two of us, but there were no more outbursts from him. It would take everyone a while to adjust. Our time post-Christmas had almost been too perfect. Maybe I was gun shy, but I worried that everything wasn't what it seemed.

Still I'd agreed to go with him to a New Year's Eve party at the Overton Hotel downtown. I wanted things to be right. I wanted to bask in his love and affection. But I also didn't want to get hurt. And my heart was warring with my head.

"Why do you look so nervous?" Heidi asked. She was fussing with my hair, having already done my makeup for the event.

"I'm not nervous," I lied.

"Yes, you are," Julia said, leaning back against the chair.

We had all convened at my house to get ready. Julia already looked stunning with her recently dyed burgundy hair piled on the top of her head and dressed in a rocking black dress.

"Things are rocky, and you have turtle head now," Heidi insisted.

"Turtle head?" I asked with a laugh.

"Yeah, you're crawling back into your shell because you're worried he'll fuck up again," Heidi said.

"I'm not worried. I'm cautious."

Heidi nodded her head. "Yep. Turtle head."

"Wouldn't you be cautious?" I demanded.

"I don't know," Heidi said with a shrug.

"He just abandoned me for a week. I'm trying to take it easy."

"Just try to have fun, okay?" Heidi asked.

I nodded. That was the plan. I was just going to have fun tonight. We were going to be back in a good place again. I *wanted* us to be back in a good place.

"Good," Julia said. "Now we need to find someone for me to kiss at midnight."

"Oh, me too!" Heidi said.

"Landon?" I coughed under my breath.

Heidi's eyes were round as saucers. "What? No! He's married!"

"What if he wasn't?"

"Then he'd be *your* ex-boyfriend."

"I'm dating his brother, Heidi."

"Nuh-uh. No way. This is girl code we're talking about! Sacred shit here, Em."

I laughed at her vehemence. I knew something was up even if she wouldn't admit to it, but I decided to let it slide. "Well, you know I'm good for that kiss at midnight for the both you."

Heidi snort-laughed. "Oh my God, yes, my love. Take me away!"

"Lesbian threesome. I'm in," Julia said with a laugh.

Heidi threw herself into my arms and made ridiculous kissy noises. We laughed like we were back in school together, when the world was a lot easier to deal with.

Julia just stared at us and shook her head. "You two are so hot for each other."

Heidi laughed again and kissed my cheek. "Always."

The doorbell rang, and I had déjà vu, back to the first time Jensen and I had gone on a date. I dashed downstairs with my friends following behind me. Lilyanne rushed to the door, and there was Jensen holding out flowers for her. She beamed up at him.

"Mom! My boyfriend is here!" Lilyanne called to Kimber.

Kimber groaned. "We are going to need to break that habit."

Jensen ruffled Lily's hair. "How are you doing, munchkin?"

"Fine. Thank you for asking," she said politely. "We should have another ice cream date."

"We should," he said, grinning from ear to ear.

"Good. I know how to fix the flowers," Lilyanne announced before hurrying off to her mom and dad.

Jensen stood up, and I got a full view of him in a tuxedo. I heard the other girls scurry back upstairs. They would follow us to the party later.

"Wow," he said when his gaze found mine. "You look amazing."

I smiled, grabbed my jacket, and strode toward him. If I was going to give him a chance, then I needed to give him a chance. Be the confident, sexy woman he claimed to love.

"You look pretty good yourself."

"That dress though." He ran his hands down the silky material of the emerald-green dress, which matched my eyes, that I'd borrowed from Kimber's closet.

I blushed at the way his eyes devoured me. "Thanks."

He seemed to get himself together and then gestured to the door. "After you."

When I stepped outside, I gasped. A black stretch limo was waiting on the street.

"What? Are we going to prom?" I joked.

Jensen arched an eyebrow. "Didn't you go with Landon?"

"Oh, yeah. Twice."

"Then, nope. No prom for you."

"Fair enough."

Jensen opened the door to the stretch limo, and I sank into the leather seat. He followed behind me. It was jet-black and swanky on the inside. A bottle of my favorite champagne was chilling in a bucket of ice. Soft music filtered in through the speakers, and I laughed when I realized it was Mariah Carey.

"Mariah Carey?" I asked. "You're playing Mariah Carey?"

"Look, I know she made a fool of herself, but she is our singer now."

"Oh my God, it's 'Always Be My Baby.'"

"And?"

"This is a good choice."

He had clearly put some thought into all of this. He was taking this whole business of making things right serious. Between the limo, champagne, and a nod to our first date... we were off to a good start.

He reached over to pour me a glass of champagne.

I downed it before he had finished pouring his and handed my glass back to him. "More, please."

He grinned, flashing me those irresistible dimples. "Don't get face-plant-on-the-concrete drunk on me."

"I'm a good girl," I crooned.

"Don't bet on it."

Jensen took a sip of his champagne and then set it down. "Now, before we get there, I do have your Christmas present."

"My what? But it's New Year's and I thought we weren't exchanging gifts." We had decided on Christmas Eve since our relationship had been on the rocks that we would hold off on presents.

"Yes. Then, fine, your New Year's present."

"But I don't have anything for you."

Jensen leveled me with a flat look. "I absolutely do not need anything."

He procured a black velvet box from his jacket, and I stared at it in awe. When he tried to hand it to me, I just continued to look at it. I'd never gotten anything like this in my life, and I didn't even *know* what it was. He was taking this making-up thing to a new level.

"Go on. Open it," he instructed.

I gently took the box in my hand and popped the cover open. Inside was a simple chain with a round diamond encased in a halo of diamonds. It was soft, elegant, and probably cost a fortune. It looked as if it cost more than my Forester.

"I can't…"

"It's a present. You can."

"Wow. Okay," I whispered. "Will you put it on me?"

I slipped the necklace out of the box, pulled my hair up, and then let him clasp it into place. It felt like a weight sitting in the middle of my sternum, but it didn't overpower the dress. It was as if he had known. Or the man just had amazing taste in diamonds.

"Thank you. It's really too much though."

"Emery, for you, it's never going to be enough."

I leaned toward him, letting the necklace dangle between us, and then kissed him deeply. "A girl could get used to this if you're not careful."

"I'm not planning on being careful. Kid gloves are off. You might have to endure fancy dinners and random presents and unplanned trips on my private jet. This is the man I am, Emery, as much as the man I am when I'm with you. I'd like to have you in both worlds."

I nodded, suddenly speechless. Jensen was offering me his world. I'd be a fool not to take it.

The limo stopped in front of the Overton, and we were whisked out and down the breezy walkway inside. The room was already packed with people, but I could see that much of his family was already there. We meandered over to their table, and Jensen left me with Morgan before he went off to get us drinks. Apparently, our table had bottle service, but champagne wouldn't be passed out to the room until right before midnight.

"Oh!" Morgan gasped. "He gave you the necklace."

I reflexively touched the diamond. "Yes."

"It looks great on you."

"Thank you."

"I'm so glad things are going well again. Jensen gets so cranky when he's being a total idiot and refuses to admit it."

I laughed and covered my mouth.

"I'm glad things are going well too," I admitted with a smile.

"Also, I'm so happy that you're here. Seriously. The whole family is."

I just smiled, unable to convey how much that meant to me. "I think I'm just going to slip to the restroom while Jensen waits in that outrageous line."

"All right," Morgan said. "Do you want me to come with you?"

"Nah, I'm okay. I'll just be back in a minute."

Then, I disappeared into the crowd to locate the restroom in this huge ballroom. It was off some hallway, and luckily, since it was so early in the night, it wasn't full with a line. I did my business, washed my hands, and then exited, only to almost run into someone.

"Oh! Sorry," I said, trying to sidestep the woman.

"Just the person I was looking for," she said.

I glanced up at her and finally took her in. My stomach dropped. This could not be who I thought it was. "Have we met?"

"We haven't had the pleasure. I'm glad to rectify that. I'm Vanessa."

She stuck her hand out, but I just stared down at it in shock. When I didn't say anything, she dropped her hand, looked down at my necklace, and then back up at me.

"Vanessa, as in…"

"Yes, Jensen's Vanessa." The way she said it was soft and seductive, as if she belonged to him and he belonged to her.

She was stunning, like drop-dead gorgeous. Her hair was a soft blonde color, and it came down nearly to her waist in supermodel waves. She had a good four or five inches in height on me, and she was in a black dress that accentuated her rail-thin figure. But it was her face and the honey color of her eyes that had clearly gotten her modeling jobs. She was exotic but familiar, striking but down-to-earth. She confused the senses.

And I hated her on sight.

"What are you doing here?" I demanded.

"Well, I came here to be with Jensen."

"Too bad. He's here with me," I said, getting territorial on instinct.

"Ah, yes," she said, eyeing me up and down like I was a piece of trash and she was considering how to dispose of me. "Are you the flavor of the week?"

"Nope. I'm his girlfriend. So, you should probably just leave. I don't want to have to deal with you when we're having a perfectly good night together."

"Girlfriend," Vanessa said, breaking into this little musical laugh.

No one laughs like that! No one!

I shrugged. "Believe what you want to believe. I really don't care."

"But how could you be his girlfriend when he stayed with me all last week?"

My heart stuttered. I'd known that Jensen had seen her last week, but I hadn't known he'd *stayed* with her.

"I knew he was in New York and that he saw you. I doubt he stayed with you."

"I saw you walk in here with him, but he never even mentioned you once," she said, digging the knife in deeper.

"Jensen told me he saw you and that there was *nothing* there. I know that you cheated on him. I know that he divorced you for it. If you came here for a catfight, consider me tapped out."

I turned and strutted away, back down the deserted hallway. I felt fierce. I felt like I was on fire. I was in control. I didn't know why Vanessa was here, but I had handled her like a champ. I'd go tell Jensen, and he'd tell her to get the fuck out. The end.

"But did he tell you about Colton?"

My feet stalled. *Who the hell is Colton? And why did he matter?*

"Of course he didn't," Vanessa said with a staged sigh. "He doesn't tell anyone. Why would he tell you?"

I turned slowly and faced her. I wanted to ask her the question, but it was stuck on my tongue. Something was telling me that I didn't even want to know. I didn't want to deal with this.

"Just face it. You could never compare to me," Vanessa said with a sweet tilt to her head. "How could you compare to the mother of his son?"

Twenty-Nine

Jensen

"She should be back already," I said to Austin.

I'd left Morgan flirting with Patrick when I found out where Emery had gone off to. But that had been a while ago. I'd had enough time to get our drinks from the crazy line and return.

Austin shrugged. He'd been drinking nonstop, and I just wanted to slap the drink out of his hand. He had a problem. He'd brought a flask with him to church. I needed to send him to rehab or something. He needed to be sober, or he'd end up choking on his own vomit, like our father after an overdose. I didn't want that for him. And I'd been so lost in my own mess to see it. New year and all that, and I'd get him help.

Right after I found Emery.

"What could be taking her this long?" I asked.

Austin shrugged again. "Don't know, man. There's probably just a line. You know how the girls' restroom is."

"Right, line," I murmured but didn't believe it.

I didn't know why exactly. Maybe I was just paranoid. After the week we'd gone through, I'd been trying to be on my best behavior. I had a big surprise for her. I was finally going to tell her everything. It would be such a relief when it all came out.

I was just about to go find the restrooms and make sure everything was all right when Emery appeared out of the crowd. She looked...shaken. Visibly shaken. As if she had seen a ghost.

She had her hands clenched in low at her sides, and her eyes were wide, darting here and there and everywhere. Her stride was fierce, like she was anxious to be away. Her shoulders were tight. Something had happened. Something had definitely happened.

"Hey," I said, instantly stepping toward her.

Whatever had hurt her...I would destroy it. This was supposed to be our night.

"I want to leave," she said immediately. She wouldn't even look at me.

"Emery, what happened?"

"I said I want to leave," she said, raising her voice.

"Okay, okay. I'll get your coat."

I reached for her jacket without a word and ignored the concerned looks on my friends' and family's faces. They knew what had been going on with me and Emery. They knew not to interfere.

I handed her, her coat, and she snatched it out of my hand.

"Let's go."

"Emery, what happened?" I asked. I followed behind her as she hurried from the room. I reached out and grabbed her elbow to stop her. "Please, talk to me."

She jolted away, as if I had burned her. "Why don't you ask Vanessa?"

I furrowed my brow in confusion. "Vanessa?"

244

"Yes, your ex-wife. She can help you out."

My mouth opened and then closed. "She's here?"

"What do you think?" she asked before storming back toward the door.

I followed, but my gaze was wandering around the room as I tried to figure out how my life had crumbled to ashes in a matter of minutes.

Why is Vanessa here today? What did she hope to accomplish?

I hadn't even mentioned Emery the week that I was in New York. She couldn't know that I had a new girlfriend, because I knew she'd try to wreck our relationship. Whatever her motive, I was not going to let her win.

We were almost to the door when Vanessa seemed to materialize out of thin air. I could see that she had made an effort. She was here for a reason, and the look on her face said that reason was me.

Emery noticed her presence, and her hackles rose. "I'm leaving with or without you."

"With me," I said automatically.

"Fine," she said, passing into the foyer.

Vanessa reached me just before I followed Emery. "Hey, where are you going?"

"What are you doing here?"

"I came to see you, baby."

"Colt was supposed to come tomorrow with the nanny. That is what we agreed on. Not that you would come here and bombard my girlfriend at a party that I never invited you to!"

"Well, you forgot to mention this *fling* to me, so I thought I would come spend time with you," she said, placing her hand on my sleeve.

"Vanessa, just fucking stop. You know I don't want to spend time with you, and you've clearly offended my girlfriend. I love her, and I choose her. Just her. Only her." I snatched my arm back, feeling extra disgusted with her at the moment. It wasn't enough that she had cheated on me with my own friend, but now, she was trying to ruin everything else, and I wouldn't stand for it. "I think you're scum on the bottom of my shoe. I wish you would stop trying to ruin my fucking life."

"Jensen," she murmured, her voice dipping an octave.

"You're in my life for one reason, Vanessa. One." I held up my finger. "Colton. That's it. Otherwise, you can go to hell."

I turned on my heel and walked away from her. The last thing I wanted was for Emery to think that I wanted to talk to Vanessa or that I had more interest in what she had to say than Emery hurting. Because that was the furthest thing from the truth. I sprinted out of the building and found Emery hovering by the valet stand.

She dismissively waved her hand at me. "I already called for a cab."

"No. We have the limo." I gestured to the valet to have the limo come around for us.

"I can't—"

"Emery, please. I don't know what Vanessa said, but she is just trying to get between us. There is nothing between me and Vanessa. Nothing."

"She said you have a son," she said in a deadly whisper.

Her eyes were bullets targeted on my face. She was waiting for a reaction. She was waiting for me to deny it. My heart sank. This was not how I'd wanted her to find out. I'd wanted to tell her tomorrow the best way that I knew now. Fuck, Vanessa ruined everything.

"I do," I said, dropping my hands. "I do have a son."

She shook her head and glanced away from me. "I cannot believe this. All the opportunities I gave you to tell me. This whole second-chance business, and you didn't think I should know?"

"It's not that, Emery. I was going to tell you. I'd been planning to tell you tomorrow."

"Well, you blew it. Vanessa is here. She's in Lubbock. She found me and cornered me and tried to make me feel worthless. And you know what? She didn't succeed. She said some horrible things, but I knew where you and I were, and I was giving us a chance. But then I found out...nope, *you* weren't giving us a chance."

The limo pulled up in front of the stand at that time. The driver jumped out and opened the door for Emery.

She shook her head. "You take it."

"Please," I begged. "Please just let me explain. I gave you the opportunity to explain. Give me that same chance. We said we'd try this together. I want to do this together. After we talk, if you think I've relinquished our second chance, then I'll just...drop you off at home. But I won't let you go. I'll keep fighting for us because you are the only woman I have ever met who has made me feel like this."

She swallowed and looked away from me. Tears glistened in her eyes, but she wouldn't meet mine. She was torn. I could see it. She was willing to hear me out, but she didn't think I deserved another chance. I would have to prove her wrong. Because this was all a mistake. A misunderstanding. We could get through this. I would make sure of it.

Without another word, she sank into the limo. That was her answer. Yes. Yes, she would try.

I deflated in relief. I knew that this needed to happen. I'd just thought I'd have more time. I also...hadn't anticipated her being on the defensive when I finally told her.

It felt like control was slipping out of my fingertips, and I just wanted to be able to hold on tight. It just seemed, with Emery, I was never in control. A feeling I was unaccustomed to. But I was beginning to realize, this wasn't a power struggle; it was just two people in love. And I needed to stop trying to hold on to my past and move forward with my future.

I took the seat next to her in the limo.

She scooted over so that she could face me. "Why didn't you tell me that you had a son?"

247

"We've only been dating a couple weeks, and I'm a very private person. I wanted to make sure that this was the real deal. I don't introduce people to my son who are going to leave his life. I don't think it's fair to him. Since he lives in New York with Vanessa, that's where his life is. I fly to New York all the time actually. Nearly every single holiday and at least once a month so I don't have to uproot his life. I'm fortunate enough to be able to do that."

"So…you thought that I would leave your life?" she asked.

"Honestly, until this week, I didn't know." I ran a hand back through my hair and tried to ignore the death glare she was sending me. "But I changed my mind this week and wanted to make it right. Colton was supposed to fly in tomorrow with the nanny so that you could meet him. I had no clue that Vanessa was going to show up unannounced or why she decided to come a day early."

"I think she made it perfectly clear to me," she grumbled.

"I promise there is nothing going on with me and Vanessa. Our relationship centers entirely around our son."

"I just hate that I found out from someone else."

"I was planning on telling you tomorrow," I repeated with a sigh.

"Too little, too late," she whispered.

"Honestly, Emery, I was going to tell you *tomorrow*. I wanted to get through our date and have an amazing time with you. I even gave you my mother's necklace."

Her hand dashed to the diamond hanging around her throat, and her eyes shot to mine. "You gave me your mother's necklace?"

"Yes. Morgan and Sutton have most of her pieces, but she left me a few. She wanted them to go to the woman I loved, and I gave one to you. I'm sure that's why Vanessa freaked the fuck out. She's seen it before."

Emery retracted her hand from the necklace at the mention of Vanessa. "And you really didn't know that she would be here?"

"No. Fuck, no. I don't want her here. She obviously just wanted to fuck with me." I cleared my throat. "You told me that you wanted to do these things together. I was going to give you that opportunity."

"I think it's sweet that you wanted me to meet him," she said softly, "but I just don't know why you wouldn't tell me before I met him, like…I don't know…the day you said you saw Vanessa in New York. You were clearly there to see Colton, not her, right?"

I nodded. "I was."

"Yet you didn't tell me. You told me the whole story about Vanessa cheating on you with Marc, how your ex-wife and Cheaterpants horribly ruined your life, but you left out the part where you had a son in the mix of it all. It's like I know only half of your story. I got the abridged version of the book. You could have told me at anytime, and you didn't. Did you think that I wouldn't be understanding?"

"No," I said immediately. "Emery, that's not it."

She wrapped her arms around herself and shook her head. "I think I just need to cope tonight, Jensen. I don't fault you for having a son. I love Lilyanne, and now, I understand why you're so good with her. But I just fear that you'll never really trust me. Maybe you'll never trust anyone again."

Her words lingered between us.

Half an accusation, half a prayer.

I didn't know what to say to that. *Had I not trusted her? Had I really been trying to push her away?* I'd been planning to tell her, yet that hadn't been enough. Landon had known that when he had confronted me two weeks ago. Even if I had told her tomorrow, she would have been upset. I could see that now. Falling in love with someone and leaving out the most important thing in your life was showing no trust at all.

I could see the hurt and despair in her eyes. That I had claimed to love her, yet I had fed her lies about my life.

She turned her face away from me, and I was struggling to find words when her phone started ringing from the pocket of her coat.

"Kimber," she whispered when she checked the screen. Her mouth opened slightly in worry. She picked up the phone right away. "Hey! What's going on? Is everything okay?" There was silence as I waited for an answer. "Yes. Yes. I'll be right there. Do you need anything? Okay. Don't worry about it."

She hung up, and I knew what had happened.

"She's gone into labor?" I asked.

"Yes. I need to get home, so I can drive over to the hospital."

"What about Lilyanne?"

"My mom is watching her."

"Then, I'll have the limo drop you off."

"No—"

"We're going straight there," I insisted.

"Okay," she said.

She didn't argue at all, which was a sure sign of how worried and excited she was for Kimber.

I told the limo driver where to go, and we sped off to the hospital. The rest of the ride was silent. She was brimming with nerves about her sister, and I couldn't bear to bring up what had happened with us and what we were going to do next.

The driver stopped in front of the entrance to the hospital wing where the maternity ward was.

"Thank you for dropping me off," she whispered.

"You're welcome. Tell Kimber good luck."

"I will."

She reached behind her, unclasped the necklace, and held it out to me. "You should keep this."

"It was a gift."

"It's your mother's. I only want you to give it to me if this works out. And, right now…"

She dropped the necklace into my palm, and I suddenly felt cold.

"Right now what?"

She started to slide away from me, but I reached out and pulled her in close.

"What does this mean for us?"

She shook her head. "I don't know. I can't think right now. I just need to be with my sister."

"I understand. That's what's important." I placed a soft kiss on her forehead. "We'll figure the rest of this out another time."

"Yeah," she said, sad and distracted. "Another time."

With a weight on my chest, I watched her disappear. I'd thought tonight would be the start of everything new. I'd thought, tomorrow, she would meet Colton and see why I loved him so much. And, now, I was left wondering if we were even going to make it to tomorrow.

Thirty

Emery

Tears streamed down my face as I stood in front of the elevators. The hospital ward was empty. I was sure the ER was packed with drunken accidents, but here, in this part of the hospital, it was deserted. And I was grateful.

I couldn't seem to stop crying. My breaths were coming out in short spurts, and my chest constricted. I felt like I was hyperventilating, unable to get enough air in and hiccuping to try to recover.

My heart ached. My chest ached. My head ached.

Everything hurt.

Walking away from Jensen hurt.

I hadn't wanted to do it. But I'd meant every word that I said. He didn't trust, period. And I couldn't be with him if he didn't trust me. That left us at an impasse.

After the mess back in Austin, I'd thought moving home and trying to figure out what I wanted in my life would be easy.

I'd spend time with Kimber and Heidi. I'd find a real job. I'd discover what I wanted.

Instead, my heart, mind, body, and soul belonged to Jensen Wright.

I should have stayed sworn off of men.

I should have stayed far away from the Wrights.

Then, I wouldn't be standing here with a heart threatening to shatter.

"Fuck," I whispered, jamming the button to go upstairs. I scrubbed at my face.

No more tears.

No more.

Kimber would notice. I was sure of it. But I was here for her now, and that was what was important. Meeting my new niece.

I took the elevator up to the fourth floor and was directed to my sister's room.

"Knock, knock," I said, entering the room.

Kimber was lying in the bed with Noah hovering next to her, holding a cup of ice chips.

"Hey!" she said with a genuine smile. "You made it."

"I made it."

"Are you okay?"

"Totally. I'm so excited to finally meet the little one!" I put on a big smile and pushed the last couple of hours out of my mind.

"Well, it's still going to be a while," Noah said. "Water hasn't even broken, but she's dilated and having contractions at a regular interval. Same as last time."

"I'm here for an all-nighter then."

"You look like you came straight from a party. Did you give up your midnight kiss for me?" Kimber asked.

I glanced up at the clock and realized it was only ten thirty. We'd totally missed our New Year's kiss. Not that I was exactly up for a steamy kiss right now.

"Meh. Don't worry about it. I know you brought a couple of extra outfits. I'll just steal your clothes and send Mom back with more when I take over for Lily."

"You are going to send Mom here?" Kimber asked hysterically.

I cackled, finally feeling an ounce of buoyancy. "Now, you admit your true feelings! She's crazy, right?"

"I just don't need coaching! I already have two doctors. Sorry, Noah."

"No offense taken."

"Ohhh!" Kimber yelled. She doubled over as a contraction hit her full force.

And then I went into full-on sister mode. Kimber gave me something to focus on. I was able to be helpful and be there to make her smile and laugh through the worst of it.

Right after midnight, my phone started ringing and I saw that it was Heidi. "Is it okay if I take this?"

"We're going to be here a while," Kimber said. "Go ahead."

I walked out of the room and found a quiet place to answer. "Hey Heidi."

"Em! Where are you?" Heidi asked. "I found the hottest guy for my New Year's kiss, and I want you to meet him."

"I actually left."

"Oh, you and Jensen left early for some sex," Heidi said. I could tell she was drunk.

"Actually, no. Kimber went into labor, and Jensen and I got into a huge fight."

"Kimber went into labor!" Heidi cried, sobering up. "Should I leave? And wait, what fight? What happened?"

"No, don't leave. We're going to be here all night. I can text you when the baby comes."

"Okay. But what happened with Jensen?"

"His ex-wife Vanessa showed up at the party and told me that Jensen had a son."

"Well, of course he has a son," Heidi said. "Duh."

I froze in place. "What do you mean of course he has a son, Heidi! You knew? Why wouldn't you tell me something like that?"

"Jesus Christ, I didn't know that you didn't know, Emery. Everyone knows he has a kid. He's like this absentee father, who spends all his money on child support and only sees his kid for the holidays. What did you think I meant when I said that he flies to New York every holiday?"

That conversation all those weeks ago when Heidi had said that came back to me. God, I hadn't even known what she had meant, but now that I did, I felt like an idiot.

"Fuck. Really everyone knows?" I asked.

"I mean it's not a secret that he had a kid. I swear I thought you knew before you even hooked up with him."

"I didn't."

"Shit, I'm sorry. I would have said something, but I figured you knew and thought it was no big deal. It's not like this is his first hook up post-child."

"Yeah," I said softly. It sure wasn't. "It just...I don't think he's an absentee father, Heidi. I think he's really involved in his son's life. He said he's very protective of people meeting him. He wants me to meet him, and I just don't know if I want that. I don't think he really trusts me."

"Maybe he thought you already knew about his son like I did."

I shook my head. "I don't think he did. We would have talked about it."

"Well, now I feel even shittier. What are you going to do?"

I leaned my head back against the wall and closed my eyes. "I have no idea."

"Look, when you and Jensen started this, it was just supposed to be a fling. It's only been a few weeks since you've been together."

"Yeah. That's true. Why would he share crucial information with a fling?" she asked miserably. God, I knew that I wasn't a fling to him, but this whole trust thing was just taking me to a bad place.

"You're not a fling anymore. So, if he wants you to meet his kid, then this is a good sign, Em," Heidi said. "Just because you didn't find out the way that you wanted doesn't mean that he doesn't trust you."

"Maybe."

"Okay. Worry about Kimber right now and deal with Jensen tomorrow. Maybe you'll have a clear head then. We can talk more if you need to work through it."

"Thank, Heidi."

"You're the best."

"Don't forget it."

We ended the call, and I took my time getting back to the hospital room. I couldn't believe that Heidi had known… that everyone had known. I knew I was out of the loop on Lubbock gossip, but I thought I would have heard something like this. But no, I had closed myself off from the Wright family so much that I didn't even know this one piece of information. And Jensen hadn't trusted me with it.

I just hoped Heidi was right and that by tomorrow I would know what to do. Because right now, I had a long night ahead of me. A long, tiring night.

Thirty-One

Jensen

Leaving Emery at the hospital was much harder than I'd thought possible. Her words had put my entire life in perspective. I was the one letting Vanessa continue to ruin my life. And I wouldn't do it any longer. I wouldn't be ruled by her dictatorship in our relationship. I didn't care what she wanted or what she thought she could threaten me with. Colton wasn't a game piece in an adult battle. And I refused to let her use him in such a manner.

He was a six-year-old boy. Vanessa using me and our past as weapons only hurt him. And the last thing in the whole world that I wanted was to hurt my son.

I spent the rest of the night fighting with myself to go to sleep. Even for a half hour. But it never came. At an ungodly hour, I finally stumbled out of bed and decided to do something about it. I texted Vanessa to find out where she was staying and then drove the Mercedes over to the hotel downtown.

I parked the car out front and took the elevator to the top floor. I knocked on the door and the nanny, Jennifer, answered the door. She was a twenty-something live-in that Vanessa had hired last year full-time.

"Hey, Jensen!" Jennifer said. "Oh, Colton has been talking about you nonstop!"

"Hey Jennifer. Good to see you too."

I stepped inside, but before I even fully entered the living room, I heard the familiar ring of, "Daddy!"

Colton launched himself from the couch in the living room and straight into my arms. I picked him up off the ground and swung him around in a circle.

"Hey, champ," I said, squeezing him tight.

I could never get enough of this. I could never have enough hugs or enough of these moments. Him living in New York was a vise on my chest at all times. I hated it. The week I'd seen him before Christmas wasn't long enough by far. He'd been in Paris with Vanessa for the two weeks before that, and it had been so hard to let him out of the country. Even if he had done it before, I still worried. Having him here with me always made me less nervous.

Most days, I still couldn't believe that I had moved back to Lubbock. I'd had to admit that the two years I'd lived in New York were bad for the company. It had been a devastating decision, one I could never take lightly. But I also couldn't take Colton out of New York. I wanted what was best for him, and even if Lubbock had good schools, I'd be stripping his known environment from him and taking him away from better schools.

On days like today, I wanted to not care.

"God, I missed you so much," I told him as I moved him to one hip and carried him into the living room.

"I missed you, too! Are you coming home with me and Mommy and Nanny Jenn?" Colton asked. He was an adorable kid with unruly dark hair and big brown eyes that got him anything he ever wanted.

"Home?" I asked, setting him on his feet on the couch. My eyes jumped to Jennifer's. She shrugged helplessly and the nodded her head to the bedroom as if to say leaving was Vanessa's idea.

"Yeah, Daddy. Mommy said that we're going back to New York today. I want you to come with us. You can meet my new art teacher when I start school again."

I grinned down at him. Colton loved art. Vanessa had sent me pictures of the dinosaurs he had drawn after I'd taken him to the American Museum of Natural History. I wanted to take him all over the world and feed his addiction. But I definitely did not want him to leave today.

"Going to have to talk to your mom about that," I told him.

Just then, Vanessa walked into the room. She leaned her hip against the wall to the kitchen and crossed her arms. Her eyes were guarded and wary. It was a look I was used to getting from people today. Vanessa's was warranted after the way I'd spoken to her at the New Year's Eve party. She'd deserved it, but I didn't like to argue with her. It wasn't good for Colt to see us angry even if simply being in her presence pissed me off.

"You're leaving?" I asked. "I thought you were staying for a couple of days."

She shrugged. "Changed my mind."

"Hey, Daddy!" Colton said, still holding my hand. "Look at my new drawings."

I gave Vanessa a look that said this was not over and then sat down on the couch next to Colton.

"This one is a pterodactyl," he said, showing me a flying green dinosaur. Then, he showed me another one with horns. "This is a triceratops."

"Wow. These are really good, champ."

I inspected the one he was working on now. They were good for his age. It made me proud, how much he loved this. He was excelling in school, but I never wanted to suffocate my kid's love like my father had.

"Are you going to be an artist when you grow up?"

"No, Daddy, I'm going to be just like you."

I laughed, and then life flashed before my eyes of Colton being just like I was with my father. I shuddered at the very idea. God, I hoped I wouldn't ruin him.

"You can be and do whatever you want."

"I'll fly on planes then!"

"Like a pilot?"

"No. I'll run my business in the air."

I chuckled again. There was no deterring him. Perhaps, it was normal for your child to want to grow up to be just like you. At least at this age. I knew he'd grow up to have huge dreams, and I wanted to be there to encourage every one of them.

"You know, little man, I have someone very special that I want you to meet when you're ready. Would you like a new friend?"

"Yeah!" Colton agreed. "I love friends. Do you think he'd color with me?"

"Jensen!" Vanessa snapped from the kitchen.

Vanessa clearly was unhappy with the idea that I was going to introduce him to anyone. And I was sure she was pissed that it was coming on the heels of meeting Emery.

"I'm sure she would color with you," I said. "But I'm going to go talk to your mom for a minute, okay? Maybe I can make you waffles afterward?"

"Yes! Waffles are my favorite. I'd like them with strawberries and whipped cream."

"Extra whipped cream," I agreed easily.

I kissed him on the cheek and then left him to his drawings. Jennifer moved into to play with him while I stepped up to Vanessa.

"We need to talk." She strode into the bedroom of the suite without another glance.

I took my time, following her inside and closing the door. I took over the space, stretching in height and crossing my arms over the bulk of my chest. She might want to have this conversation, but I wasn't going to give her any concessions.

She whirled around on me and then took a step back. I knew that look on her face. I'd made my point. I wasn't going to give an inch to the woman who frequently took a mile.

"You are not introducing your latest fling to Colton."

"She's my girlfriend, Vanessa. I can, and I will introduce her to my son."

"Jensen, absolutely not! You don't even know if she's going to be in your life past tomorrow! I won't allow you to disrupt his life like that."

"Let's get to the bottom of this, Vanessa. You don't like that someone new is in my life, and you don't want it to disrupt your delusions. This has nothing to do with Colt."

"I don't like that you're going to introduce him to someone that might leave. That's selfish."

I ran a hand back through my hair and sighed. "You're right, Vanessa. Under any other circumstance, it would be selfish. But it has been four years since we divorced. It's not unreasonable for me to meet someone new in that time."

Vanessa rolled her eyes. "She's not someone new in your life. She's another fling. I know you have them all the time. I know the signs."

"Emery is different."

"Really? How did you meet?" she asked, crossing her arms.

"At Sutton's wedding."

"Let me get this straight. You met her a month ago, probably banged her that night, didn't tell her about Colton, and now think you're ready to introduce her to him? I don't think so."

"What I do in my free time is none of your business. Emery is my girlfriend. You may not like that Vanessa, but that's not about to change. Good try showing up last night and trying to break us up though."

"I was just trying to tell her the truth. You're the one who was a raving jackass," Vanessa spat.

"The truth. Right," I said sarcastically. "You were trying to break us up. Even though you were, I am sorry that I spoke to you the way that I did." I had been harsh in the moment. Normally I never would have spoken to her that way, but after seeing Emery's reaction, I'd lost it. "I didn't come here to argue with you about last night. I just wanted you to understand where I'm coming from."

"Oh, I understand where you're coming from," she spat. "You're thinking with your dick."

"I can't handle this Vanessa. I'm tired of arguing. I apologized for how I treated you, but you can't dictate who Colton meets. Emery is in my life, and Colton is my life."

I turned and opened the door to go back out to see my son. I knew that I needed to talk to Emery about again. I wanted to make things right and get us on the same page.

"I'll tell Marc," Vanessa spat.

I shook my head. I'd heard that one before. "Empty threats, Vanessa."

"They're not empty threats," she spat. "I will tell him.

"I don't believe you. If you think meeting Emery isn't in his best interest, then I have no idea how you could think Marc would be either."

Then I strode away from her. After kissing Colton good-bye and promising to come back later, I left the hotel and went to go see Emery. We had some catching up to do.

Thirty-Two

Emery

Kimber's contractions went on forever with no end in sight. By the next morning, I was worn out and had barely slept. I couldn't even imagine what Kimber was feeling.

Luckily, she had finally managed to get some sleep, which was my chance to find the Starbucks downstairs and drink the entire store dry. I let Noah go first though. He'd been there longer than me, and I knew he needed to eat something even if he claimed he wasn't hungry. As a doctor, he was used to the weird hours, but he needed to be Kimber's rock. I'd take care of him for her.

While Noah was gone, my phone pinged. Heidi and I had been texting on and off all night. I swiped my phone and checked the screen, expecting another text from Heidi about the guy she had hit on all last night. But, instead, it was a message from Jensen.

Coffee and doughnuts?

It was as if he had read my mind. I wanted those things so bad. My stomach grumbled. *But did I want the added struggle of Jensen right now when I was sleep-deprived?*

He texted me again.

> *It's just coffee and doughnuts. We don't have to talk if you don't want, but I thought you could use some sustenance.*

Noah walked back in the door at that time with his own cup of coffee. "Hey, I saw Jensen downstairs. I think he's waiting for you. So, you can go ahead. I'll take watch."

I ground my teeth. Of course he had presumed to show up without checking with me first.

> *You're already here?*

> *Guilty.*

> *Fine. I'll be down. But I'm not a person right now.*

I left Noah to watch over Kimber and then headed back down to the first floor. My stomach noisily growled again. I couldn't remember what I'd last had to eat. A candy bar or something in the middle of the night. I'd been so shaken, and I hadn't even realized it until I'd gone to find something to help me power through the wee hours of the night.

Jensen was waiting in the lobby, holding two coffees and a bag of doughnuts. He looked…beat. He probably hadn't slept all night either. And this was the first time I'd ever seen him with stubble. Jensen and clean-shaven went hand in hand. But, fuck, it was definitely sexy on him. Like I wouldn't mind finding out exactly how he could use that in the bedroom. I was sure it would leave a trail of wonderful marks up my inner thighs.

Damn sleep-deprived brain was yelling at me, *Sex, sex, sex.*

I shook my head and tried to put everything back in perspective. I was standing on quicksand. If I kept struggling, I'd be swallowed up even faster. But, if I stayed still, maybe, just maybe Jensen could pull me back out.

"Rough night?" I asked when I approached him.

He grimaced slightly at the comment. "You could say that."

"Yeah. Me, too."

Jensen passed me the coffee, and we moved to a table inside Starbucks, which was blissfully quiet at such an early hour.

"Noah said that you're going to be here for a while longer."

"Looks like it."

I reached into the bag and smiled when I saw an apple fritter and a cinnamon twist inside. My two favorite doughnuts.

"Thanks for these."

"I thought that you might be hungry."

I nodded. For the first time ever, there was awkwardness between us. We had one foot in the water and one foot on solid ground. Not knowing where we stood or what would come next seemed to be killing both of us.

"I know I said that we didn't have to talk," Jensen said, breaking the silence.

"Too much to ask for, I guess," I mumbled.

"And we don't have to if it's too much, but I stayed up all night, thinking about what you said."

"Which part?"

"Me not trusting you…or anyone," he clarified. His eyes darted up to mine, and I could see the hours of anguish and self-deprecation that radiated from him. "I don't think that I ever realized until last night that I absolutely do not trust anyone other than myself. Not one person. Not even my family."

I nodded, having found out firsthand the truth of that statement.

"I wish I could say that I don't know how that happened to me, but I do." He sighed and glanced away, as if he didn't want to continue, as if the next words would rip through him. "Colton isn't my son."

I opened my mouth, stuttered incoherently, and then closed it again. I shook my head in confusion, trying to understand how his own son couldn't be his. "What do you mean?"

"I mean, Colt is Marc's son," he said so calmly that I knew it must have been killing him to admit it. "I've never told anyone this. Not even my family. The only people who know are me and Vanessa."

"Not even Marc?"

"Especially not Marc," he growled low.

My heart ached for him. *How could he possibly live with the fact that his son wasn't really his? How had he kept that secret locked up for all of these years?*

"What happened?" I asked, suddenly desperate for him to tell me the story. To finally have an explanation for why he was so guarded.

"Vanessa and I had been married for almost two years when she found out that she was pregnant. I had been living in Lubbock, taking over the company for my father after his death. I'd barely been in New York. We weren't even trying. I was still too devastated by his death to think about that. When she called and told me she was pregnant, I was ecstatic. Maybe I should have been more cautious." He shrugged, as if he had played this over and over again in his head before.

"But you weren't."

"No. I never suspected once that she and Marc were together. I was too grief-stricken and dealing with the company to consider what was going on with her when I was away."

"You were dealing with all of that, and she was banging someone else on the side," I said, furious. "What a bitch."

Jensen looked off in the distance, the memory hitting him fresh once more. "As I told you, I moved back to New York. As far as I know, their relationship stopped after that. I don't know if I believe it for sure, but I think Marc was worried Colton was his kid and cleared out. His dad wasn't doing that well, so he moved back to Austin around the same time that I got to New York." He took a long sip of his coffee and leaned back in his chair.

"What a creep," I grumbled. "So, how did you find out?"

"I was there when Colton was born. I took him home from the hospital. I changed diapers. I fed him when Vanessa was sleeping. I was there every single second that I wasn't working. Colton *is* my son in every way that matters."

I smiled at that statement. I loved the thought that Jensen had never treated his son any differently.

"Marc was in town on business for Colt's second birthday. We all went out to dinner together."

"And you had no idea?"

"None."

"How could Vanessa go out to dinner with him?" I gasped.

"I think she thought it would be fine. I really don't know. The next day, I found her sitting in Colt's bedroom, crying. I asked her why she was crying, and she said she couldn't keep lying to me. Then, she told me about her affair with Marc. It must have been weighing on her for a long time for her to actually break down and tell me." He set his cup down and sighed heavily. "We probably could have survived that. It would have taken a long time, but we could have made it. But then she told me that Colt was Marc's, and I lost it."

"I don't blame you."

"No, I mean, I *actually* lost it, Emery. I rampaged throughout the apartment. I broke furniture. I found Marc and beat him to a bloody pulp." Jensen clenched and unclenched his fist, remembering the bloodlust. "I never told him it was because of Colt though. He thought it was because of Vanessa, which is probably why he didn't press charges."

"Still…I don't blame you, Jensen."

And I meant every word. *How could I possibly blame him for what happened?* Vanessa and Marc were to blame. They had taken everything from him. Even his son. A son he had raised for two years, thinking Colt was his. No wonder he never told anyone. *How could he ear the shame? The sense of loss?*

I reached out and took his hand. He glanced up at me with surprise in his dark eyes. He must have thought that I would turn on him, like everyone else had in his life.

He deflated before my eyes. As if he had been so pent-up over the whole thing that finally telling someone else the truth had drained him. He tightened his fingers around my hand, and we stayed like that for a few minutes in silence.

"So, that's the whole story," he finally said, drawing back. "I know that you're upset with me, and you have every right to be, but I do trust you. Or I want to. I want you in my life, but I know that we have a ways to go. But, now, you know the whole story. I feel like our train got off the rails somewhere or took a wrong turn, but I want this to work. I wouldn't be here, and I wouldn't have given you my mother's necklace if I didn't want that."

He pulled the diamond necklace out of his pocket and let it dangle between us.

"This belongs to you."

"Jensen," I whispered.

He took my hand and gently laid the necklace into my palm. "It's a promise. I'm going to make this right. One way or another."

This was a lot to absorb.

He wanted to prove to me that he trusted me. That he *could* trust.

It didn't make up for what we had gone through, but it was a start.

I closed my hand around the necklace. He smiled brilliantly, the hours of anxiety from the past day falling off of his shoulder. He leaned forward and brushed his lips to my forehead. Slowly, I let a smile stretch across my face as I put the necklace back around my neck and tucked it under my shirt.

I'd given him hope…and now, I had some, too.

He stood up to leave and give me space when his phone started ringing. He gave me a sheepish look and then glanced at the screen. His face paled.

"Who is it?" I asked. I did not like that look on his face.

"Marc."

"Why would he be calling?"

Jensen shook his head as if he didn't know, but I could see on his face that he did. And it was bad.

He sank back into his chair and answered. "Hello?"

Marc's response was so loud that I could hear it through the other line. "You son of a bitch!"

"What do you want, Marc?"

Marc responded, but I couldn't hear what he said, then Jensen said, "Are you out of your fucking mind?"

"I have a right to know!" Marc shouted back.

"It's been almost seven years, Marc. This is fucked."

"What's fucked up is you lying to me for that long! I'm getting on a plane right the fuck now. I'll be in Lubbock tonight, you motherfucker."

"Marc, you cannot get near my son."

"He's not even yours!" Marc screamed.

"I am his father!" Jensen said, raising his voice in fury.

"We'll fucking see about that."

"Colton is my son, and I'll be damned if I let you fuck with his head by walking into his life. What you're going to do is irresponsible and reckless. And there's no way I will let you near him."

"Well, you don't get to decide that!"

"Like hell I don't."

Jensen slammed his phone down on the table and fumed. "Fuck," he muttered. He put both of his hands into his hair and pulled. His teeth were gritted. His body tense. He looked as if he were ready to erupt.

"What's just happened?" I asked softly, though I feared I already knew the answer from that conversation.

"Vanessa told Marc."

My heart stopped beating for a split second. I couldn't believe that Vanessa would go to such extremes.

"Fuck, I should have known. I went to see Colton this morning, and we argued. She threatened me by saying she would tell Marc, but she has said that a million times before. I told her it was an empty threat. Apparently, she took that to heart. I guess, she was so upset that I was going to introduce Colton to you that she decided that the best route was to inform his *real* father and get me out of the picture."

"You cannot stand for that! You have to do something!"

"I'll get my lawyers on the situation. They knew this was a possibility and we're prepared for it," he told me. But he sounded like he'd been hit by a truck when he said it. "I just...I have to meet with Marc tomorrow when he comes into town. Before he can see Colton, he'll have to get permission. My lawyers will file paperwork so that neither of us can go near Colton until this is resolved."

"Oh, Jensen," I said, my heart breaking for him. "You won't be able to see him at all?"

It took him a full minute before he could respond, "No."

"What do you need from me?"

"I can't ask…"

"You can."

"I just…I can handle this, Emery. I can stand up to Marc again. I can face down Vanessa for the hundredth time. I can fight for Colton, like I have been doing since he was born. I just need…want…"

"Jensen," I whispered, reaching out for him, "I'm here for you if you need me."

"I hate to ask it of you when your sister is about to have her baby."

"The baby will come soon, and then they're going to need their space. Kimber will understand. I want to help."

"I need you," he told me.

"Okay. What's the plan?"

Thirty-Three

Emery

I stayed at the hospital the rest of the afternoon at Jensen's insistence. I wanted to be there for when the baby was delivered, and I know that he had to deal with his lawyers in the meantime.

Later that day, I finally got to hold my new niece in my arms. She was as light as a feather and adorable to boot. Little Bethany Ilsa Thompson came in at seven pounds and three ounces and nineteen inches. She slept, swaddled up to her chin, with her eyes firmly shut, and everyone in the room was huddled around her.

I wasn't ready to relinquish her. I knew I was going to spoil her to death as she got older. But I also knew that her mom and dad and older sister wanted a turn. Not to mention, her grandmother kept trying to take her out of everyone's arms.

But it didn't matter. This was perfect.

Forget the last couple of weeks of madness in my life. Bethany was too perfect for drama.

Reluctantly, I handed her back to Kimber, who was setting Lilyanne up to hold her. A nurse knocked on the door just as we got Bethany into Lily's arms.

"Hey, hey, everyone!" she said with a bright smile. "Just coming to check on y'all and see how you're doing. I'm going to need to take Bethany for a little while for some tests if that's all right."

Lilyanne looked like she was about to cry, but she nodded and handed Bethany to the nurse.

"I promise I'll bring her right back to you, big sister."

Lily beamed at that. She was loving the idea of being a big sister.

"All right, it's that time," Kimber said with a sigh. "I'm taking a shower."

"About time, you mean," I joked.

"Such a kidder."

"I think I'm actually going to head out and go see Jensen. I'll be back in the morning!"

"That's cool. We're just going to be sleeping," Kimber said. "And probably eating and showering."

I laughed. "All right. Don't let her do anything cute without me."

"Promise."

I smiled at Kimber as she grabbed some fresh clothes to take into the bathroom. I knew she'd be in there for a long time after the night she'd endured. Hours and hours of labor with no respite. It had been tough, but I knew she thought it was worth the effort. We all did.

I was excited to see Jensen again. I hated what was happening to him because of Vanessa. After we had just sat down for our big talk at that. I appreciated that he had recognized that he couldn't trust and that he was working to fix it. I still wanted that man who had gone out of his way to drive me through Christmas lights, who couldn't resist asking me out—in church, no less—and who had hired someone to pack up my apartment just so we could spend the afternoon together. But I wanted him with all his skeletons out of the closet and our pasts firmly in the past. Hopefully, after this week, that would be the case.

I left the hospital and went straight to Jensen's place. The door was unlocked, and I entered the house.

"Hello?" I called into the foyer.

Jensen appeared then at the top of the stairs in dark-wash jeans and a plain T-shirt. His muscles rippled from the tightly fitted shirt, and I practically salivated at the sight of him. I knew I was here to be emotional support and help him make it through the next twelve hours, but my mind apparently had other plans.

He smiled, and those dimples did me in. "Emery," he said with a deeply relieved sigh.

"Hey," I said climbing the stairs. "We have a new baby girl in the family."

"Congratulations. I'm so happy for Kimber and Noah. What did they name her?"

"Bethany Isla. And she's adorable. I can't wait for you to meet her. Though Lilyanne might be worried about her boyfriend coming to see her sister."

Jensen grinned. "She shouldn't worry. Her real competition is standing in front of me."

I grinned and willed my mind to get myself under control. It had been too long since we slept together. And, now that I could see him clearly again, all I wanted to do was jump his bones. Except that I knew he needed something more than sex tonight. Sex might make him forget, but it wouldn't heal anything.

When I came eye-to-eye with him, I noticed how ragged he looked. Still sexy as hell but beaten down. Vanessa was trying to undo him. And, while he stood tall and had the presence of the brilliant CEO that he was, I knew him well enough to know that he was lost and crumbling into that dark place in his chest. A place from which I feared he would not return.

"Have you slept at all?" I asked.

He cocked his head to the side and stared off into space. "Sleep doesn't get anything done. There's too much work, too much to deal with for sleeping."

I sighed. I was sure that, in his head, that was true. But I also knew that his body would start to shut down, and he had to be cognizant tomorrow. To be able to face Marc and not lose control again around him, not like the time he'd beaten his face in after Vanessa had told him about the affair. He needed to be sharp.

Wordlessly, I took his hand.

He stared down at it with a mixture of awe and concern. "You don't have to do this."

"Do what?" I asked, bringing his hand up to my lips and kissing it.

"Be here."

"Don't I?"

"No."

"You're wrong."

"All too often."

"You need me," I whispered, drawing him closer to me. "So, I'm here."

"Good," he said, his voice deep and guttural. A feral sound that bordered on hysteria.

"And I know what you need."

"That so?" he asked.

I could see in his eyes that he thought I meant everything sexual. A thought that had obviously crossed my mind. I wanted that to make him feel better, but I knew he needed so much more.

I held on to his hand and pulled him down the hallway without another word.

Our relationship might have been a bumpy ride. We had secrets. We'd traded lies. We'd tried to find ways to fit the other into the mess that we'd been living in. But, at the end of the day, I knew Jensen Wright. I'd chosen him, and I'd be here for him through the worst of it.

When we entered his bedroom, I languidly tugged his shirt over his head. Lust swirled in his eyes as I did it, and I knew, if I gave in, *neither* of us would sleep ever again. We'd stay in bed all night. Lost in our own desires.

He reached for my shirt, but I stopped him.

"Uh-uh. Look but no touch," I warned him.

He fumed but dropped his hands. I flicked the button on his jeans, dragged them down his legs, and watched as he kicked them off, leaving him in his tight boxer briefs. He was rock hard for me, and it took everything in my power not to lick my lips.

I directed him into bed, and he went willingly. *What man wouldn't?*

Then, I stripped out of my jeans and T-shirt. Jensen looked ready to launch himself across the room when he saw the black lace set I'd been wearing for him on New Year's Eve. But I hastily threw on his T-shirt, which was way too big for me.

Then, I turned out all the lights and crawled into bed. He reached for me as soon as I was under the covers, pressing his dick firmly against my ass and squeezing me tight to his chest.

"You're killing me," he breathed into my neck.

"I just came here to help," I whispered.

"This is helping." He thrust against my ass, and I squeezed my legs together.

"You need to sleep."

"You think I'm going to sleep after seeing you in lingerie?" he asked, as if I were insane.

With effort, I turned to face him and saw his dark eyes filled with lust. I wanted this. He wanted this. I just didn't trust myself to stop.

With Jensen Wright, there were only two speeds—more and, God, more.

I gently placed my hand on his chest and slightly pushed him away. "You need to sleep. You're a walking zombie. I came over to help you. I don't think marathon sex is going to help."

"It's not going to hurt," he groaned.

He slid his hand up and down my side, fisting his shirt and exposing my stomach and lace thong. His hand snagged on the material, and he flicked it with his thumb. It snapped against my skin, causing my whole body to clench up.

"Jensen," I moaned. My walls were weakening.

He pushed into the space I'd put between us and ran the stubble of his chin across my shoulder and up my neck.

His voice rasped into my earlobe as he tugged on it. "Just let me make you come, Emery. I want your taste on my lips."

"Fuck," I whispered.

He took that as a yes and slipped the rest of my clothes off of me with aching slowness. First, the T-shirt went over my head. Then, he snapped my bra off and tossed it off the bed. Finally, he dragged my thong down my knees and over my feet. I shivered the whole way down. He removed his own boxer briefs next with much less care, and just when I thought he was going to give me what I wanted, he flipped me over on top of him.

His dick nudged at my wet opening, and it took everything in me not to rock back onto him. I eased down, savoring the feel of him. Just the head…just the tip…just an inch…maybe two. My body tightened around him, wanting to feel him fill me up.

But then he stopped me and pulled me off of his dick. I groaned with dissatisfaction.

"Jensen…"

"Sit on my face," he demanded.

My eyes found his in shock. "Seriously?"

"I said I wanted to taste you. This is *how* I want to taste you."

I hesitantly edged forward until my pussy was directly over his lips. Then, he clamped his hands down on my ass cheeks and ground his face up into my body. I cried out as he ravaged me from below. My hands jerked out and landed on the headboard, bracing myself as my body abandoned my control.

He licked and sucked and got the taste of me on more than just his tongue. My whole body convulsed, and I tried to pull up from his incredible assault, but he wasn't having it. He tightened his grip on me and brought my pussy closer to him. I writhed in ecstasy until I exploded from the most amazing orgasm. Then, I sat there, trembling, with him still licking me past the point of my release...prolonging my pleasure.

When I was finally sated, he flipped me backward and fell on top of me. I was so wet, he slid into me with ease. I arched my back off the bed, purring like a kitten as he took me balls deep.

Nothing else mattered in that moment. All my fears and worries stripped away. There was only here and now. There was only sex and lust and passion. We could ride the wave. We could survive the current. We could fucking rein it in with a lasso and make it our own.

He drove into me with relentless force. Meeting him stroke for stroke and falling into oblivion for the second time, I actually thought I might pass out from pure pleasure. He followed right after me, and his heavy weight collapsing over me was the best feeling in the world.

He nipped at my neck. "This is the best sleep I've ever gotten."

I laughed, low and raspy. I'd used my vocal cords properly as I came. "Me, too."

We didn't have to say anything else. Words were beyond us at this point. We had a world to face tomorrow, but for tonight, he was mine, and I was his.

Thirty-Four

Jensen

When I finally woke up, it felt like I'd slept for days. It had been so long since I got a full night sleep and days since I slept at all, period, I was shocked that I had even been functioning. The only good sleep I ever got anymore was when Emery was in my arms. Like she was right at this moment—naked and completely satisfied.

We probably should have gone to sleep like she had said last night. But, once she'd stripped me down and put me in bed, I had known there was no way that was happening. I'd been thinking about this girl nonstop—up until Marc had uttered those unbelievable words.

"Vanessa told me."

I still couldn't believe she'd done it. She had been hanging it over my head for so long that I'd become complacent to the threat. I never thought she'd actually break down and do it. Then again…it had taken her years to admit to cheating on me with Marc. Maybe I shouldn't have been surprised that it'd taken her this long to tell him the truth.

The girl was a snake. I didn't know how I had never seen it all those years we had been together. Or maybe New York had just poisoned her. Maybe she hadn't actually been cut out for the big city and modeling, and her way of coping had been to become worse than the city itself. But these were just excuses. They didn't justify her behavior. Lots of people moved to New York and didn't cheat on their husbands…didn't have a child with someone else.

I closed my eyes, wishing that I could disappear back into last night. Feel Emery's warm body against mine and pretend not to have a care in the world. But reality was crashing back down. I had to face Marc and Vanessa today. I had to claim my son. Last night had been a dream, but it was time to wake up.

Kissing Emery's forehead, I washed last night's events off of my body and changed into a crisp black Tom Ford suit. Everything about the ensemble screamed power and money. Both things I wanted to exert to the two people who had ruined my life. Marc had stolen my wife. He wasn't going to steal my son, too. It wasn't enough that I had bought out his company and was in the process of selling it off for parts like a used car. I would bury him before letting him have access to Colton. My lawyers had been working on a case against Vanessa since the day I left New York. We could handle her if need be.

"You're up early," Emery mumbled from the bed when I appeared once more.

"Six hours of sleep is plenty for me. You can go back to sleep."

"Mmm," she said, letting the sheet slip down her naked body.

"If you keep that up, you're never going to leave that bed."

She blushed a soft pink that I adored. After all our sex, she still blushed at my comments.

"I should probably check on Kimber. When do you meet Marc?"

"This afternoon. He had to fly commercial," I said with a twitch in my lips. *Oh, how the mighty have fallen.*

"Oh, the horror," she joked.

"So, I can pick you up from the hospital later if that works for you."

"Yes, as long as you think you'll be all right."

I nodded. "I have some work to do and a meeting with my lawyer before that. I'll be occupied. Plus, you helped me last night. I can face another day with you at my side."

She smiled lazily at me. "Good. I'm glad."

———

It was hours before I would get to see that smile again. Work was torture. I hadn't wanted to worry her, but the hours waiting, even when I was busy, didn't help. She dampened the pain. Only her.

By the time I finally got to pick her up again, it was like a balm. I didn't show nerves or stress. Only a few people— primarily Morgan—even noticed, but Emery seemed to have a radar for it. She put her hand on mine as soon as she sat down in the Mercedes and kissed my cheek.

"I've been thinking about you," she said with such candor.

"How are Kimber and Bethany?" I asked as I pulled away from the hospital and drove across town.

"They're great. All of them are. Ready to go home."

"I bet."

"They're getting discharged within the hour. So, they get to take the little cutie home with them."

"I remember what that's like," I said softly.

I rarely talked about what it had been like in those first two years with Colton. The facade that Vanessa had created was so great that, when she took it all away, even the happy memories were tainted with her lies.

Emery squeezed my hand and nodded. "We'll work it out."

"You're right. We will," I said, going back to that cold, detached place that fought my battles and won my wars. I would damn sure win this one.

We parked out front of the lawyer's office. I recognized Vanessa's father's car, which meant she must have left Colton with him for this meeting. Good. I didn't want Colton anywhere near this. It was going to get ugly. I didn't know what Marc was driving, but I didn't see anything pretentious enough for him.

Emery hurried around to the other side of the car and took my hand. She held it, as if we were a united front against the enemy. And I couldn't have been more thankful to have her there. She made me a better man. And, with her, I had the added benefit of putting Vanessa on edge.

As expected, when we walked into the lobby, Vanessa whipped around and glared at our entwined fingers. Her lawyer was talking on a cell phone in a corner.

"You've got to be joking," she spat. "She can't be here."

I just shrugged and gave her a cool smile. No reason to give in to her antics. We were only here because of her bullshit. We would end it here, too.

We waited another five minutes in tense silence before Marc finally showed. I was surprised Abigail wasn't with him. She went everywhere with him to temper his anger. I wondered if he'd even told her what was happening before disappearing. Instead, he only had his lawyer present with him. I shouldn't be surprised that he'd gotten someone on his own to represent his interests instead of relying on Vanessa.

Marc's eyes landed on me first. "You fucking douche," Marc spat. "You spent all this time taking everything away from me, and now, you took more than six years away from me and my son."

"We'll see," I said.

Marc stalked right over to me and got in my face. Emery squeezed my hand.

"I'm here to take my son back."

"You can try," I told him. *And fail.*

Just then, the door to the lawyer's office opened, and my lawyer, Jake McCarty, appeared. He was a short, stocky man, who had been my father's lawyer before me. He knew his shit, and he knew how to get his clients what they wanted.

"You can all come in now."

We moved into a large conference room with Marc and Vanessa on one side and me and Emery on the other.

"Does she have to be here for this?" Vanessa asked. "She's not even involved!"

"She stays," I told her crisply.

"She's fine by me," Jake said with a nod at Emery. "Considering my client has made it clear that he wants Miss Robinson in his life and eventually in Colton's life, I think her presence makes sense for this."

"Never happening," Vanessa hissed.

"We'll see," I said calmly.

"After going over everything in the last twenty-four hours, I got a judge to approve my request that no new people could be introduced into Colton's life until we have this all sorted out. That includes you, Miss Robinson, and Mr. Tarman. Unfortunately, due to the nature of the concern over who is the father to Colton Wright, I've also asked my client, Mr. Wright, not to have contact with Colton until we have this all resolved. All of this is, of course, temporary, barring no complications in the proceedings. Is that all understood and acceptable?"

The other lawyers agreed with the terms even though Marc looked ready to explode that he had come all this way and had no access to Colton. I was pleased with that even though I was pissed that I couldn't see my own son.

"Additionally, I've requested a paternity test be taken immediately to determine who is Colton's biological father. That test should be administered at this location," he said, passing paperwork to both me, Marc, and Vanessa, "within forty-eight hours."

"My client disagrees that a paternity test is necessary," Marc's lawyer said. "He was the only one sleeping with Ms. Hendricks at the time in which Colton was conceived. There is no doubt in his mind that Colton is his."

"If there is no doubt, then he won't have any problem with the test," Jake said dryly. "And, furthermore, if he is so certain, why is he just now coming forward?"

Marc's lawyer glanced at Marc, as if to say, *Want to go to bat?* "When Ms. Hendricks told my client she was pregnant, she said the child belonged to Mr. Wright, and she was going to stop seeing my client. He chose to believe her, but it appears that she has been lying to both of them this whole time."

Vanessa gasped, as if Marc's lawyer had slapped her. Either way, she was the villain. I approved.

"Regardless of Ms. Hendricks's actions or comments during or after the pregnancy, a paternity test is mandatory to determine the custody situation for Colton. Our first priority is his continued health, especially his mental health. The last thing we want to do is introduce new people to him without first being sure that what we are doing is legal. If your client wishes to have any contact with Colton, then he must submit to a paternity test."

"I'll do it," Marc said, cutting his own lawyer off.

"Good. Then, we will reconvene after the results have come in, and then we can determine what will happen next."

Marc and Vanessa glared at me before filing out of the room and leaving the three of us alone.

"That went as well as expected," I told Jake.

He shook my hand and nodded. "The test takes a few days, Jensen. Don't do anything foolish in the meantime."

"Foolish?" I countered.

"Like kidnapping your son."

I couldn't deny that I'd thought about it. I wanted to steal Colton away and never have anyone interfere in our lives again. But I wouldn't. I would be a mess and in a total panic if Vanessa ever did such a thing. I could never do that to her, no matter what she had done to me. And I could never hurt Colton like that.

"I won't."

"Good. I might recommend that you take some time off. Just get away for a few days. I can handle the heavy lifting from here, and you should just try to take your mind off of this until we get the results in. If you stay here, I suspect you'll do something else foolish...like assault Marc Tarman," Jake said with a measured look. "Again."

"I think, this time, he wouldn't be so generous," I said, thinking about how he hadn't pressed charges all those years ago.

"No, he wouldn't," Jake said flatly.

Emery's hand went into mine again. I hadn't realized I'd been clenching my fists.

"I'll take care of him," she said.

My solid rock.

God, I believed her.

Thirty-Five

Emery

"There's one thing I don't understand," I said as we left the lawyer's office behind.

"Just one?" Jensen asked.

"Well, probably a lot of things but one in particular."

"What's that?"

"Why didn't you ever get a paternity test done?"

"You mean...if I thought that Colton was Marc's all along, why didn't I confirm it?"

"Yes."

That had been bugging me from the start. He had just let that stand without confirmation. It would have driven me crazy.

"For a couple reasons. Proof could have only hurt me. Proof could have taken him away. Proof could have shattered our reality. If I got a paternity test, and it said, as I suspect it will in a couple days, that Colton is Marc's son, then I could lose him. But if I never got one done, then Vanessa only had the threat to hang over my head, and nothing else.

"That makes sense. You didn't want her to take him away. So, you never gave her the proof she needed to do it."

"Right, but the other reason is because I didn't need a paternity test to tell me that Colton is my son. I didn't need the confirmation. Colton *is* my son. Regardless of biology or anything else. He's mine. I love him."

My eyes widened, and a smile stretched my face.

"I didn't need proof when I held him in my arms every day and watched him grow up. I had all the proof I needed when he kissed me good night and called me Daddy."

A tear glimmered in my eye, and I wrapped my arms around his waist, drawing him into a hug. He held me tight and placed a kiss on the top of my head.

"You're a good dad, Jensen Wright."

"It is what I have always endeavored to be."

I released Jensen and wiped my eyes. "Don't ever let them take that away from you. No matter what."

He warily stared down at me. "If they take my son from me, I will no longer be a good person. There'll be little hope for anything else."

He moved past me and took the driver's seat in the Mercedes. It took me a couple of seconds to get composed. I couldn't imagine what he was feeling or how he was handling this right now. My heart went out to him, and I truly feared that, if all went as I suspected it would, with Marc's test coming back as Colton's father, that Marc and Vanessa would wreck him.

With a gulp, I followed Jensen into the car. We drove across town to the lab specified on the form. I told Jensen I would wait in the lobby while he got his test done. It took forever. I wasn't sure why since all he had to do was a normal cotton swab or a blood test. But that was a doctor's office for you.

I flipped through my phone and read a few magazines while I waited. By the time he finally came out, I had a full plan of action for the few days we'd have to wait until the tests came back.

"Painless?" I asked as we exited.

"Yeah. Now, the waiting begins."

"I have an idea about that."

"Hmm?" he asked, distracted.

"I thought we might disappear for a bit. Not too long but just to get your mind off of things."

"Are you really sure I should leave?"

"I think it would be good. Plus, your lawyer agrees."

"Yeah, but what if Vanessa does something crazy or Marc interferes? What if I'm not here?" he asked.

"We won't go far. I promise."

He sighed, knowing I was right. "All right."

"You could come meet Bethany when I stop by my place to get clothes."

"I'd like that."

Jensen drove us to Kimber's place in a hurry. He took corners so fast, I thought we were going to go flying. But I didn't tell him to stop or slow down. I knew what had kindled this aggression.

Heidi's car was in the driveway when we showed up. And she greeted us at the door with baby Bethany.

"Hey, cutie," I said, accepting her like a present.

"About time you showed up!" Heidi said with a grin. "Hey, Jensen."

"Heidi," he said with a smile.

She gave me a strange look, as if she couldn't figure out what was up with us. How could I blame her? I was sure she was wondering what the hell was happening with us. Last she had heard, we'd gotten in a fight on New Year's Eve, and now, he was showing up to see the baby. There was a lot I needed to explain, and there was no time like the present to do it.

"She's so cute," I said with a grin.

"Isn't she?" Kimber said from the couch. "Noah's at work, and Lily is upstairs, napping."

"Beautiful," I confirmed. I turned my attention to Jensen, who was looking down at Bethany like she was the most exquisite thing. "Do you want to hold her?"

"If that's all right?"

"Of course," Kimber said. "You're great with Lilyanne."

He nodded, and then I passed him the little bundle of joy. He immediately softened. I knew he was thinking about Colton at this age. He couldn't see his son right now, but it must have felt nice to hold a baby regardless.

"I'm going to go pack."

"Pack?" Kimber asked.

"I thought y'all might like some space with Bethany home and all. I'm going to go stay with Jensen for a few days."

"That's sweet, Em," Kimber said, "but not necessary. I don't mind you staying."

"I know, but I don't want to be in the way when you want to bond. I'll be right back."

Heidi followed me upstairs and leaned against the doorframe as I stuffed clothes into my overnight bag. "Your shit is still in boxes from Austin. Are you ever going to unpack?"

"Not until I move in with you," I told her with a grin.

"Seriously? You think I want you in my apartment?"

"Of course you do. I'm awesome."

"Move in whenever you want, whore. But give me the deets on you and Jensen. Fighting. Not fighting. What gives?"

I shrugged. "Things were put into perspective. He went out on a limb for me, and I want to trust him and see this through."

"Way to vaguebook. Give me the down and dirty."

"I can't," I told her, facing her. "I love you—you know that—but this isn't my secret to tell. Until Jensen is ready to tell it, I don't want to mess up his trust. We're kind of on new ground here…and I like him too much to lose that."

Heidi held her hands up. "That's fair. I'm not trying to pry. Okay, I am. But I don't want to fuck up your relationship. Everything okay?"

"Honestly…we'll find out in a few days."

"Seems grim."

"You've no idea."

"Okay, okay. Well, fill me in when you can, and let's set up a plan for you to actually move in. You'd better not be that girl who moves in with her bestie and then sleeps at her boyfriend's house the whole time."

"You know I've got time for you in my bed."

Heidi snorted. "I love you. So, where are you going?"

"Surprise. Will you check on Kimber the next couple of days? I really don't want to smother them, but I'll miss my niece."

"You know it."

I finished filling up my bag, slung it over my shoulder, and then retreated downstairs. I hugged Kimber, who was cooing over Bethany asleep in Jensen's arms. It was almost comical really. He was such a big guy, and she was so tiny. Yet he held her as if she were the most precious cargo.

"She's gorgeous, Kimber," Jensen said before passing her back. "Congratulations to you both."

"Thank you," she said, smiling down at her daughter.

"I'll see you in a couple of days. Call me if you need me," I said to Kimber.

"Okay," Kimber said, giving me a hug. "Love you."

Jensen and I retreated back to his Mercedes.

"You going to fill me in on where we're going?"

I grinned as we drove to his place. "You haven't guessed?"

"Coming up blank."

"Back to our first date."

He smiled the first real smile all afternoon, and his eyes raked over my body. "The cabin."

Jensen's cabin in Ransom Canyon was exactly the way I remembered it. Chic furniture and hardwood floors. Sheepskin rugs and modern appliances. A roaring fireplace with soft music filtering in through a surround sound stereo system. It was everything I could want in a place that was both somehow high-end and old school.

It brought back memories of camping when I'd been in school yet exuded a realm of luxury I'd never understood until Jensen.

Here was where we had first had sex, giving into desire and never thinking forward from that moment. If I had known then where we would be standing now, I probably would have thought I was insane. No way would I be Jensen Wright's girlfriend. He'd been out of my league. I'd merely been a conquest…and happy to oblige for a night. Yet…here we were.

"Maybe we should go back," Jensen said doubtfully.

"Look, I know you're worried," I told him, divesting myself of my jacket and tossing it on the back of the couch. "I'm worried, too. But you need to get your mind off of things just until we know the test results. If not, all you'll do is worry yourself to death…and probably do something stupid."

He ran a hand back through his hair. His eyes were haunted. "You're probably right."

"I'm definitely right."

His eyes slid back to me. "And how exactly are you going to get my mind off of things?"

"I had a few ideas."

"Does the first start with you stripping in front of the fire again?"

I smirked. "That's like the third idea."

His hands slid up my sides. "We should move it up the list."

Then, he wrapped his arms around my thighs and hoisted me up into the air. I latched on to his neck, holding myself in place. He effortlessly carried me to the sheepskin rug where we had first had sex.

"Help me forget," he breathed against my neck as he lay me back on the rug.

He didn't have to tell me twice. If he wanted sex, I was there, but I knew he wouldn't really forget like this. It would dampen but not change how he felt. I knew that talking was the only thing that would get us there. However, I was all for talking after.

I slipped my shirt over my head and reached for the button on his jeans. Pushing myself into a sitting position, I stripped off his jeans and then ran my hand over the edge of his boxer briefs. He groaned, even before I slipped under the material and took the length of him in my hand. He grew in size at my careful ministrations. Then, I leaned forward, removed his boxers, and licked him from base to head. He definitely was not thinking about anything else now.

I brought him almost to climax with my mouth before he wrestled me to the ground, removed my clothes, and rammed into me. His eyes were full of emotions now. Lust, desire, heat. He wanted me, and I wanted him.

My hand reached up and brushed his cheek. "I love you," I murmured.

His pacing slowed, and he eased forward onto his elbows, so he could look directly into my face. "I will always love you."

He kissed me, slow and purposeful, matching our lips to his strokes. I twined my legs around his body, reveling in the sensation. Before I knew it, my whole body convulsed, and I was coming with him deep inside me. He tipped his head back and followed on the heels of my orgasm.

It felt like more than just sex.

More than just fucking.

It was deep and personal.

He had touched my soul.

Devoured my heart.

And brought us both back to life.

Jensen Wright had rewritten my world.

We both lay back on the rug, spent...for now. My breathing was irregular, and my heartbeat was skyrocketing. Yet all I wanted was to start up again. I was insatiable for this man. And it terrified me that we had come so close to stepping away...to saying that this was too much.

Love was hard.

It shook you to your core.

It remade you into a different person.

But that was what made it beautiful. Knowing that no one else in the world could ever make you feel like you did in that moment. Accepting the pain and really experiencing what it meant to be together.

It moved mountains.

It certainly moved me.

"How are you doing?" Jensen asked, kissing my shoulder.

"Never been better."

"Mmm," he agreed.

"I think I want to teach," I told him out of nowhere.

"I bet you'd be amazing at it."

"My mother, of all people, suggested I do it, and now, I think it sounds like the right choice."

"Is that what you want then?"

"It was the only thing that really made me happy in grad school. I thought it would get easier. All the research and papers and such, but it was the classroom that made me happy. I just...thought that was normal."

"Maybe it was just telling you something," he said, twining my dark hair around his finger.

"Maybe it was," I whispered. "I've never really told anyone that. It was anathema to what everyone thought I should be focusing on in grad school. No one talked about loving the teaching side."

"Well, I think you should stop caring what they think and follow your heart."

I glanced over at him. Naked and satisfied on a sheepskin rug with nothing but Jensen Wright in my sight.

"I think I have."

"You are my heart," he said. He took my hand up to his lips and kissed each individual knuckle. "And I can't thank you enough for being here right now through all of this. I know that things haven't been easy. You could have left at anytime. Yet you are here with me through the hardest moment of my life. No matter what happens, Emery, when I walk out on the other side of this...I want you to be with me. I want you to be mine."

I touched his face and drew his lips to mine. "I am."

Thirty-Six

Jensen

Emery and I had spent the last four days in my cabin, locked away from the outside world. As stressed as I was about what was to come, Emery was right. I'd needed to get away and to try not to think about anything for a while. I couldn't do anything to change the situation while we waited for the test results to come back in. All I could do was stress. So, here we had been, just far enough away for me to relax some.

I was still on edge, but Emery wouldn't let me stay there. At least not for long.

We were coming down from our morning sex on the fifth day when I got the call.

"Tests are in," Jake said. "Showtime."

"Do you know what they say?"

"They're sealed. We'll find out at the same time as everyone else. But be prepared."

I nodded and then hung up the phone. "Time to go."

Emery stretched out in bed and yawned. Her tits looked amazing in the morning right after I fucked her brains out. "Right now?"

"Test results are in."

"Fuck," she said, jolting up. "Let's go."

"We have to get everyone together at once before we can go through the sealed paperwork. But we should get over there as soon as possible."

She jumped out of bed and hurried to clean up the mess that we had made while we were here. Clothes were scattered all across the room, hastily discarded in our den of iniquity. Neither of us had minded. It was easier to let everything go and just enjoy how much we fucked than to consider what was coming next.

But, now, that time had come.

We put the place back together in record time and were out of the cabin. It was a quick drive back to Lubbock and to reality.

After this moment, I would definitely know that Colton was Marc's son. I didn't know what I would do with that information. It would be up to Vanessa if she wanted to try to change the custody agreement. But this was a day I had been dreading for a long time. A day I'd hoped would never come.

We made it back to my lawyer's office in good time. He had already spoken to both Vanessa's and Marc's lawyers, and we would be reconvening within the hour. I chose to wait. I couldn't leave, knowing that we had the results waiting. I'd spent years waiting for this moment. I could wait another hour.

Vanessa and Marc showed up separately and warily looked at each other. I wondered what they had done in my time away with Emery. I hoped it had driven them both as crazy as it had me. But they hadn't had the benefit of amazing sex to forget about it. The way they were looking at each other, I was sure they hadn't indulged, which made me grin.

"What?" Vanessa snapped.

"Nothing," I said, purposely glancing between them. "Just had an amusing thought."

"Your thought was so clear on your face. Maybe turn off the broadcast."

I shrugged. Of course she could read me. I'd wanted her to.

Jake reappeared a few minutes later with the information in his hands, and everyone took their seats. Marc was jittery. I could tell by the way he kept fiddling with his hands. He'd done that in school, too. Vanessa looked stoic, as if her relationship with her son didn't depend on this moment. Emery squeezed my leg under the table, and I met her gaze only briefly. I was glad she was here to ground me. I didn't know what I would look like otherwise.

Rattled and a mess.

Neither of which I ever showed to anyone else anymore.

"Thank you for joining us again on such short notice," Jake said, beginning the meeting. "We just received the paperwork from the laboratory that did the paternity test. This is the first time any of us will be seeing it.

"As stated before, Ms. Hendricks has claimed that Colton's father is not her ex-husband, Mr. Wright, but Mr. Tarman instead. This allegation, if true, will begin a change in the custody agreement to potentially allow Mr. Tarman rights to see his son. If the allegation is false, the custody agreement will remain the same unless Mr. Wright or Ms. Hendricks wants to return to court to renegotiate. Is that clear?"

Everyone but Emery said, "Yes," around the table, anxiously staring at the paperwork.

He bent back the metal brackets holding the envelope secured and then opened it. A stack of papers came out, and on the top, were the results. I held my breath as Jake read through the document. You could have heard a pin drop in the room.

303

"The paternity test came back positive for…Mr. Wright." Jake turned to face me with a giant smile on his face. "Jensen, you're the father. Colton *is* your son."

Vanessa exclaimed from across the room, and I heard Marc cuss. But it was all background noise to me. It was like being sealed in a vacuum.

Colton was my son.

He was mine.

My boy.

I nearly broke down at the very thought that, after all this time, all this worrying, all the arguments and debates and complications…Colton had been mine all along. I'd been so sure that Vanessa was telling the truth. She had been so sure of the truth. I had let her hang it over my head for years. Years!

But she was wrong. Or she had lied. She had lied to my face all those times. Told me countless times that I hadn't even been in New York the month that she got pregnant. My schedule hadn't always overlapped with hers, but I'd believed her. She'd had no reason to say otherwise. Colton had been two years old before I even knew about it. By then, the exact travel dates had been lost on me. I could see them on my work schedule and the flight schedules, but we hadn't always had sex every time I was there. It had been impossible to determine if I was Colt's father.

Now, I knew that I was.

Colton was mine.

Emery's arms were around me, and I stood, lifting her into the air.

"I'm so happy for you," she whispered through the vacuum.

"God, I love you," I murmured back, forgetting everyone else in the room.

I set her back down on her feet, cupped her face in my hands, and kissed the breath out of her. This was the moment I had been born for. The knowledge that I had the woman I loved here with me now and that I would never have to worry about my son again. It was euphoric.

"What the fuck, Vanessa?" Marc cried, jarring me out of my moment. "Why would you drag me into this?"

Marc's and Vanessa's lawyers were looking at the document, but it was clear from their faces that they agreed with Jake.

"I swear, it was you, Marc. I swear," Vanessa said. "Jensen wasn't even in town that month. We weren't together. You know that."

"You just wanted the drama. Fuck!"

"I really believed it was you," she whispered. Tears brimmed in her eyes. "I did."

"You lied to all of us, Vanessa," I said, drawing her attention to me. "You lied to me, to Marc, to everyone. But even worse was that you deluded yourself into believing it. You're never holding this over my head again. I'm free. Free of you."

At those words, Vanessa completely lost it. She broke down into tears and covered her face in her hands. Vanessa had been holding onto this fact for so long, thinking it was a way to keep me. As if she had thought for a second that I would still hold a flame for her after all she had done.

But it was over. There was nothing left. And she had no more control.

"If this satisfies everyone, we'll leave the custody agreement as it stands and deny Mr. Tarman's request for access to Colton," Jake said. "If we want to take this further, then we'll see you in court, Ms. Hendricks."

Vanessa shook her head, blubbering about how she'd sworn she knew. She'd thought this would fix it all.

"Sounds good to me," I said to Jake.

Sure, I would love to get custody of Colton and have him live here in Lubbock with me. But I didn't want to go to court with Vanessa over it, and I wasn't willing to disrupt Colt's life.

He was happy in New York, and he had a great school there. *I* wasn't the type of person to do something like that just to make someone else miserable. That was all Vanessa.

We filed out of the office and stood in the foyer. Vanessa was shaking, talking to her lawyer.

Marc approached us. "I see you've taken everything from me now. Vanessa, Colton, the company."

"Interesting how you put that," I said. "All I see is that you were trying to take things from me that never belonged to you. And the company was just for fun."

Marc glared and looked ready to throw a punch. Instead, he turned to Emery and grinned. "When he gets tired of you, give me a call."

Emery arched an eyebrow in disgust. "Not even in your dreams."

He laughed. "Oh, be sure, he'll tire of you. He bores easily."

"Unless you want a repeat of that time I found out you had an affair with my wife, I would step away," I growled. "Now."

"Don't even waste your breath on him, Jensen," Emery said. "He's just trying to provoke you because he's jealous. You have the world at your feet."

I turned to face my girl and smiled. She was right. Of course she was right. "I want you to meet my son."

"I'd love to meet him."

I took Emery's hand then and left the lawyer's office. I knew there was more to take care of, and I definitely had to get back to the office. But first things first. I needed to set all of this straight. Vanessa might be upset about it. Frankly, I didn't care for Vanessa's opinions any longer. Emery was in my life, and she was here to stay.

We showed up at the hotel right after our meeting, and I took Emery up to the top floor. I knocked on the door and Nanny Jennifer answer.

"Jensen! I'm surprised to see you here," she said. "I thought Vanessa said that you couldn't see Colton for right now."

"Change of plans. Just got it approved by the judge that I have full access back."

"Oh, that's wonderful." Jennifer smiled at Emery. "And you must be Emery."

"Hi, nice to meet you," Emery said, holding out her hand.

"Let me go check on Colt for you two."

I turned to Emery. "Can you stay here for a minute. I want to talk to him first."

"Of course," she agreed.

"Colton, your dad is here!" Nanny Jennifer called.

I walked into the suite just as Colton came running. "Daddy!"

He launched himself into my arms, and I hugged him tighter than I'd ever squeezed him before. *My son. Mine!* No one could ever take him away again.

"Hey, champ," I said. I set him back down. "Remember how I told you that I wanted you to meet a friend of mine?"

"Yes. A *girrrl*," Colton singsonged.

I laughed. "Yes. A girl. She's my girlfriend, and her name is Emery."

"You have a girlfriend?"

"Yep, and I want you to meet her. I think you'll like her. Are you ready?"

Colton looked down at himself and gave me a thumbs up. *God, I loved him.*

I took his hand, and we walked together to the front of the suite where Emery was waiting.

"All right, champ, this is my girlfriend, Emery," I said to Colton.

Colton stood very still and smiled up at Emery with the brilliance that only a child could have.

Then, I looked up in Emery's big green eyes. "Emery, this is *my* son."

"You're very pretty," he said with a Wright grin.

Emery laughed. "Why, thank you. It's so nice to meet you. I've heard so much about you."

"Dad said that you were going to be my new friend."

"I would like that very much."

"Are you going to come visit me at home?"

Emery smiled and looked up at me with a question in her eyes.

"Yes," I answered for her. "She will most definitely be visiting you in New York. I'm going to bring her as often as I come to visit."

"I'd like that," Emery said as much to me as to Colton. "I'd like to spend all my time in your lives."

We moved back into the living space and took a seat. I picked Colton up and planted him on my knee. Emery sat next to me, and I wrapped my other arm around her.

This was our life. It wasn't perfect. It was far from easy. But it was ours. And I loved them both more than words for being a part of it.

Epilogue

Emery
Eight Months Later

"Heidi, have you seen my black pumps?" I called into the living room.

"Which ones?"

"The closed-toe ones. Roundish."

She appeared in my bedroom a minute later, holding a pair of shoes in her hand. Curse of living with someone who could pretty much wear all the same sizes as me. Except jeans, because she was a giant compared to me.

"Gimme those."

I put them on my feet and looked in the mirror at the knee-length black skirt and black top I was wearing with the heels. "How do I look?"

"I'd fuck you," she said with a laugh.

"Oh God, I hope all the high school boys aren't going to think that."

"Um…hell yes, they are."

At that moment, a knock came from the front door, and I groaned, trying not to think about high school boys wanting to fuck me. I'd had enough torture for one lifetime on that front. Before I even reached the front door, Jensen popped open the door with his key to the place.

"Hey, babe," he said, giving me a kiss. "Are you really wearing that on your first day?"

"Why? Do I look like shit?" I asked, concerned.

"No, you look hot as fuck. Every kid in the place is going to want to bang their teacher."

I groaned. "Ew. Should I go for flats?"

"Only if you change into the heels for me later." He winked.

I plucked the shoes off my feet and shoved them into his hands. Then, I dashed back into my bedroom and slipped on a sensible pair of black flats. I grabbed the official-looking teacher bag that Jensen had gotten for me as a congratulations for landing my first high school teaching job.

I'd spent all last semester substitute teaching to build up hours for the certification that I needed to be able to be in the classroom. Then, I'd applied to what felt like a million jobs all over Lubbock, and somehow, against all odds, I had gotten a job teaching European history at my old high school. My life could not be more ironic.

"Come on, before you're late to class," Jensen joked, smacking my ass on the way out the door.

"See you later, Heidi!" I called.

"Have a good first day at school, darling!" she yelled back.

Jensen had the truck, which calmed my nerves. I couldn't imagine driving the Mercedes or the flashier sports car he had recently purchased to Lubbock High School. Sure, there was some oil money at the school...and there had always been the Wright family, but I wasn't part of that elite inner circle—or, at least, I kept telling myself that.

Because, when the billionaire CEO himself dropped me off in front of the school, I felt pretty inner circle.

Things with Jensen had been much smoother sailing since the post-holidays madness. I spent a couple of nights a week at his house. We flew to New York once a month to see Colton, and he started spending a weekend here every month. I knew Jensen wanted more time with him, but he also didn't want to interfere with Colton's schooling. Vanessa had mellowed out. I wasn't sure if it was the large quantities of Xanax she was taking or what, but she just stopped fighting us when we came into town. After eight months, she must have finally decided I wasn't going anywhere. And I wasn't.

"Thanks for dropping me off," I said.

I was trying not to be nervous even though it was really my first official day teaching high school students. I'd been a TA in college and taught my own introductory history class, but for some reason, high school had felt more daunting than college. Maybe because I'd found out who I was in college, and I had been so scared of high school.

"Have a good first day," he told me, leaning in and giving me a lingering kiss.

"Is anyone actually ready for their first day of high school?"

"You survived once before. You can probably make it a second time."

"And with the right brother this time."

"Ha-ha!" he said with a roll of his eyes. "I'd better be the right brother."

"The one and only," I whispered against his lips.

"Good. Now, get in there, and then later, we can enact all my naughty teacher fantasies."

I blushed despite myself. It didn't matter how much sex we'd had. I couldn't seem to keep it together.

"God, I love you," he said.

"I love you, too."

I kissed him once more and then hopped out of the truck.

I adjusted my skirt and took in the world I was about to enter. I never thought that I'd be back. It was kind of cool to think that I could start over here. I entered the building with more optimism than I'd thought possible.

The day went by lightning fast. Way faster than I remembered high school going when I had been there. But, before I knew it, my first day was over. I had over a hundred and fifty names to remember that had completely flitted out of my brain. But I'd survived.

There was Jensen, waiting for me, when I left. Of course, he was in the flashy Corvette. Bright red and low to the ground with the top down. I shook my head and laughed as I approached the car that all the students were staring at.

"Miss me?" he asked with a grin.

"Every moment."

"Good." He popped open the passenger door, and I dropped inside. "So, where do you want to go to celebrate your birthday?"

I dropped my head into my hands and groaned. "Oh my God, how did you find out?"

"Heidi." He sat down in the driver's seat and then obnoxiously revved the engine.

"Bitch." I shook my head in disbelief. "I don't know. Let's just stay in and work on those fantasies."

He grinned. "Thought you'd say that."

The drive back to his house was unbelievably short in his new car. It blew my hair all around my face, but it was exhilarating. I could see why he loved the thing, and he was already talking about getting something sleek and distinctly European. He was addicted.

He parked in the garage and took my hand as I stepped out of the car.

"I am so *not* a birthday person," I informed him with a sigh. "I do like cake though."

"I was made aware of this. But I don't care. You'll celebrate with me if I want you to."

"Just be warned, I will retaliate!"

He laughed and drew me in for a kiss. "I'll take all the punishment you're willing to offer."

We stepped in through the garage and straight into the kitchen.

Jensen flipped the lights, and suddenly, a whole group of people jumped up and screamed, "Surprise!"

I put my hand over my mouth. "Oh my God!"

There were party streamers all over his kitchen and out through the foyer. A giant party cake that read *Happy Birthday, Emery* with a bunch of lit candles sat in the middle of the island. And all around it were my friends and family and Jensen's family.

My heart expanded enough to hold them all. I might not have been a birthday person before, but today changed that. I'd never had good birthdays growing up. They'd always been filled with disappointment—kids missing parties, no one showing up, and all that. But right here was exactly what I'd always wanted.

Heidi was jumping up and down next to Landon. They both looked ecstatic that they had been able to surprise me. Austin was across the room from Julia but kept glancing her way. She was making a point not to look at him so much that it was clear she wanted to look over. Instead, she beamed extra hard at me. Morgan was leaning into Patrick, and Sutton was holding her new baby boy, Jason, in her arms. Maverick was at her side, indulging her. Then, there was Kimber, Noah, Lilyanne, and Bethany all standing to one side with my mother, of all people.

But it was the one other little face who nudged Lilyanne and smiled back at me that surprised me the most. Jensen must have gone to great lengths for this entire thing because Colton was even here.

Jensen wrapped an arm around me as Heidi pushed me toward the cake.

"Make a wish," Jensen said.

I stared down at the cake and realized that I already had everything I wanted.

What I had always been searching for.

Home.

I took a mental snapshot of the beauty before me, at my new reality, and then I leaned forward and made my wish.

The End

Acknowledgments

This book came out of the idea from a total stranger, who I can now call a friend. Thank you, Kristina, for telling that random story to my husband.

And, of course, the long list of incredible people who helped me make this book what it is today: Rebecca Kimmerling, Anjee Sapp, Katie Miller, Polly Matthews, Anjee Sapp, Diana Peterfreund, Lori Francis, Rebecca Gibson, Sarah Hansen for the amazingly hot cover, Sara Eirew for the sexy photograph, Jovana Shirley for the incredible editing and formatting, Danielle Sanchez for keeping me sane plus your marketing guru genius, Alyssa Garcia for beautiful graphics, and my wonderful agent, Kimberly Brower, for all her amazing work.

Additionally, the much-needed love from authors who kept me up late at night writing and supported me along the way: A.L. Jackson, Lauren Blakely, Kristy Bromberg, Corinne Michaels, Tijan, Rachel Brookes, Rebecca Yarros, Sloane Howell, Jessica Hawkins, Staci Hart, Belle Aurora, Kendall Ryan, Meghan March, Jillian Dodd, Jenn Sterling, S.C. Stephens, Laurelin Paige, Kandi Steiner, Claire Contreras, and many more!

All the incredible bloggers who worked tirelessly day in and day out to get content to readers just because you love books so much, I see you. I appreciate you.

As always, thank you so much to my husband for dealing with me being sick, wanting to write three books at once, late nights, and deciding to take up piano and working out in the same month. I love you and the puppies to the moon and back.

Finally, and most importantly, YOU! That's right. You, as the reader! Thank you for reading this book. I hope you loved it, and I can't wait to give you more amazing books to follow.

About the Author

K.A. Linde is the *USA Today* bestselling author of the Avoiding Series and more than fifteen other novels. She grew up as a military brat and attended the University of Georgia where she obtained a Master's in political science. She works full-time as an author and loves Disney movies and binge-watching *Supernatural* and *Star Wars*.

She currently lives in Lubbock, Texas, with her husband and two super-adorable puppies.

Visit her online at www.kalinde.com and on Facebook, Twitter, and Instagram @authorkalinde.

Join her newsletter at www.kalinde.com/subscribe for exclusive content, free books, and giveaways every month.

CPSIA information can be obtained
at www.ICGtesting.com
Printed in the USA
BVOW08s1053150317
478540BV00002B/107/P